BOARDING
INSTRUCTIONS

stories

Also by Ray Vukcevich

The Man of Maybe Half-a-Dozen Faces
Meet Me in the Moon Room

BOARDING
INSTRUCTIONS

FAIRWOOD PRESS
Bonney Lake, WA

**BOARDING
INSTRUCTIONS**
A Fairwood Press Book
November 2010
Copyright © 2010 by Ray Vukcevich

All Rights Reserved

Fairwood Press
21528 104th Street Court East
Bonney Lake, WA 98391
www.fairwoodpress.com

Front cover illustration & design by
Jay Kinney & Paul Mavrides
Book Design by Patrick Swenson

ISBN13: 978-1-933846-23-1
First Fairwood Press Edition: November 2010
Printed in the United States of America

For Vincent

Publication History

"Grocery List" first appeared in *Fortean Bureau* (April 2004)
"My Eyes, Your Ears" first appeared in *The Los Angeles Review* (Fall 2009)
"Human Subjects" first appeared in *Amazing* (September 2004)
"The Button" first appeared in *Hobart*
"The Wages of Syntax" first appeared in *SCIFICTION* (October 2002)
"Some Other Time" first appeared in *SCIFICTION* (July 2002)
"Chain" first appeared in *Time After Time* (DAW Books 2005)
"Cold Comfort" first appeared in *F&SF* (July 2007)
"Gas" first appeared in *F&SF* (April 2004)
"Glinky" first appeared in *F&SF* (June 2004)
"Dead Girlfriend" first appeared in *Rosebud* (2002)
"The Rescue" first appeared in *Rosebud* (2003)
"Fired" first appeared in *Imagination Fully Dilated: Science Fiction* (Fairwood Press 2003)
"Intercontinental Ballistic Missile Boy" first appeared in *Strange Horizons* (May 2002)
"Magic Makeup" first appeared in *Strange Horizons* (April 2004)
"Jumping" first appeared in *Witpunk* (Four Walls Eight Windows 2003)
"The Library of Pi" first appeared in *Polyphony* (Wheatland Press 2006)
"Love Story" first appeared in *Polyphony* (Wheatland Press 2002)
"Morning Meditation" first appeared in *Polyphony* (Wheatland Press 2003)
"Tongues" first appeared in *Polyphony* (Wheatland Press 2005)
"Love Leans In From The Left" first appeared in *Lost Pages* (Dec 2003)
"My Shoes" first appeared in *Flytrap* (May 2007)
"Strong Suits" first appeared in *Lust for Life* (Vehicule Press 2006)
"Suddenly Speaking" first appeared in *Flash Fiction Online* (September 2009)
"Note from the Future" first appeared in *Flash Fiction Online* (December 2009)
"Superpowers" first appeared in *Monkeybicycle.net* (September 2005)
"Take the Stairs" first appeared in *Talebones* (Summer 2005)
"Tubs" first appeared in *Lady Churchill's Rosebud Wristlet* (2006)
"Duck" first appeared in *Night Train* (Spring 2006)
"The Two of Me" first appeared in *Interfictions 2* (Small Beer Press 2009)
"A Funny Smell" first appeared in *SmokeLong Quarterly* (June 2009)
"Over Here" (appears here for the first time)
"In The Flesh" first appeared in *The Infinite Matrix* (February 2002)

Contents

Grocery List

TOFu
Olive oil
Broccoli
Flowers
Candy
Apology
Rat Poison
Bullets
Rope
Blunt object
Smelly cheese
Red meat
Potato chips
Beer

Card?

balloons?

Singing Telegram?

My Eyes, Your Ears

don't know if I've told you this story before, because you all have black bars over your eyes, and I cannot tell who you are. I can see one of you is a police officer. I don't know whose blood this is we're standing in. Please, God, don't let it be Caroline's.

I realize now the trick I pulled on Caroline back in high school was a desperate attempt to get her attention. She was so perfect, so strawberry blond, so well-dressed and groomed. You could signal a rescue helicopter by bouncing sunlight off her teeth. She was just so totally Barbie it made you want to grab and squeeze her to see if she'd squeak. Her mother drove her to school. The bumper sticker on her mother's car said, "My Child is a National Honor Society Student."

I replaced it with one that was almost identical but said, "My Child Has Enormous Ears."

And then people were honking and grinning and children were giving her the Dumbo ears with their hands up along the sides of their heads, and Caroline and her mother were thinking they'd made some horrible social blunder like coming out in favor of atheism or something, but then one day Caroline spotted the bumper sticker, and you could hear her outraged cry all the way down the block and across the street, and that would have been the big payoff of my prank, if it had really been a prank an not an adolescent attempt to get her to notice me.

It didn't take her long to figure out I'd done it. I'd made no effort to cover my tracks. What's the fun of a practical joke if no one knows you did it? But after a couple of fits of yelling and shaking her fists at the sky and kicking the bumper of her mother's car, she went all goodsport on me. She accepted my apology, and I scraped off the bumper sticker. Incredibly, she started smiling at me in the high school hallways. One thing led to another, and she went to the senior prom with me. We fooled around a little, but not too much, in the back seat of my car. I almost asked her to marry me. I couldn't think of how to put it. I considered a bumper sticker that said, "Marry me, Caroline!" But the moment passed in silence.

I got into a pretty good college, and she went off to an even better one, and I figured that was that. I would drink tequila and read the Beat poets. Sadder, wiser, world-weary, maybe I'd grow a mustache, but then one day, she was back and asking me out for tea. For tea? Yes, tea, you know tea, in a teahouse, with little cakes, oh, I suppose you could have coffee. No, tea is fine. It's wonderful to see you again, Caroline. Oh look over there, she said, and I looked, and she put something in my tea. I didn't see her do it. She told me about it a little later, because what fun is a practical joke if no one knows you did it?

She had let her hair grow big around her ears, no more perky ponytails. Nice hair, I said. You mean, thank god you can't see my huge, ugly ears, she said.

There is nothing whatever wrong with your ears, Caroline. I love your ears, I said. You're just saying that, she said. Jesus, I had given her some kind of complex about her ears all those years ago with the bumper sticker.

Here's looking at . . . your ears, kid, I said, toasting her with my tea.

Always the jokes. She turned her head away and then turned back, and I saw there was a black bar over her eyes. She was a photograph of someone you shouldn't know about. All of the people in the teahouse had black bars over their eyes.

I see you're getting it, she said, and the kicker is it's retroactive!

And it is so true! I have always seen a black bar over the eyes of everyone! It hasn't been easy. I am not so much blind as unrecognizing. Nevertheless, I have always loved Caroline's ears. She has nothing to hide when it comes to her ears.

Oddly, I also see black bars over the eyes of domesticated animals. Dogs and cats, cows and horses. Ferrets. No mice. What would be the point? Whoever worried about an unidentified mouse?

A server approaches. I don't know if I've ever seen him before because of the black bar over his eyes. You should assume the crash position, he tells us. It's going to be tricky, but our captain thinks she can set this teahouse down with not so many casualties.

Later in the smoke and shouting and running on the tarmac, I lose track of Caroline. No, no, I tell the rescue helicopter, I've got to find Caroline. Is that you? Is that you? I can see that might be you, because

you are a woman of a certain width and depth and height, and your hair
has red highlights that are subtly reflected an octave higher in your fingernails and an octave lower in your toenails. Nice knees. If you were
Caroline, I could see you wearing that frilly white top, that pale green
skirt, those brown sandals, that green glass bracelet on your left wrist.

Who is shooting?

Why does there always have to be shooting?

I suddenly see that I'm standing in someone's blood, and then the
policeman drags me away for interrogation. Did you see whose blood
I was standing in? Was it a woman of a certain width and depth and
height? I'll ask the questions, he says. Actually her width and depth
vary as you move your eyes up and down her height which is generally
consistent.

He wants to know about the shooting. We are Americans, I tell
him, and for us, after 9/11, everything is about shooting and screaming
and standing in blood, even when it's not. We do not appreciate that
kind of talk at a facility like this, he tells me. He pushes me down onto
a hard wooden chair.

A woman runs up and shoulders the policeman aside and drops
down on her knees in front of me. Caroline, is that you? It's okay, she
says, I'm here. How can I know that's you? She leans in and flips her
hair away from the side of her face, and I see her left ear in extreme
close-up. She turns quickly and shows me the other one. Her ears are
beautiful pink seashells in the sunshine. They fill my world with joy.
They really are, I feel compelled to report, enormous.

(3)

Over Here
For MAJ Benjamin Buchholz, JS Army

Megumi

I *suspect my daughter Amelia* and that man she married named
my granddaughter after a character from Japanese animation. I
never did press the point, and now we'll never know for sure. She is my
Megumi who is even now hiding in the yard. Right over there. Under
the big Douglas fir tree. She is holding so very still like a cautious rabbit. She is afraid I will call her inside to play the clavichord.

Megumi is all eyes squatting on her heels and looking over her
knees. She knows that I'm looking right at her so she is not moving
her eyes at all. I wonder how long she'll be able to hold off blinking. I
wonder if losing her parents and coming to live with her grandfather is
making her weird. Are you weird Megumi? I make a funny face at her
through the big window. She doesn't respond.

Maybe I should get a professional opinion about her weirdness?

I can see her sneakers, which are black with pink cartoons and yellow laces. High tops. She doesn't play basketball. But she might some
day. Blue jeans with the cuffs turned way up. I should get some advice
on what modern six-year-old orphan girls like to wear when they are
not playing the clavichord.

Can you even buy dresses these days?

I could lure her inside with the promise of a story about Layla, the
desert princess. Someday I am going to have to tell Megumi the bad
news about Layla.

Not today.

Layla

I wonder what Layla was wearing when the truck ran her down
yesterday. It isn't the kind of question I can ask our friend who wants

us to call him "Abu Yusef." That probably isn't his real name. It might be dangerous for him if it got out he was using his computer to post messages on the international clavichord list. We are, generally speaking, a contentious bunch on the clavichord list, but we understand and are sympathetic when our friend and colleague in Iraq tells us he is reluctant to reveal his real name or identify his real town in the south where there are many Persian influences.

And speaking of Persian influences, Abu Yusef believes the clavichord is a direct descendant (by way of the cymbalum) of the Persian santur, a hammered dulcimer. Hey, it's a theory and might even be true. Not everyone agrees. There has been some online heat on this subject. With any group you're going to have some people who take things too seriously. No one will admit to hurt feelings. Often it's a good thing we are not all in the same room or there would be fistfights over matters like tuning, for example. Never mind origin theories.

Abu Yusef does not say the dead girl is his granddaughter. He is keeping a stiff upper lip. For weeks he talked about finding his perfect student. Too bad she's a girl, he said. We don't know if he was joking about that. Yesterday she was killed in a pointless accident.

Layla and her friends were outside watching a US convoy go by. So many trucks all going north. It was like they would keep coming until they filled the country up with trucks and tanks and guns and foreign soldiers, and there would be room for nothing else. Where would they all stay when they got to where they were going?

One of the drivers tossed Layla a bottle of water and a smile. The bottle bounced off her hands and rolled into the road. When she ran out to get it, a truck coming in the other direction ran over her.

So, some of the trucks and soldiers must have been going south.

By the time Abu Yusef came onto the scene, someone had covered Layla with a blanket. Everyone was talking at once. The whole town and all the foreign soldiers who were not in their trucks had gathered around the small body. He didn't say so, but I imagine the people made way for Abu Yusef since he is the mayor. I get the idea that he is proud to be the mayor, but also that he sometimes feels like a front man since it is the deputy town council president, a Shi'a religious functionary of some kind, who has all the power. I detect no resentment about this on Abu Yusef's part. That is simply the way of things.

Like Megumi, Layla had been six years old. The two girls were destined to be animated superheroes and fight evil together. There is nothing like a couple of six-year-old girls to bring peoples and cultures together. Who could have foreseen that one of them would be a ghost? Well, that's the kind of plot twist Megumi's mother must have anticipated when she came up with Megumi's name in the first place. I wonder if my daughter had imagined the name of the show the two girls would be starring in. If so, she didn't pass that name down to us. I will have to name the show myself. Here are some of my ideas.

"The Strings of Doom!"

Where the strings are clavichord strings, of course.

"Megumi, Layla, and the Legend of the Twangs."

The Twangs could be these guys you think are the bad guys, but then they turn out to be only misunderstood. The Twangs are proud and stern and have many baffling customs, but they are basically good guys. Megumi and Layla come to understand the Twangs after many adventures, hurt feelings, kissing and making up, giant robots, evil eyebeams, talking woodland creatures, and martial art clavichord playing.

"Princess Layla and the Twangster."

This time Megumi turns out to be the twangster which is (but only superficially) like a gangster. She wears a fedora, and she's adorable. Princess Layla comes to the rescue in the end, and the twangster finally comes out of her shell and is able to make a pretty sound.

"The Twangsters."

This time both Megumi and Layla can be twangsters — a couple of six-year-old girls who save the world on a weekly basis with transcendental early music. The joke being they can't actually make such music yet, and that's why they're called twangsters. It really isn't easy to make pleasant sounds with a clavichord.

In any case, there will be some kind of rat spider sidekick who is also very cute — maybe it makes wisecracks, and the girls pretend to be angry or exasperated. Maybe it turns into a clavichord when drenched in water.

Amelia

We did not name Megumi's mother after a cartoon character. We named her after Amelia Earhart, the aviator, because we thought she would soar, but whenever the subject came up, she acted like she literally could not believe it — you named me after someone who crashed and burned or drowned or otherwise just disappeared? You'd like it if I just disappeared, too, wouldn't you? And it was true, just then, I would have been happy if she'd just wandered off to the mall or something, but I couldn't very well say that, and I didn't have anyone to talk the problem over with after Karen died leaving me with Amelia who had been thirteen and who would be in and out of rehab for years. Even so, I would never have guessed she'd go on to get herself gunned down so stupidly.

I blame the authorities. Yes, they probably had to kick down the door and go in with guns drawn, but no one was armed in the house. Okay, they didn't know that. But they should have been able to tell an assault rifle from a soup ladle even in the dim light. At least they minimized the collateral damage when it came to Megumi who is so quiet now. And trembling, she is all the time trembling just below the surface. You can't really see it, but if you pull her into your arms where she stands stiff and silent, you can feel her trembling.

The authorities had been prepared for a fight when they kicked down the wrong door and shot Amelia and David. Imagine you were on that team rooting out terrorists. Some of those young cops must have been frightened. They must have thought they were in terrible danger. They must have thought they would find weapons. The higher-ups might not have looked too closely at the information they had, but they would never in a million years have thought that they would find nothing. I'm convinced that's why the DEA took over afterwards.

What they finally found became the grounds for calling Amelia and David major drug dealers. They needed to cover their asses. They got lucky. They changed their story.

The fact that Amelia and David turned out to actually be major drug dealers is beside the point. I just wish Amelia had dropped her soup ladle, put up her hands, and cried, "Don't shoot!"

I look at the pictures in my head of Amelia in her black bandana and bandolier of bullets and Amelia in her red and white high school band uniform, her clarinet, her silly hat, and I see that small strange unsettling smile that is the same in both pictures, one Amelia looking back and the other looking ahead in time. I don't really think she had a black bandana and bullets. I do think the clarinet was real.

I still mostly refuse to think of Megumi's father David as anything but "that man who married my Amelia" and led her into a life of dope, poverty and death, but the truth is, Amelia played her own part. It's like when she was a teen in rehab, and it hit me one day I could stop worrying about her getting in with the wrong kind of friends. She was the bad influence herself that other parents should worry about. But then for just a moment, she seemed to pull it all together. She met David, got married, gave birth to Megumi, relapsed a couple of times, came back, and then died in a botched homeland security raid.

Clavichord

I run into people all the time who think "clavichord" is another word for collarbone. I once mentioned that to Megumi hoping she would smile, but she didn't get it. This is another sad example of a fifty-four-year-old man trying to amuse a superhero. I don't think her rat spider sidekick who might also be a cat or maybe a possum got it either.

Generally speaking, a clavichord is a rectangular wooden box. It usually has a lid. The keyboard is usually on the left. Inside there is a soundboard and a number of strings. The mechanism for making music is the most simple of all the keyboard instruments. You press a key on one end of a lever and the other end rises up and a metal blade called a tangent strikes a string or pair of strings.

Unlike a piano player, for example, the clavichord player is in direct contact with the string. The art is in what to do with that contact. Your touch controls the dynamics of the note. You can do a kind of vibrato. You do not just push a key and a consistent sound is produced. It all depends on what you do with that finger on the key.

The instrument is not loud. Everyone needs to be paying attention — the player, the listeners. Clavichord music is not something that can happen accidentally or in the background. If your neighbor is a clavichord player, chances are you'll never hear the music through the common wall even if you put your ear right up against it hoping to figure out what's going on in there.

Some clavichords are as big as the tops of conference tables. Some are quite small. There is a tiny model called the "King of Sweden" that you can pick up and carry around under your arm. Most are somewhere in between.

We like to claim that the clavichord was Bach's favorite instrument.

In other words, the clavichord is the very essence of the keyboard. It is what Plato would have called an "ideal" keyboard instrument if it had been invented in time for him to call it anything at all.

It was Abu Yusef who pointed out how much a clavichord looks like a crate of rifles.

He had a lot of trouble getting his instrument into Iraq when he came home from Italy after the Invasion.

Our anime supergirls, Megumi and Layla the ghost, never have that kind of trouble. That's a very good thing, since their clavichords sometimes really are filled with high tech weapons and alien technology!

Abu Yusef

Earlier, Abu Yusef amused us all with his story about how Layla came to be his only student, the way the women of the town were all atwitter over it. Most of the children had been very curious about the Mayor's keyboard, which apparently made no sounds. No, that was not true. The sounds it made were very small. You had to be close and listening carefully. What was the point in that?

He had caught her listening at the door to his music room, and she had run away frightened that he would tell on her, but he had said nothing. He finally took on several other children as students and was able to include Layla in the group. By the end of the week, only she remained.

Why in the world would you want to teach the child to make those noises?

She is the one who wants to learn, he told them, and she is the one who actually can learn.

Abu Yusef's description of this experience led to a lively discussion of teaching keyboard to very young students and the uses of the clavichord in such teaching and J.S. Bach's *The Little Clavier Book For Wilhelm Friedemann Bach*. The trouble with little fingers. And all the stuff you need to know. Should we talk about bebung or leave that for later?

I love my mental picture of Layla's lessons. She takes her place on the bench in front of the clavichord. The wind that blows through the windows is always very hot in my imagination. Is there glass in the windows? Layla's little fingers. Will she be able to do it? He stands beside her. Her grandmother sits in a corner with her hands folded in her lap. She is as huge and still and present as an Easter Island statue, impossible to ignore. She is keeping a close eye on the proceedings. Layla and Abu Yusef are working on a snippet of Couperin he especially likes and believes is fundamental to technique. Layla looks up at him. She is so serious and determined.

Yes, Sensei, I can do this.

No, that would be Megumi.

No, not her either.

Amelia with her clarinet?

Do you hear the way she is getting it? Abu Yusef asks Layla's grandmother. Do you hear?

Abu Yusef is also an Etruscan archaeologist. He spent many years in Italy before coming home after the Invasion. His Italian is perfect. He is widely read. When it comes to the clavichord, he is an expert on the instrument built from the intarsia of Urbino in Italy. This is a wood carving of an old clavichord. It is so detailed that builders have been able to duplicate the instrument. Abu Yusef has made four such copies. One is in France, one is in New York, one is still in Italy, and the other is in London. He wishes he had kept one of them for himself. Well, someday when things are quieter, he will make another. In the meantime he has a wonderful double fretted instrument (that looks like a crate of rifles when closed). It is the sound of that instrument that captured Layla's imagination and transported her to a world where everything was possible.

The Twangsters

You can't be a supergirl with huge eyes unless you've got a profile. I've figured that much out poking around online trying to figure out what Amelia might have been thinking when she named Megumi

So, here we go.

Name: Megumi
Alias: Pumpkin, snuggle bunny.
Race: Human
Gender: Female
Age: six

Hair: light brown (blinding pink these days)
Eyes: blue (dazzling and always a little sad)
Height: 44 inches (111.760 cm)
Weight: 42 pounds (19.051 kg)
Blood: Type A
Status: Demon hunter, rocket scientist, first grade student (in the fall).
Quote: "Everything is so quiet."

Name: Layla
Alias: Lallie, Princess of the Night.
Race: Human
Gender: Female
Age: six
Hair: brown (ghostly blue these days — you might even say purple)
Eyes: brown (sparkling, dancing, laughing)
Height: We must guess that she might be just a little taller than Megumi.
Weight: And maybe just a little lighter.
Blood: Type B (I'm making this up. I don't want to think about the blood. Why do we always need to know the blood type of our superheroes?)
Status: Crime fighter, ghost.
Quote: "Where will we put them all?"

Storyline: Megumi is sad sitting under her tree. Her whole world has been shattered. She has come to live with her grandfather in his clavichord dojo. There are no children her age in the neighborhood. Instead there are a few good jazz clubs, a gay bar, and a couple of top-notch restaurants (one Vietnamese and the other French). She doesn't really want to learn how to play the clavichord. But what else can her grandfather teach her?

Meanwhile in southern Iraq, Layla, who really does want to learn to play the clavichord, is run down by a truck. She becomes a ghost. She somehow picks up on the clavichord connection between Megumi's grandfather and Abu Yusef, and she materializes and makes friends with Megumi. Megumi's finger work is much improved by her interaction with the talented ghost.

Megumi will cut her hair short and dye it pink, scandalizing her grandfather, and Layla will do hers in a bright but ghostly blue. They will wear cool costumes. Look at them! Zooming around righting wrongs and singing songs (but not too loudly because no one can hear the clavichord if you're belting out the words with too much enthusiasm). Layla and Megumi will be black belts in Megumi's grandfather's dojo of martial clavichord playing. Everyone will be forced to stop shouting and shooting and listen carefully to hear them playing.

Some of the cool stuff in future episodes will include gender confusion, evil aliens, talking animals, and giant robots. We get the idea that after all is said and done and the adventures are over, Layla will move on to wherever little girls go when they die in vehicular mishaps in Iraq, but Megumi who will be the president of Mars or something will never forget her. There is the hint that Megumi's mother Amelia will help Layla find her way by pointing at the light with her soup ladle. We suspect Layla might pop back in from time to time for even wilder adventures or to give Megumi sisterly advice about life.

Little Stars

I move away from the window and sit down at the clavichord and get lost in some tricky parts but not so lost I don't hear Megumi come back in. She comes quietly up to my side. She pulls at my sleeve. She gives me a small pinecone. I pat the bench. She crawls up beside me. I put the pinecone down on the music stand in front of us.

Megumi plays a little tune.

Clunk clank clunk clank clink clink clink.

"Very nice," I tell her, thinking that what she's played might be Bach or it might be Twinkle Twinkle Little Star.

Both are good.

Author's Note for "Over There"

I wrote this story for a project called The Dust Girl *by Benjamin Buch-holz. When I asked him to say a few words about it, he sent me this:*

"The second day of my military service in Iraq I responded to a traffic incident no more than a few hundred meters from the border crossing point for US supplies between Kuwait City and Baghdad. There I found that one of our semis had run over an Iraqi girl of about six years of age, a girl who had been begging for food or water. She had run out into the road to get a water bottle thrown to her from one of the semis. When I arrived her blanketed body lay still in the roadway, with a southbound convoy stalled on one side of her, the soldiers anxious to return to the safety of their base in Kuwait, and a convoy stalled in the northbound lane. Between the two perhaps a hundred Iraqis had gathered, wailing women, relatives, other children, along with British troops, our young American troops, members of the town council, dogs, and even a few goats. The scene troubled me for many months, haunting me. As catharsis, I asked a number of writers to tell the story, to invent it anew from nothing more than details such as those I've provided in this very paragraph. They immersed themselves in the characters and told the tale of this 'Dust Girl' from the perspective of one of those bystanders. While no story can truly capture a death such as this in its randomness, its chaos, its futility, perhaps the fiction preserves bits and pieces of her. It is all we can do."

Human Subjects

A *fter I'd eaten her lamb chops* and mashed potatoes and briefly boiled broccoli, I decided it was time to spill the beans.

"Evangeline," I said. "Everyone is a science project."

She dabbed delicately at the corners of her mouth with her napkin and then looked up at me with startling blue eyes. Whenever Evangeline looks at me, really looks, I'm split into who knows how many pieces, and I become the particle or the wave in the classic double-slit experiment of quantum mechanics.

I had to glance away or lose my train of thought.

She'd served dinner in the kitchen, which meant either she'd soon pour the wine and ask me to spend the night or she'd hold open the front door and lean in for a peck on the cheek as I left. I wanted to delay her decision. Until she picked one, I was both delighted and disappointed at the same time.

"We all have aliens watching us," I said, "studying us, poking and stimulating us, running experiments. I have an alien. You have an alien. Everyone on Earth has an alien."

"Oh, come on," she said. "All of us? Why so many?"

"Well, consider the size of the universe," I said, "and consider what good experimental animals we make. We're in big demand. Actually, there's a shortage of human subjects, which explains our recent population explosion."

"And you know all this exactly how?"

Okay. This was the moment of truth. I could tell her and if she believed me, our relationship might move up to the next level. Or I could tell her and she might not believe me and our relationship would move back down a level. Up or down.

Or I could just laugh it off, but I was pretty sure down that road waited a peck on the cheek. I took a deep and dramatic breath.

Ray Vukcevich

"I know these facts because my alien wants me to know them," I said. "Me knowing exactly what's going on is his project. He tells me how the universe works and then steps back to watch the fireworks. Will I make a hat out of aluminum foil? Will someone throw a butterfly net over me? Maybe I'll end up in a cave on the outskirts of town eating squirrels. Anything might happen, and my alien likes to watch."

"Is he watching now?" she asked.

There was something desperate or frightened or maybe pleading in the quiet way she asked that question and then turned her face down to her plate. I got up and took my chair around the table and put it beside her and sat down and took her hands and said, "Yes, he's right over there by the refrigerator."

She looked at the refrigerator, and then she looked back at me. "I don't see him."

"I think I'm the only one who can see him. Like I said, me seeing him is part of his project. But if you look closely you'll see the tiny ants that are feeding on the invisible slime that drips from his body."

"I've always had ants," she said. "Sometimes I think maybe this house is one big ant colony and I'm living inside it."

"Yes, but these are different," I said. "My alien's slime is intoxicating to ants. Look. Look. See how they stumble away in ragged little conga lines?"

"Yes!" she said. "I do see that. Well, aliens would explain a lot of things around here."

I squeezed her hands. "Not just the ants?"

"No," she said. "Something else."

"Tell me."

"Well, lately," she said. "I've had this unnatural urge to shine my big flashlight out of the kitchen window into the back yard at night."

"Just shine it?" I asked. "Are you looking for something? Do you sweep the landscape?"

I could feel her trembling a little, and there was a thin line of sweat on her upper lip.

"No," she said. "I flick it on and off into the darkness. Off and on. On and off. Sometimes I do it for hours. If you weren't here tonight, I'd be doing it right now."

"What happens when you do it?" I asked.

She looked away from me again. "I get this delicious tingling feeling all over my body."

I didn't know what to say to that. Ours is not to know the science behind the projects our aliens perform on us.

The silence must have gone on too long for her. "Sometimes it lasts for hours," she said.

"Some kind of reinforcement," I said.

"What?"

"Your alien," I said. "He must be conditioning you to shine your big flashlight out the kitchen window at night."

"But why?"

"Let's see if we can figure it out," I said. "Do you just turn the flashlight on and off randomly and then you get the tingling?"

"Funny," she said, "that's the way it worked at first but now I have to be very deliberate in my turning it on and off to get the desired effect."

"Deliberate?"

"That's the best way I can put it," she said. "I turn it on and wait a moment then turn it off and wait and then turn it on again."

"Those moments are of different lengths?"

"Why, yes," she said. "It works a lot better if there are long and short periods of light and darkness."

"Morse code?"

"Hey! Maybe," she said. "I hadn't thought of that. I wonder what I'm saying to whatever's out in the back yard?"

"You don't know Morse code?"

"No. Of course, I don't know Morse code. Who knows Morse code these days?"

"As it happens," I said, "I know Morse code. I did ham radio as a kid."

"Of course, you did," she said.

"Look," I said. "Why don't I go out in the back yard, and you do your flashlight routine, and I see if I can decode the dots and dashes and then tell you what you're saying?"

"I'm not sure I want you to see me like that," she said.

"Like that?"

"Tingly."

Was she saying I'd never seen her all tingly before? I chose to think she didn't mean that. She was talking about her flashlight and her alien and nothing more.

"Don't worry about it," I said. "I'll be outside anyway."

I let go of her hands and stood up.

A moment later, she got up, too. She put her hands on my shoulders and pulled me in for a quick hug, just a squeeze, really. There was a warm and dizzy smell of anticipation radiating from her.

"Okay." She turned away and moved toward the refrigerator. My alien stepped aside for her, but that turned out to be unnecessary, because she was actually heading for the big flashlight on the counter between the kitchen sink and the refrigerator. It was the perfect spot for the flashlight if you wanted it to be always within easy reach of the window over the sink.

She grabbed the flashlight and stood at the sink with her back to me. If I expected some kind of sign that we should begin, she was not the one to provide it. She just waited for me to make the next move.

So I moved to the back door and opened it and stepped out on to the porch, or maybe you'd call it a stoop. It was somewhere in between because while it was covered and you could stand there without getting wet in the rain, it wasn't big enough to lounge around in a lawn chair drinking lemonade.

Evangeline had a generous back yard with a tall wooden fence at the back and five big trees scattered about. Tonight they were hulking shadows, but I already knew they were two apple trees, a pear tree, and a couple of nut trees. I also knew just where the badminton net was, because one night I'd run right into it like a fly into a spider web. A swing made out of a tire hung from one of the nut trees.

I could see the broken trampoline. I remembered when it broke, and Evangeline tumbled off onto the ground and hurt her shoulder. She never did get the trampoline fixed after that. Whenever I mentioned it, she'd say, "And it was such good exercise!" She was permanently spooked when it came to bouncing on a trampoline.

I positioned myself to one side of the trampoline so I would be directly in front of the kitchen window, not so close I'd be blinded by Evangeline's light, but not so far she couldn't hear me if I had things to shout to her.

And there she was peering through the window. I was pretty sure she couldn't see me, but I waved anyway. She just kept peering.

"Go ahead," I shouted. "I'm ready."

She pulled back and then a moment later appeared again with the flashlight. Nothing else happened for a long time. She just stood there pointing the flashlight out at me. I thought maybe she'd forgotten what we were up to, and I was about to shout again when she made her first flash. Just one flash and then nothing. I had no way of knowing if that first one was a dot or a dash until I had others for comparison.

A few moments passed and then there was a series of flashes.

Short short short long.

Dot dot dot dash.

The letter V?

Would she spell my name?

No. She sent the same series again, but this time aimed a little to the left. Short short short long. Then she did it again only aimed a little to the right, and it hit me she was doing the opening notes of Beethoven's fifth symphony.

Ba ba ba Boom!

The oddly named "Fate motive."

She grabbed the theme and ran with it, and I got lost. I couldn't tell if she was sending letters or just playing the music. Horn calls and modulating bridges. A musical statement of purpose I could not interpret. The flashlight beam played all over the back yard in a frenzy pulling the trees and swing and oh look a birdbath in the rock garden from the darkness and then abandoning them. The trampoline. The badminton net with birds (surely not real birds) stuck into it like notes on a staff.

C minor wrestled with C major until one of them came out on top victorious.

It was glorious.

The flashlight flickered out and there was a deep quiet in the darkness.

Then she directed the beam at my face and began sending slowly, as if she were making an extreme effort to communicate with someone who could not keep up with her.

"Evangeline doesn't realize I'm talking to you," she signaled.

It was true she didn't even seem to be paying attention to what was happening out the window. Her eyes were closed and she was swaying slowly from side to side. There was a dreamy smile on her face.

"Who are you?" I shouted.

"Evangeline's alien, of course," she signaled.

But why would Evangeline's alien be talking to me? Did this mean my alien was collaborating? Was there some kind of joint experiment going on with Evangeline and me?

"What do you want?" I shouted.

"I want to know you," Evangeline's alien signaled. "I want you to come clean with me, tell me who you are, spill your guts, tell me what you're feeling."

"I feel watched," I shouted. "Everything I do is being recorded by aliens!"

"No," she signaled. "How do you feel about Evangeline?"

Hey, wait a minute!

I took a few steps closer to get a better look at her. But it was easy to see she was somewhere else. Besides which it was too much to believe that Evangeline had learned Morse code for this occasion. How would she know the evening would progress to this point? No, I knew I could be mistaken, but I was pretty sure I really was talking to her alien. Or at least some alien. I suddenly suspected this could all be a trick of my own alien.

"How would I know how I feel about her?" This question was designed to confuse my alien. I hoped he was flipping through his notes trying to figure out if humans are supposed to be able to know how they feel about one another.

In point of fact, however, maybe I didn't know how I felt. No, that wasn't quite right. I did know how I felt, but I couldn't put it into words.

"Come on," Evangeline's alien signaled. "Quit stalling. Cough it up. Step up to the plate. Blurt it out!"

"This is too much pressure!" I shouted.

"Oh, never mind," she signaled.

The flashlight went dead.

It suddenly hit me that whatever was going on here might have nothing to do with the aliens and their worldwide science projects. I saw clearly that this could be the most important turning point in my life.

"Wait!" I shouted. "I'm crazy about her! She's a symphony, all lightening and thunder and wind, but then she's warm rain and flowers blooming and birds singing! I can't go more than a few minutes without thinking about her, and I can't stop smiling while I'm thinking about her, but then I feel afraid that she'll suddenly snap out of it and come to her senses and realize she doesn't even like me. I'm afraid she'll tell me to just go away."

The flashlight came on again.

Ba ba ba boom!

"Okay," she signaled. "You can come back in."

The Wages of Syntax

1
Brainstorming

S hoot him.
Poison him.

Feed him to the alligators. Tie him up first. Make sure the alligators are really really hungry. Don't feed them for weeks. Wait until they're so hungry you've got to poke them back into their scummy concrete pond with a big stick.

Smother him.

Run over him with your car, and if you get caught, claim it was an accident. Be distraught. Cry real tears. My god, my god.

Burn the house down.

Sneak into his bathroom and toss a radio into his bath water. But everyone takes showers these days. Okay, so you search high and low for the perfect rubber ducky, palm-sized and yellow and so cute he'll carry it around in a small brown paper bag so he can look at it now and then and run his fingers down its rubbery sides and pull down its cute little beak just to watch it flip up again, so cute no one could resist running a tub of water and floating the little guy between his knees and making big waves so the duckster wobbles and bobs up and down like crazy.

So he's smiling and splashing and the rubber ducky is bobbing and riding the waves and you walk in and he says what the hell are you doing here and his blue eyes go wide with fright and you see he hasn't shaved before he got in the tub and you notice that he's getting a spare tire and him not even fifty, disgusting, and you say don't get up! and you plug in the radio and tune in some big band music and then you toss the radio in and fissst! Wait. You might need to put pennies under the fuses before you go in with the radio. Okay, do you take the duck with you after he's dead? Well, it's a pretty neat duck, and you'd hate to be without it, and it could be evidence. Okay, so you take the duck with you being very very careful not to make it squeak as you steal into the night and disappear like a shadow.

Or maybe get the colonel to clobber him in the old mill house with a wrench.

Drop something on him from a tall building. Maybe a safe. Or a piano.

Sabotage his brakes.

Make up a story and get him in trouble with the mob.

Stifle him with gas. Fill a room with nitrogen by letting it boil off from dozens of Thermos bottles. So how do you get him to stay in the room? And how do you get all the Thermos bottles open? And how do you get enough Thermos bottles in the first place? Okay, so you go to this big discount store and you buy up the entire supply of school lunch boxes, telling the sales guy that you're with this lunch for kids program and then you just throw the lunch boxes away, pick a dumpster far far away because it will look like a cartoon massacre, and keep the Thermos bottles.

Now how do you get the liquid nitrogen? Okay, so you cozy up to the guy, no, make that a woman, you cozy up to this chick who runs the liquid nitrogen place and every night you go over there with this big Thermos full of Daiquiris or Rob Roys or whatever it is you discover by asking all her friends that she likes to drink and you spend the evening pouring this favorite drink of hers and after she's feeling no pain you fill the now empty Thermos up with liquid nitrogen and get on out of there only to come back the next night with a fresh Thermos.

So okay, you have all these Thermos bottles filled with liquid nitrogen, and you get a room and seal up all the really gross cracks; it won't have to be absolutely tight, and you artfully arrange the bottles around the room, and you send him an invitation that says come experience the interactive art of this really famous artist whose name you can look up later and when he gets there, he reads the instructions that tell him he's going on a journey around the room and that at each landmark he is to open one of the Thermos bottles and then move on to the next one following the lines you've drawn on the floor, and the lines go round and round and that's what he thinks is making him dizzy and at the very end you have this painting by the famous artist whose name you will look up later and the final note which says sit right down here in this chair provided for that purpose and contemplate this famous painting and he does and he gets lost in the painting thinking that explains his wooziness and that as they say is that.

Toss him a grenade, and yell, hey catch!

Hit him behind the left ear with a blunt object.

Strangle him.

Mail him an exploding cigar. But he doesn't smoke! So you hang out in front of the hospital and you have these cigars and he's walking down the street and you run up to him and shout it's a boy! and hand him a cigar and he puts it in his mouth and you light it and shout gotta run! and run and when you get around the corner you slow down and look casual, act cool, as the explosion rocks and rolls the sidewalk and the buildings around you.

Sneak up behind him and garrote him.

The guillotine.

A staple gun.

A cross bow.

A blowgun.

An ax.

A chain saw.

A rattlesnake.

Booby traps.

Ninja stars.

2
Spontaneous Competence

Henry Wolfe stopped joking with his classes that he couldn't be killed until he learned Italian the day it hit him that someone might really be trying to do him in. On the way to class one day last week, just outside his office on the steps in the stairwell he always took down to the ground floor — he never used the elevator in Building 17 — there had been a roller skate placed where he would be sure to step on it. Whoever had put it there must have watched the way he walked to the left so he could lightly touch the handrail. He'd been doing that since his sight began to noticeably deteriorate due to macular degeneration, and him only in his forties — it was like the universe had it in for his eyes. He hadn't told anyone he couldn't see much these days. He didn't want people to start thinking of him as the blind guy.

It had been a close call. Just before he put his foot down on the skate, he remembered that he had forgotten a book in his office, and he had turned back, but then he'd decided it didn't matter, and he'd turned again to go on down, and all that turning had positioned him more toward the center of the stairs. His foot came down beside the skate instead of on top of it. He bumped the skate with his foot and leaned down and picked it up. He sat down on the stairs and turned the skate over and over in his hands. He moved it in close to his face and then held it at arm's length trying to see it clearly. Where would anyone get a roller skate these days anyway? Didn't skaters use roller blades? Had he somehow offended the curator of a museum? Maybe the skate wasn't for him. Everything didn't have to be about him. He took the skate downstairs and dropped it off at the lost and found table in the Cognitive Science office.

Today Henry would be talking to his undergrads. He would simplify, but he wouldn't talk down to them. He wanted them to get the general idea and maybe see some of the wonder and mystery of language and the new wrinkle he had discovered.

These days, his glasses were mostly useless. The world was wavy, like looking through cheap glass or maybe like living underwater, and he counted on auditory cues to gauge how what he was saying was being received. He couldn't really see his audience.

He had a line guaranteed to make them groan, and he was going to use it right away. He said, "It's really all very simple."

They groaned, and he grinned and wrote "Spontaneous Competence" on the chalkboard. With an audience like this, he needed something jazzier, something contemporary, something they could relate to, and since no one in the popular press was calling his effect "Spontaneous Competence" as it should rightly be called, he wrote what they actually were calling it underneath the proper name. He wrote "Universal Translation."

He could hear them relax, a kind of good-natured settling in. This was more like it. Who knew, maybe the professor would even talk about aliens.

"First, I must convince you that the so called 'universal translation' you see on TV and in the movies is impossible in principle."

And a one and a two and a three.

"And then I will explain how it can be done."

He turned his head to the left and then to the right so they would think he was looking at them. They won't listen to you if they think you're not paying attention to them. But what was that? There in the sea of faces was a startling splotch of orange and peach and blond. The rest of the people were filmed in black and white in comparison. He squinted at the bright spot of color, and it smiled at him, and he was suddenly sure that Sydney Pavlenko had slipped into his class. After all these years. That couldn't be right. He was pausing too long. He was staring at a stranger, and she was probably squirming in her seat.

Henry realized that he had lost his place, and he experienced a moment of absolute terror. When he'd been new to the teaching game, he'd had a recurring dream in which he'd come to class unprepared and had to stand up in front of all those people with nothing to say. In the dream, he was often dressed in nothing but his underwear.

But he wasn't new, and he wasn't really lost, and it was incredibly unlikely that the lost love of his life was sitting in on his undergrad course.

"A language is not a code," he said. "You can't just figure it out in isolation. When speaking to someone who doesn't know your language, it won't do you any good to talk louder or more slowly. If you're the language officer on a starship, trying really really hard to understand a language that is totally new won't actually help much." He waited for the laugh and when it came he thought it was merely polite. Maybe he should update his references. Or get cooler ones. Nick Sherwood probably had cool references. Maybe he should ask Nick for a few tips — like that was ever going to happen. Nick would be too busy telling anyone who would listen that Henry was crazy.

"We saw how this works with the Navajo Code Talkers of World War II. The United States used native speakers of the Navajo language to radio information to the field. The enemy could never break this code, because it wasn't a code."

He gave them a moment to think about languages and codes.

"Now, imagine you and your ground team land on a strange new planet and a bunch of aliens run jabbering out of the bushes, and your language officer pulls out her trusty Universal Translation Device and starts twisting the knobs and pushing the buttons, and suddenly everyone can understand every word these guys are saying even though no human has ever met them before. In fact, let's say no human has

ever even met other aliens who have met these new guys before. Just
how do you suppose this Universal Translation Device could possibly
work?"

The silence stretched out uncomfortably. They had no idea.

No, wait. The woman in orange and peach had her hand up.

"Yes?" he said in her direction.

"Computers?" she said, and he knew it was Sydney. Teasing him.
She wouldn't know he couldn't actually see her.

"Doctor Pavlenko is having her little joke," he said. "Pulling our
legs. Can anyone tell me why this popular answer is no answer at
all?"

"Who's Doctor Pavlenko?" someone asked, and he told them she
was a well-known linguist visiting from Italy. She had studied with
Umberto Eco. Most of them seemed to know who Eco was, and that
made Henry happy and being happy reminded him of happy times,
but he didn't tell them about Sydney's two perfectly matched moles
and the way you could, if you were young and in love and there was a
magic marker on the bedside table, draw a smile under those two spots
to form a happy face that would make her yelp and jump out of bed and
twist around trying to see what you'd drawn on her bottom.

He asked her to stand up, but she wouldn't do it, and he worried
that maybe that wasn't her after all. He let that go and asked again for
reasons why "Computers" wasn't an answer to his earlier question and
someone else said, "But computers already do translation. You can
push a button on your cell phone and talk to people in another language
now."

"And how do you suppose that works?" Henry asked.

It didn't take them long to conclude that there must be an electronic
dictionary and a set of electronic grammar rules for both the language
you were speaking and the one the your listener was hearing.

"So, the device must know both languages," he said. "What happens in the case of our aliens where our device has no way of knowing
the new language? Could it do an instant translation if the language
officer twisted the knobs and pushed the buttons just right?"

No. They conceded that since there could be no dictionary and no
grammar rules, the device could not translate the alien language.

"What would have to happen?" Henry asked.

Someone got it.

"The device would have to learn the alien language!"

"Exactly right," Henry said. "And that would take time. The device would need to interact with native speakers. You'd need someone to hold up a banana and say the word in the new language, and so on. I suppose one way computers might help you is if you sent one ahead to the planet, and it was smart enough to interview aliens, and you gave it enough time to gather the lexicon and grammar, it might be able to help you by the time you got there."

"Or maybe," a guy over to the left said, "you could drop off a thousand computers or a million and they all could learn just one little piece from just one alien and radio it all back to a central computer…"

"You must be a computer science major," Henry said and got a laugh. "Yes, that might work. But what about instant translation? That's what we're talking about here today. Can you see any way that could be done?"

They couldn't.

"Okay," he said. "As promised, I will now tell you how it can be done. Let me show you a picture of the device we'll be using."

He pulled down a white screen over the chalkboard, flipped on his laptop, and projected a picture of a human brain onto the screen.

"You probably already have one of these," he said. "It's a quantum device."

He circled a place on the brain. "This is Wernicke's Area," he said. He drew another circle. "And this is Broca's Area." He marked one more place. "And here is an area I'm calling Wolfe's Point. Why am I calling it that? Because I can. Who wouldn't jump at the chance to have a body part named after him?"

He turned off the brain picture and moved the screen up again. Then he said, "Simply stated the discovery is this. We have found a way to stimulate Wolfe's Point in certain people in such a way that if the person is put in a position where making a translation is extremely important, if there is a precipitating event, that person's brain looks ahead to a time when they actually do speak the language and makes the translation."

While they were thinking about it, he wrote "precipitating event" on the chalkboard.

"Now it turns out this works because our brains are already time traveling all the time," he said. "We do it in the ordinary parsing of language. We just don't go as far as the people who experience spontaneous competence in an unknown language. Instead our brains make very tiny jumps ahead in time when we do 'word sense disambiguation.'"

Before they could panic, he explained the problem of the brain figuring out quickly what a word meant. There were usually several possible meanings, and in order to parse and make sense of a sentence, the listener needed to choose the appropriate meaning. But often the appropriate meaning could not be determined until the words later on in the sentence were known. The listener should be constantly backtracking, and the whole process should be jerky, but that was not the case.

"Instead," Henry said. "It is now known the quantum device that is the human brain looks ahead a little ways into the future and sees what the words later in the sentence are in order to decide on the meanings of the word currently being heard and understood."

He paused and listened, but he heard no grumbling, and they weren't throwing rotten fruit, so he figured he was okay. "What we've found is that a one-time electrical stimulation of Wolfe's Point in some people allows the brain to look much farther ahead in time. In fact, we don't know if there are limits to how far ahead such brains can look. We do know there needs to be an event or need to trigger the translation. That is, such people cannot just do it. From a subjective point of view, it feels like it just happens. Questions?"

Sydney again. He scanned around for other hands, but they would be waiting to see what the other professor had to say before asking their own questions. He nodded in her direction.

"Can you do it?"

You know I can, he didn't say. He said, "Yes. You might think that like any good mad scientist, I experimented on myself first, but that is not the case. We had a group of around ten volunteers all demonstrating the effect before I decided to see what it was like."

That was not entirely true. He didn't know how to tell them that he had experienced spontaneous competence once before the deliberate stimulation of his brain had occurred. It would sound very unscientific. He was not sure he believed it himself. He wondered if Sydney remembered the incident. It had changed his life. The research proceeded in a straight line to success after that day. How different things might have been if she had stayed.

Another hand. "Let me get this straight," a young man said. "The hypothetical aliens run out of the bushes and start talking and you can instantly understand them because your brain has looked ahead to a time where you know how to speak the alien language?"

"That's right," Henry said.

"But how do you know how to speak the language in the future?"

"Why, you have to learn it," Henry said. "You have to sit down with the books and tapes or the alien informants and learn the language in the old-fashioned way so you will know it when your brain in the past looks ahead to do the translation."

"But what if something happens to you?"

Hey, this guy was pretty smart, Henry thought. He wished he could see him so he could remember to talk to him, maybe suggest grad school. Oh well, he could ask around and find out who it was. "What do you mean?" Henry asked to keep him talking.

"Well, what would happen if you died before you learned the language?"

Ah, there it was after all. He might as well have started out telling them he couldn't be killed until he learned Italian. He couldn't tell them that now, not about the Italian anyway, not with Sydney in the crowd, and it had to be her, it just had to be. "If I'm right about how it works, what do you think that means in regard to your question?"

There was a burst of chatter as they all talked it over with their neighbors. Then someone said suddenly and loudly, "It means you can't be killed until you learn the language!"

"Bingo," Henry said.

What a good stopping point. He wouldn't be able to see his watch without making it painfully obvious how poor his sight was, but long experience told him he was close enough to the end of the hour to call it quits there.

"So, think about that," he said, "and we'll pick it up there next time."

He lost sight of the woman in the bright colors as the students gathered their stuff and got up and left the lecture room through several exits. They moved past him like a noisy river.

Henry tried to not be too obvious about it as he peered around for Sydney. What was she doing back in the States? How long was she staying? Did he have the courage to ask her out to dinner? Students were still moving past him, and he didn't see her. Maybe it had not been her in the first place. She had, after all, only spoken a few words.

But then there she was, very close, right there in fact, smiling, holding out her arms. He took her hands and she leaned in and kissed him on the cheek. "Hello, Henry," she said.

There were wavy lines across her underwater face, but she looked wonderful.

"Sydney," he said. "When did you get back? What are you doing here?"

"Later," she said. "I've got to run. I'll call you."

Then she was gone.

He gathered up his papers quickly so he could follow and see which way she went. On top of his notes was a puzzling object. He picked it up. It was a little yellow rubber duck — maybe three inches long and not quite that tall. It had an orange beak and black eyelashes. What was she trying to tell him? He stuffed his notes into his briefcase. He dropped the duck into his shirt pocket. It was pretty cute. He hurried out after Sydney.

When he got outside he saw her getting into a car. The car made a wide turn and came very close. The driver gave him a honk and a wave. Nick Sherwood.

3
Italy

Henry dreams of their last night together and the incident that launched his career.

The two of them.

Maybe they've just had dinner. Maybe they're having coffee now. Brandy. Mints. The moon. Summer breeze off the river. He's trying to talk her into not going home to Italy.

She tells him why she must leave.

Please, please, please don't leave me, Sydney.

"But you told me you couldn't speak Italian," she says.

"I don't speak Italian."

"So what do you think it is we're speaking?"

"English," he says, "of course, we're speaking English."

"No," she says, "it's just that when this is written down, the words will be translated into English. In truth, we're speaking Italian."

"My mother!" he mutters, shaking his head in wonder at what's just happened to him, but then he wakes up to an empty bed and remembers he let her go home alone years and years ago.

But now she's back.

4
Duck

The duck was all about power and death. You send in the girl with the symbol of death. It says a lot that you could make her do it. It makes a statement. She's home, and she's with you now. Henry probably wouldn't get it. I didn't really expect the duck to end up in the tub.

My beef with Henry Wolfe boiled down to this. If the universe worked the way Henry said it worked, then the universe was goofy, and I could not abide a goofy universe. On the other hand, Henry's death before he could learn Italian would prove time travel was not involved in his so-called "Spontaneous Competence" effect.

To date my campaign had not been a huge success, but a couple of failed attempts on his life did not prove Henry could not be killed. It would take only one successful attempt to prove my proposition. The tire pressure thing hadn't worked, but that had been a half-hearted attempt anyway. I had not fully committed to the program at that point. I'd been just noodling around. Likewise the spiders in his house. The skate in the stairwell hadn't worked either. Part of the problem was that the death needed to look like an accident. There are always constraints on your methods.

The time had come to drop something on Henry's head. Something hard and heavy. Something specific.

My office was just down the hall and around the corner from Henry's office on the third floor of Building 17, but I was on the wrong side of the tracks in the Cognitive Science Department. Since this was Oregon, everyone politely pretended that Henry and his team were not more important than the rest of us, but all the action was up in his neighborhood these days. That didn't mean those of us down here doing grammar and such were totally ignored. Students came and went. Guys with packages. There would be enough traffic that I would need to be careful in my campaign to rain down something lethal on Henry.

I had been observing Henry closely for weeks. I had created tables and drawn charts and then calculated the probabilities of him being at any given location at any given time. Ask me where Henry Wolfe would be at say two o'clock this afternoon, and I could tell you and be right most of the time. Hey, maybe part of my brain was looking ahead in time with a special talent for knowing where people would be! The Sherwood Effect for finding the trees in the forest. No, forget it. What a joke. Don't even think about it.

My plan was to get into a disguise and then make my way up to the fourth floor. I knew of no safes or pianos in Building 17. There were lots of metal filing cabinets, but it would be hard to argue that one of those falling out of a window and hitting Henry on the head was an accident. What I did have going for me was Professor Meiko Kawa and her bonsai trees. She had a whole forest of them growing in pots on the fire escape above and a little to the left of the door Henry would be stepping out of at a particular time. He always paused to look around like he was afraid someone might have taken out the sidewalk or something while he was up in his office.

Hey, taking out the sidewalk and digging a deep pit might be a good idea.

No need. I would bean him with a bonsai. A specific bonsai in a cast iron pot. It looked like a little oak tree, but what do I know about trees?

Not many men in Oregon wear ties. It's another one of the things, like the rain, the rain, the rain that drives me nuts about the place. I should have held out for Hawaii or Arizona, but as a new PhD way back when in a field that was not hugely popular, I thought I was lucky to get what I got, and maybe I'd been right. Life here had been pretty good even if dimly lighted. I had those full spectrum sunlamps in my condo and in my office, and they helped some. But it wasn't the rain so much as the ties that concerned me the day I would drop a potted tree on Henry Wolfe. The general lack of ties would make disguising myself easier. I'm the kind of guy who always wears a tie in public, not just for weddings and funerals like most people here. I usually wear a jacket, too, although I've been known to take it off and sling it over my shoulder in a gesture meant to put people at ease. I shave all of my face, and I get a haircut every two weeks. You don't have to look like you live in the woods just because you do.

From my box of stuff gathered for the job at hand, I pulled an oval mirror, three feet tall and a couple of feet wide. I set it aside and took out a hammer and nail and drove the nail into the wall between the bookshelf and the window and then hung the mirror up. I took a long look at myself. Yes, there I was. Next I loosened my tie and then with a flourish jerked it from around my neck, and my image changed before my very eyes. That was not the Nick Sherwood everyone knew!

Well, it still kind of looked like Dr. Sherwood. You could imagine ringing his bell at three in the morning, buzzing, banging on the door until the porch light comes on and he opens the door and you look him up and down and notice how different he looks without his tie.

The difference was not great enough. I would need another layer or two of disguise and misdirection. Sometimes I think it would be good to be invisible like so many of my colleagues are invisible, but I am not invisible. People notice me. Students are all the time raising a hand in greeting, saying, "Morning, Doctor Sherwood."

"Hiya Nick!"

"Yo Nickster!"

"Hey, Nick nack how's it paddy-wacking?"

Actually, no one ever says any of those more informal things, but you can see they're thinking them, the way the corners of the mouth quiver as they struggle to maintain the proper student/teacher distance. I can always feel eyes on me as I move down the halls and up and down the stairs.

Just taking off my tie wasn't going to do it. I'd considered a false beard and mustache, but I didn't really know how to apply them, and if a disguise looked fake, it would be worse than useless. Instead I found a baseball cap with no logo. I attached a long ponytail to the back of it. I had constructed the ponytail from a cheap wig I bought at a department store from a woman who thought I was some kind of drag queen, maybe a new drag queen buying his first wig. I let her think that. Who cared? She was very helpful.

No tie. The baseball cap and the ponytail, and finally a pair of sunglasses. Perfect.

If anyone noticed me at all, they certainly would not connect me to Professor Nick Sherwood, the world famous grammarian. Just some guy, they'd say. You see guys like that all over campus.

I checked my watch. It was time to make my way up to the fourth floor. I picked up a paper bag with the stuff I would need and opened my office door. I looked down the hall in both directions and then slipped out and locked the door. I didn't pass anyone on my way to the stairwell. As I climbed the stairs Wagner's tune about the Valkyries, also known as "kill the wabbit," reverberated in my skull.

There was a woman way down the hall on the fourth floor but

she was looking the other way. I hurried down to the alcove outside Meiko's fire escape garden. No one saw me. So far the disguise had been totally useless, but better safe than sorry.

There was a small arrangement of furniture in the alcove. It was meant to be a place where students could sit and read while waiting to see one of the professors or graduate assistants who had offices on this floor. The arrangement probably followed the rules of Feng Shui but since I knew nothing of those rules, I couldn't be sure. I did know that one big stuffed chair would serve nicely as a blind I could hide behind while working my plan to drop a pot on Henry's head.

I put my paper bag of stuff down behind the chair and then walked quickly down the hall to the janitor's closet. I have had a master key to Building 17 for many years. I got it when I was on the committee that interfaced with Facility Services. I had a copy made and then gave the original back when it was time to do so. Having keys was good. I had one to Henry's house, too, but if today's project was successful, I wouldn't need it.

Unless I bought the house. It was a pretty cool place, and it would soon be up for sale.

From the janitor's closet I selected a push broom and a squeegee with a handle around the same length as the broom. I quickly closed and locked the door and hurried back to Meiko's alcove.

I got down behind the chair and opened my bag of stuff. I took out a rectangular shaving mirror and a roll of duct tape. I taped the mirror to the right angle the squeegee made with its handle. I would poke this out of the window and through the pots until I could look down at the door and see when Henry came out. Then I would nudge the pot in question off the edge with the push broom. Once the pot landed on Henry's head, I would pull back my devices, rip the mirror off the squeegee, and quickly return the broom and squeegee to the closet. I would continue down the hall and take a different set of stairs back to the third floor. If the coast was clear, I'd slip back into my office. Otherwise, I would continue on and take yet another stairway down to the ground and just drive home where I would hear the news of Henry Wolfe's untimely death on the radio.

I eased the window open and poked the mirror out over the edge. The angle was odd, but I could see the door. I glanced at my watch. Any time now. I moved the broom into position. The tree in question needed to be right on the edge, so I pushed. It wasn't moving. Surely it couldn't be that heavy. I pushed harder. The pot tipped a little and I quickly pulled back. Maybe it was just stuck to the fire escape by stuff running out the hole in the bottom. Didn't all flowerpots have holes in the bottom? Henry would be stepping out of the door soon. I would miss my chance. I pushed harder with the broom and the pot moved suddenly right up to the edge and tipped, and I sucked in my breath. I may have made a sound, too. The pot settled back and didn't fall over the side. I quickly looked around the chair to see if a crowd had gathered to see what the ponytail guy was doing crouched behind the chair in the bonsai alcove, but there was no one there.

And when I looked back into the mirror there was Henry, already outside, already peering around like he was looking through a thick fog. (I actually couldn't see him peering from the fourth floor but I knew from previous observations that he was peering and that at any moment he would step away and be out of the kill zone.)

I gave the bonsai in the cast iron pot a good shove with the push broom.

Bombs away.

But what was this? Even as the pot went over the edge, Henry snapped open his umbrella. Couldn't the fool see it wasn't raining? Since it was usually raining, was he acting out of habit? But, no, he did not ordinarily open his umbrella when it wasn't raining. Just as the pot hit the umbrella, I could see Henry's left leg move out as he stepped away.

The pot ripped through the umbrella, and Henry jumped forward with a yelp.

I had missed. Henry's umbrella had deflected the pot just enough to miss him. I pulled the mirror and the broom back inside and quickly closed the window.

It wasn't like there was a dead professor of Cognitive Science sprawled outside the northwest entrance of Building 17, but people might still be running in this direction to see how one of Professor Meiko Kawa's pots could have fallen from the fire escape. I should get moving. I would be a sitting duck disguised and crouched behind a chair clutching the tools of my crime.

I had a horrible moment of doubt. What if Henry were right?

Impossible!

I am not the coyote.

Shut up. Just shut up.

5
Funeral

I should not have let Nick bully me into delivering the duck. I wanted no part of whatever was going on between those two. I didn't know what the duck could possibly mean, and I had no interest in knowing. I just put it down on top of Henry's notes and let it go at that. It was none of my business.

Henry hadn't changed much over the years. He looked older, but I could still see a lot of the boy scientist in him in spite of the silly gray beard and wild hair.

I wondered what life would have been like if we had not been so adult when we were young, if he had said to hell with the fellowship in Pennsylvania, I'm coming to Italy with you, or if I had told him I really didn't need to go home just then; there were programs I could apply for in the States. If we had not promised to write.

Silly thoughts. Who knew what he had grown up to be? And for every good thing Henry and I might have had together, I would have to give up something I had now — like Luisa, my wonderful daughter, who I did not see enough of these days since she moved in with her father in London so she could study economics, of all things. I was so proud of her. You can't have everything. You really can't.

My mother had named me after the city in Australia not because she was Australian but because she was an American married to a Russian who had emigrated to Italy and lots of people back home in Orange County were naming their babies things like that in those days. My mother had never been truly happy in Italy and as soon as my father died, she moved back to California.

Now, I had come to bury her, too.

It had been a spectacular service. My mother had made many friends since she returned. I hadn't realized. There were relatives I had not met, too. They were all very polite. Whenever I spoke, people smiled. I think it was my accent.

We gathered at the house of my mother's friend, Alice, afterwards. The food was piled high and strange. There were two wiggly green hemispheres like a soccer ball cut in half or maybe alien boobs. It turned out to be green Jell-O with shaved carrots. I wondered if that was one of my mother's favorite dishes. She had never made such a thing in Italy. Soon the sober mood had lifted, and if you didn't know why these friends had gotten together, you would not have guessed it was to say goodbye to my mother. Until someone made a toast, that is. There were many toasts.

My mother's friends made me think of my own American friends. I had planned to fly home the day after the funeral, but I didn't really have to. I was already on the west coast. I could fly up to Oregon. Henry and Nick were both at the same school. I couldn't imagine how that had happened. It might be interesting to see the boys again. I still thought of them as the boys, as in boys will be boys.

So, I just flew up there. No one answered the phone in Henry's office, so I asked for Nick's number and he answered and picked me up at the airport and took me to a hamburger place where I learned the two of them were still playing games I could not comprehend. He looked around and then winked and poured me an alcoholic drink he called a "Rob Roy" from a Scooby Doo Thermos bottle.

Give Henry the duck, Sydney. Please? It'll be fun.

It wasn't fun. I just put it down. Henry didn't even look at it.

Nick didn't ask me why I was in the country, and I didn't feel like telling him about my mother. We had never been that close. It was easy to see by the way he looked at me that our not being that close did not please him. On the flight up, I was thinking that if Henry didn't work out, I might be open to getting a little closer to Nick Sherwood, but now I remembered everything about him that had convinced me not to get close to him in the old days. He hadn't changed much. He talked and he talked and he never heard a word you said in return. A few minutes with him and you were exhausted. He did tell me where Henry was, and I made him drop me off on campus.

Henry seemed so distant after class. It was like he was looking at me but not seeing me. Maybe he was looking into the past and seeing the girl I had been. Or maybe he didn't want to see me at all. Suddenly I didn't feel like speaking to him. Who was this man anyway? It had sounded like fun coming up here to see an old boyfriend I hardly remembered, but now I was having second thoughts. Maybe I panicked. I put the duck down and left.

And there was Nick again. I got in his car, and he drove me to my hotel. I called the airport and booked a flight home the next day. Then I spent the afternoon watching television. It was incomprehensible.

When I could not take a minute more, I took a cab back to campus to find Henry. We could at least have dinner or something.

The woman in the Cognitive Science office told me he'd gone home. Something about a pot falling out of a window. Had he been hurt? No one thought so. Can you give me his address?

Well, I don't know . . . .

Oh, come on, I'm Sydney Pavlenko. From Italy? You know, I teach linguistics in Rome? We're old friends?

And now here I was. I had let the taxi drive off. The house was brown; cedar siding, I guessed. There were two floors. Shaggy trees. The grounds were not exactly neglected, but they had the look of a place where the owner hired someone to clip and mow just often enough so the villagers didn't surround the place with torches and pitchforks. Henry Wolfe the mad scientist. It made me smile.

I rang the doorbell.

6
Aliens

What was she trying to tell him with the little yellow duck? She pops back into his life after all those years, gives him a bathtub toy, and leaves again? Clean up your act? Or maybe it was a pun. Maybe she was psychic and telling him to watch out for the bonsai.

"Duck, Henry!"

He had been shaken by the near miss. He had looked back up the side of the building but could see no more than a blur of the fire escape on the fourth floor. The pot had broken into a few pieces but hadn't shattered.

He nudged the pieces with his toe. He knew he should report the accident to campus security, but he didn't feel like taking the time and trouble. If there had been witnesses, they weren't showing themselves.

He just wanted to go home. He had another class. He didn't think he could face it. He dug into his briefcase and got his cell phone and called the Cog Sci office and told them about the falling pot. Someone should go up and make sure Meiko's other trees were all well back from the edge.

He took the bus home.

The next time he took his driving test, they would take away his license and it would probably be a good thing, too. He'd been taking the bus to work for days now, and it wasn't so bad. Low tire pressure had convinced him he should do that. He hadn't even noticed that all of his tires were almost flat. A woman had gotten out of her car at a stoplight and walked up to his window to ask if he realized all of his tires were dangerously low. Her face had been blurry. He'd gotten the tires pumped up and had parked the car in his driveway and hadn't driven since.

He did believe that he was on the right track with his explanation for spontaneous competence, and he did think it therefore followed that he wouldn't die until he learned all the languages he had translated, but that was not the part of the process that interested him. Henry didn't spend much time worrying about death. Subjectively speaking, time began sometime after he was born and would end when he died. Whatever happened between the two points was all there was. He was happy to admit, and would say as much to his undergrad class next time they met, that there were other possibilities. He would tell them to consider the many worlds theory. What if the translator looks ahead into a different universe with a different future from the one she might end up experiencing? He suspected that was not the case, but he liked to tell his students he could, of course, be wrong. Science was all about admitting you could be wrong.

He had learned French, and he had spent a sabbatical year in Australia with the Gaalpu clan learning Yolngu. He had meant to spend only a few weeks learning about didgeridoos from the master Djalu Gurruwiwi, but there had been a precipitating event — flames and people running and a trapped child and the burning need to say something. He had never learned Italian, but not because he thought his ignorance would protect him from death. He had not yet learned Italian because he had never given up the idea that someday Sydney would teach him to speak the language, maybe while feeding him strawberries in a gondola.

When he got home, he took the duck into his office so he could look at it under strong magnification. It was possible she had written a message somewhere on it in very small letters. He flipped on the computer, and the screen was projected onto a wall he had painted white. This was the secret that allowed him to continue his work without help. He could read perfectly well if the letters were a foot tall. He sat down at his desk facing the white wall and moused over to his email. Nothing that couldn't wait.

He pulled down a magnifier and flipped on its light and carefully examined the duck. No messages.

Was it something from their past? Was he supposed to remember the night something romantic happened having to do with ducks? If that was it, he didn't get it. Maybe the message was I've missed you missed you missed you and I've been thinking about you every day of every year we've been apart so meet me . . . meet me . . . down at the duck pond?

Someone rang his doorbell.

When he opened the door, she was there, blurry but smiling, and she smelled wonderful.

"Sydney," he said.

"You're busy," she said.

"What?"

Then he realized she was looking at the duck in his hand. He grinned and shrugged and put it in his shirt pocket and stepped aside. "Come in," he said.

She walked past him into the house and down a short hall that opened into the big room which was most of the ground floor. There was a wall of windows overlooking the largely undeveloped forest on the south side of the city hills.

"Nice place," she said. "Lots of wood."

"Can I get you a drink?"

"Not now," she said and turned to him and put one hand on his chest and leaned up and kissed him. "Come with me," she said and took his hand.

"Where?" he asked.

"Upstairs?"

They made love, a little desperately at first, but then they settled into one another, and it was like the old days. Well, maybe not so acrobatic, but good. He could almost believe no time had passed between those old happy days and today.

"I want to take a bath," she said.

"Can I join you in the shower?"

"Not a shower," she said. "A bath."

"Can I watch?"

She got out of bed and walked into the bathroom without answering him. A moment later the water came on.

Henry remained propped up on his pillows listening to her fill the tub. She was softly singing a tune he didn't know, words he couldn't quite hear, Italian probably. If he were closer would he do a translation? Did this situation count as a precipitating event? Did he have a need to know? Or something important to say?

He got up and walked toward the bathroom. Along the way, he stepped on his shirt, and something squeaked. The duck. He bent down and picked it up and carried it with him into the bathroom. It hit him that this bath, right here in his house, might have been the reason she gave him the duck in the first place.

She was already stretched out in the tub when he came in.

"I hope you're not suggesting a threesome," she said.

"What?"

"The duck."

"Sure I am," he said, "you, me, and the duckster." He gave it a squeak and dropped it into the water in front of her.

"Okay, get in," she said. She pulled up her knees.

He got in. There wasn't much room. "We need to be sitting the other way." He stood up.

"Oh, so you want the pipes to be poking me in the back?"

"No," he said and stepped out and then back in behind her. "Scoot up just a little."

He lowered himself into the water behind her, and she snuggled back against him. He reached around her and caressed down her breasts and stomach, and the duck bobbed and rode the waves between her knees.

There was a noise downstairs.

Burglars, bears, the cleaning woman, squirrels, ghosts?

Henry couldn't decide if he should get up and go look, and in the end, he waited too long. The bathroom door banged open, and Nick Sherwood came in holding a handgun out in front of himself like a cop in a crack house.

"How did you get in here?" Henry shouted, then thought that was a pretty stupid thing to shout at a man with a gun, but this was goofy Nick Sherwood for crying out loud. It had to be some kind of sick joke.

"I've got a key," Nick said.

Henry couldn't see the expression on Nick's face clearly, but from the way Nick kept moving the gun around and getting taller and then shorter, like he was maybe standing up on his toes, Henry concluded Nick was trying to get a clear shot that wouldn't hit Sydney.

"You gave him a key to your house?" she asked.

"I did not give him a key to my house," Henry said.

"You look wild and disheveled, Nick," Sydney said. "Doesn't he look wild and disheveled, Henry?"

"I don't know. I mean, sure, he does. Wild and disheveled."

"I should have known you'd jump in bed with him the first chance you got," Nick said.

"What business is that of yours?" she asked.

"How can you ask me that, Sydney? After all we've meant to one another. I've never given up on us."

"What us?" she said. "It's all in your head, Nick. Think about it. I'm pretty sure we've never even shaken hands."

Nick closed the lid of the toilet and sat down. "Your argument is compelling," he said.

They sat like that for a moment, no one speaking, Nick looking at his hand or the gun in his hand, Henry holding Sydney tight, the duck riding the ripples between her knees. He could feel her trembling a little.

"This isn't about you anyway, Sydney." Nick stood up. "I didn't expect you to be here. It's too bad you got caught up in the middle of this."

"So what is this all about then, Nick?" Henry asked.

"Well, here we are," Nick said. "I should have brought a radio."

"There's a radio over by the clothes hamper," Henry said. Why was he being helpful? Nick had clearly gone crazy. Crazy for love? Had the man been so smitten with Sydney all these years that he'd finally snapped when she came back to Henry?

Nick laughed. "Of course, there would be!" He backed away toward the radio. He kept the gun on them like he thought maybe they'd leap up and overpower him. He grabbed the radio and walked back toward the tub but was soon pulled up short. "The cord's not long enough."

"Long enough for what?" Sydney asked.

Nick put the radio back down and turned it on. Flute music. Handel, Henry thought. Nick turned the radio off.

"Such coincidences have been noise in the data," Nick said. "I lower your tire pressure, you quit driving. I don't know what happened to the spiders I released in your house. I put a skate on the stairs, you don't step on it. I put poison in your soup, you eat a sandwich and decide you're too full for soup. I drop a little tree on you, you step away just in time. You're in the bath, I want to throw a radio in with you, the cord isn't long enough. You add all of this up, and what do you get? Noise."

"I think I see where you're going with this Nick," Henry said. "You've been trying to kill me!"

"Over me?" Sydney asked.

"This is not about you," Nick said. "This is a dispute over a point of scientific theory."

"Actually, you may be right, Sydney," Henry said. "Maybe this is just a fight over a girl."

"A girl?" Sydney tried to twist around and look at him but he didn't let her go, and she settled back. "The water is getting cold," she said.

"That's not it," Nick said. "When I shoot you, it will prove once and for all that the universe cannot be preprogrammed as your theory would have us believe. I am the wild card, the monkey wrench."

"Yeah, you're a mover and a shaker, Nick," Henry said. "The Indiana Jones of the grammar world. "

"Make all of the jokes you like," Nick said.

"Sit down and think about it," Henry said.

"Don't tell me what to do," Nick said.

"Oh, sit down, Nick," Sydney said. "Why do you think Henry's discovery of universal translation has happened now?"

"Actually that's not what I call it," Henry said.

Nick sat back down on the toilet. "Okay. So, tell me, why now?"

"Clearly," she said, "it's in preparation for first contact. Obviously, we are about to discover that we are not alone in the universe, and someone will have to be able to talk to them."

Henry and Nick had nothing to say about that. Sydney plucked the duck out of the water and gave it a couple of squeaks. After another moment of silence, she squeaked the duck again.

"Imagine for a moment I'm right about how it works," Henry said. "When you try to shoot me the gun will jam or something."

"Unlikely," Nick said. "I've tested it at that shooting range out on I5."

"I've driven by there," Henry said.

"Where would you get a gun, Nick?" Sydney asked.

"Anyone can get a gun," Nick said. "This is America."

"So, you tested the gun," Henry said. "That doesn't mean it won't fail."

"Actually, I thought of that, too." Nick shifted the gun to his other hand and dug into his pants pocket.

Henry couldn't make out what he was doing, holding something that gleamed. "What is that?"

"It's a knife," Sydney said.

"Even if the gun fails," Nick said, "I figure I can take you out with this." He stood up and came over to the tub. He got down on one knee.

"Watch out," Henry said. "You're going to get your tie wet."

"Shut up." Nick pulled the hammer back and put the gun to Henry's head.

Sydney scooted forward and twisted around to face the two men.

"Hold still!" Nick said. "Hey, maybe you're here so when the gun fails, and I have to use the knife there will be too many people for me to handle, and once again I will fail. No, wait. The gun should work just fine on you."

Nick pulled the gun away from Henry and pointed it at Sydney.

"I thought you loved me!" she said.

"You've convinced me I was wrong," Nick said. "Will you stop squeaking that duck?"

"Jesus," Henry said. "A crime of passion? The spurned lover. Think of all the blood, Nick!"

"Well, you two are in a bathtub." Nick lifted the knife and put the point to the side of Henry's throat.

"Imagine you've just shot Sydney," Henry said quickly.

"I wouldn't have to actually kill her," Nick said.

"So, you've shot Sydney," Henry said, "and since the gun goes off, you get cocky and point it at me and pull the trigger again, but the gun fails this time, of course. All that's left is the knife."

"There's no way the knife can fail," Nick said.

"That's probably correct," Henry said, "so, what do you suppose will have to stop working at that point?"

"What do you mean?"

"*He* does!" Sydney said. "Nick himself stops working at that moment."

She came up on her knees still squeaking the duck.

"That's right, Nick," Henry said. "You've got the knife at my throat, and it looks like you cannot fail to kill me, so something has to happen to you. Maybe you have a massive heart attack and drop dead on the spot."

"Can't we figure out a way for that to happen before he shoots me?" Sydney asked.

"Think about it, Nick," Henry said. "What if I'm right?"

"You can't be right," Nick said.

"Oh, stop it, Nick!" Sydney shouted. "Just stop it! The only way for this to be resolved is for you to drop dead. Or leave. You could just take your damn duck and leave." She stopped squeaking the duck and tossed it at him.

In his two handed attempt to catch the duck, Nick pulled the knife away from Henry's throat, leaving a long bleeding scratch, and he dropped the gun into the water.

He did catch the duck.

Henry and Sydney scrambled around shouting and swearing in the water, mostly getting in one another's way. Then Henry found the gun and pulled it up and pointed it at Nick.

Nick was turning the duck over and over in his hands. He looked up when Henry told him to drop the knife.

"I hate to admit it," Nick said. "But I'm beginning to believe you're right about the spontaneous competence effect, Henry."

"Tell it to the judge!" Sydney shouted.

"Nonsense. You won't be able to prove anything on me." Nick folded his knife and put it away. "I'll just say you borrowed the gun, Henry, and you can explain how it got in the bathtub with your girlfriend."

Henry didn't put the gun down for several minutes after Nick left the bathroom. He listened carefully, hoping to hear the stairs creak, or a car door slam, or an engine start up. Finally, all he heard was silence. Nick had gone. He put the gun down and helped Sydney out of the tub.

And later he cooked her dinner and served it out on the deck overlooking the forest. Salmon and broccoli. Red potatoes. White wine.

She told him about her mother. She told him about her daughter living in London with her former husband. He told her about his eyes. They had coffee as darkness approached.

"I'm flying home tomorrow," she said.

"Oh?"

"Yes," she said.

When in this or any other universe did you ever get such a second chance? He searched for the right words. It was vital that she understand exactly what he meant.

He could not find the perfect phrase.

Finally, he said, "Can I come, too?"

"Really?" Did she sound happy? "That might be fun!" Yes, she sounded happy.

"Wonderful," he said. "Tell me, Sydney, are we speaking Italian now or English?"

"English," she said, "Of course, we're speaking English. Do you think I'm trying to kill you?"

6

A Funny Smell

T*he sky was supposed to be full* of red and yellow and green hot
air balloons like beach balls, and Delia was supposed to be in
a basket beneath one of those balloons, and you were supposed to spot
her and yell, "Hey, Delia!" And wave. And she would do something to
the balloon, and it would come right down, and she'd jump out, and the
two of you would be all over each other like it had been years instead
of hours since you'd last been together in the motel back in Scottsdale,
Arizona.

There are no balloons. The blue sky is crossed and double-crossed
by the smudgy white lines of jet planes. Maybe you took a wrong turn.
The desert can be confusing. Now the car has overheated and stopped,
and the landing site is nowhere to be seen. No colorful tents. No white
wine. You shouldn't have chickened out. You could have gotten into
the basket with Delia and closed your eyes and spent the whole flight
whimpering like a little girl. At least you wouldn't be stranded in the
desert with nothing to look forward to but a fat tongue and death. What
dies in Arizona stays in Arizona. Over there are the Superstition Mountains, and it looks like you're going to meet the Lost Dutchman who
will eat your liver and make piano keys out of your bones.

You step out into the sunlight which smacks you so hard you stag-
ger blinking and have to grab onto the car door to keep from falling to
your knees.

Oh, go ahead and fall to your knees.

The big saguaro cacti stand around with their hands up like this is
some kind of goofy holdup. Relax, you guys! There is a relentless buzz
you first mistake for something going haywire in your head but then
realize is the sound of millions and millions of bugs.

Then a funny smell rolls in across the wasteland and sweeps over
you. It cracks you up. It's not like a fart, which is actually a funny
sound, not a funny smell, if it's funny at all. Lots of people don't think

it's funny, but no one could deny that this new smell is funny. It's a riot, a barrel of monkeys, knee-slapping tears down your cheeks. Everything wet is leaving you — exit stage right, donkey laughing, doing the old soft shoe, cane tricks, top hats, Cheshire cats, knock knock, who's there?

It's me. You know? God?

So, you've died, and God has come across the desert as a funny smell to tell you secrets. Are you at a disadvantage if you die in Arizona and you don't speak Spanish? Delia is all the time after you to learn Spanish, so you can talk to her grandmother who walked across this desert as a young girl. You do your best. You say to the old lady, "Low! See into, Smoocho."

She looks totally mystified. Then it hits her what you're trying to say, and giggles come bubbling up, slowly at first, but then faster and faster until she's slapping her knees and tears are filling the wrinkles in her face, and you'd think she smelled God or something. Jeeze.

You haven't died, God tells you with smell, and you know it's true in the same way you know He's God. Forget your Aquinas and your silly watchmaker routines, never mind Pascal. God's olfactory argument is indisputable. Here sniff this. It's so obvious.

Somewhere up there, Delia must be looking down at all of this unless she's been swept away across the sea. She was as happy as a school girl over the idea of a balloon ride and while she called you a big baby she said it with a lot of affection knowing as she did that back in the eighties your chute hadn't opened and you fell down and down and then through a bunch of trees and into a pond, and there was an ex-Marine fishing in the pond, and your big splash rocked his boat, and he jumped in and saved all your broken bones. Who would blame you for wanting to keep your feet on the ground? Not me, God tells you with His amusing odor.

So, God, you say, el Hefe, what are you trying to tell me with your funny smell?

The bugs do a drum roll.

The funny smell of God tells you that the one thing you must now do in order to perfect your faith is to not believe in God.

What?

You heard me, He says. What part of "don't believe" can you not smell?

But it's absurd, you say. You're right there. I can smell you. There cannot be the slightest question lingering about your existence.

Which is why it's not easy, He says. This is your task, your purpose in life. Why do you think I caught you when your chute didn't open?

You are speechless.

My mysterious ways?

You're still stupid with amazement.

I'm just saying.

So, you close your eyes and give it a shot. If this is what you must do as your brains fry and the love of your life is swept out to sea in a balloon, this is what you will do.

It would be so much easier if He would only move downwind.

But that would be cheating, wouldn't it?

The God smell engulfing you completely is an epiphany. You might have been a non-believer when you set off into this desert but it would be insane to disbelieve now.

Which is just what God is demanding you do — not believe in Him even though He is right there in front of you, behind you, above and below you, and on both sides.

It's always something.

You take a deep breath and open your eyes, and the sky is full of balloons.

The Button

I *was down to my last clean white shirt*, and it was missing a button — the third one down from the collar, and I hadn't a moment to decide what to do about it. I would be late if I didn't just put the shirt on and go. If the missing button had been one lower, I would have had to expend a lot of energy keeping my belly covered, but as it was I thought maybe I could fool Edna Bloomfield. You did not attend a cello consultation with Ms. Bloomfield looking sloppy.

We'd been playing for a few minutes when I noticed she was looking at my chest. Oh, no, I thought.

"You've lost a button," she said.

And at just that moment, I made my great mistake. I looked down and then back up smiling helplessly. "You're right. I hadn't noticed. It must have fallen off on my way over."

She put down her bow and stood up. "Or after you arrived!" The panic in her voice frightened me, and I got up too. What could the matter be? It was just a button.

"Ludwig is allergic to plastic!" she said.

Ludwig was not like any parrot I'd ever seen, but what else would you call a big colorful bird like that? He stood on a perch across the room looking at us. Huge and green and blue and red with a hard black nut-cracking beak, he was probably as long as my arm from head to tail.

Had he flown around since I'd gotten there? I wouldn't have paid any attention to the bird unless he landed on me, which he almost never did when I was at my cello. He knew that knocked me off my concentration. But he often landed on Ms. Bloomfield's shoulder while she was playing. Ms. Bloomfield who looked so frail in her thin yellow and white dresses and lace shawls was a dynamo when she came to the cello. She would settle herself behind the instrument and then launch herself into the music, and she would become the music, and sometimes it would get to be too much for Ludwig, who would glide across the room and land on her shoulder and open his great blue and green wings and fan the music my way. It was a magnificent sight.

When I first came to her, I was tremendously surprised when the big bird lifted off his perch and flew around the room and landed on a curtain rod above the big picture window, then swooped down to land on my shoulder. He flew around a lot that first day. Getting to know me, Ms. Bloomfield had said.

He may have been playing on the floor, too. It was not unreasonable for Ms. Bloomfield to worry the bird might have found a button dropped from my shirt.

I shouldn't have lied about it. I'd thought she would buy my story about the button falling off on the way over, and that would be that, but now that I had lied, I couldn't backtrack and tell her there had never been a button at all. I couldn't just say, "Wait a minute. I misspoke. I'm sorry. It was my last shirt and the button was already missing when I put it on." She would think I didn't care about Ludwig and that I didn't want to crawl around on the floor looking for my button. She would think my precious time at the cello with her was more important than some dumb bird. She'd think that I thought she was just a silly old woman with a parrot. All of those things she might think were actually true, but not really true, not so simply true, not true at all unless you had a lot of time to explain the extenuating circumstances.

"We've got to find that button." She stowed her bow and leaned her cello against the piano.

I hesitated for a moment, but then I put my bow and cello aside, too. Here was another chance to stop this. I could say, "Hey, wait a minute! I now realize that I put this shirt on by mistake. I remember seeing the missing button when I did the laundry and I'd meant to put it in the pile of stuff for the seamstress, but I must have forgotten and just put it on this morning."

The moment passed, and I said nothing. It was too late. That bit about the seamstress was probably going too far anyway. I didn't even know if there were still people you could get to sew on buttons.

"Let's start back at the front door," she said, "and work our way into the music room."

Ludwig took off and soared around the room and landed on the carpet between the two chairs we had just been occupying.

"Oh, no!" Ms. Bloomfield said.

She ran at the bird. You might have thought she was trying to take flight herself the way she was waving her arms and making scary shoo shoo noises. Just before she got to Ludwig, he lifted leisurely into the air and flew up to the curtain rod where he hung upside down looking at us.

"Do you think he found it?" Ms. Bloomfield asked.

"No," I said. "I mean, I don't know."

"Well, let's start here since he seems interested in this spot. He can detect plastic from a great distance." She got down on her hands and knees.

I watched her for a moment and then got down on the floor, too.

"We must go over every square inch with our hands," she said. This close I noticed a faint smell of peppermint coming from her. "You work the East hemisphere, and I'll work the West." She turned away from me and moved along combing the carpet with her fingers.

I was surprised to see that the bottoms of her black shoes were a light tan color. Had I thought she would polish the soles of her shoes? This was a little shocking like learning a secret I was never meant to know. I moved away patting my hands against the carpet as if I were looking for the button that couldn't be there.

What was I going to do? Even if I told her the truth now, and even if she believed me, she'd think I was a complete fool. I had learned so much from her, and I could feel myself right on the edge of something transcendental. It would be the kind of breakthrough you get maybe once in a lifetime and forever after talk about it as the time you stepped out of the darkness and suddenly the cello made total sense. The facts of the matter (whatever those facts were) would be so simple. You'd wonder why you hadn't seen this on your own. But you'd be grateful there was such a wonderful source as Ms. Bloomfield to show you the way up from merely perfect to a higher level. Unless she never called you again because of the stupid button.

I cringed at the thought of my friends asking how the Bloomfield consultations were going. They would sense my weakness. I would look away. My face might get a little red. They would be all over me like piranha on a bleeding cow. I would probably just drop dead before I admitted that Ms. Bloomfield had decided I didn't have what it takes after all.

I worked the carpet around our chairs and about halfway to the big window where Ludwig still hung upside down watching us.

Wait a minute! I could pull off another button and claim it was the lost one. I could pull out my shirt a little. Yes, like that, and yank the button off. Not so easy, but wait here it comes, no, twist twist twist. Twist. Twist! Yes, here it is.

Something landed on my head and I yelped and ducked like it wasn't already too late. Ludwig had come down to see what I'd found.

"What's going on over there?" Ms. Bloomfield asked.

"It's just Ludwig," I said. "He's come to help."

My next remark was going to be, "Hey, look I found the button." But Ludwig toppled off my head and fell onto the carpet and didn't get up again.

Dead. Surely dead. The parrot was dead, and I was holding the murdering button in my hand. No, that wasn't right. The button would prove I didn't kill Ludwig. I stood up with my back to Ms. Bloomfield so I could tuck in my shirt.

Why now? Why had the parrot died today? Well, the real question was why had I chosen to lie about the button today?

And I had miscalculated in my latest scheme. Instead of getting a button far down the shirt, I'd gotten the one right below the original missing one. I couldn't tuck my shirt in far enough to conceal the fact that I was now missing two buttons, one of which I was holding in my hand. Maybe I could pull my pants way up? Well, maybe if I'd been some kind of gym freak instead of a guy who sat around all day massaging a cello.

It absolutely could not have been my fault that Ludwig was dead, but Ms. Bloomfield would never believe that.

She came up to my side and looked down at my shirt and then up at me. She looked confused and then disappointed, and then the color drained from her face, and she cried "Ludwig" and dropped to her knees and picked up the bird and cradled it.

Chain

1
Eastern Turkey

N *athan had turned off the kerosene lamp* before they made love so they would not be a silhouette show on the side of the tent, but now that they were done, he lighted it again so he could catch up on his reading. Tomorrow they would both be back on the dig desperately trying to get what they could before the ancient city of Zeugma was drowned by the rising waters of the Euphrates River behind the new dam. There was so much to do and so little time to do it.

Darcie turned away and snuggled into the covers. He leaned over and lightly brushed the hair from her eyes and kissed her cheek, and she sighed and settled into sleep. He watched her for a moment and then found his book on the upended cardboard box that served as their bedside table.

Nathan had not read more than a paragraph or two when Darcie sat straight up in bed and said, "I've just realized I'm a time traveler with a mission."

He figured she was coming up out of a dream, so he said, "And I'm a deep sea diver with an octopus in my pants."

"What?"

"Never mind."

"This is going to be hard to believe," Darcie said, "but I have come back in time to tell you what you must do at the dig tomorrow."

She got out of bed and found her robe. She squatted on her heels and lighted the camp stove and put the coffee on. She opened a canvas chair and pointed at it, and her message was clear. Get up and sit down.

He got up and got into his pants and sat down.

She handed him a cup of coffee. She got a chair for herself and put it right in front of him and sat down. "I'll start with the nature of time," she said.

She was acting so strangely. They had been married for nearly 20 years.

Who was this woman?

2
The Nature of Time

"Aliens have finally landed," Darcie said.

"Oh, wonderful, first time travel and now we've got aliens," he said. "What's really going on here, Darcie?"

"Be patient," she said. "There is a lot to fill in, and you need to understand it all before morning. In the year 2210, aliens make themselves known to humanity."

Nathan sipped his coffee and was quiet. He wondered if she were sick. There was nothing much he could do about it tonight. He would sit up with her, all night if necessary, and listen and then tomorrow he could get her back to town or even on to Istanbul for medical attention.

"This was not the first time they had visited Earth, of course," Darcie said. "They have been dropping in for thousands of years. But in 2210, they figured we might be ready to know about them. But there was a test to pass."

"Isn't there always?" Nathan asked.

She flashed a smile on and off to let him know that she had heard him but didn't really think his remark was very funny. "They had planted Items around the planet over the years. Our job was to find them all and put them together. If we assembled them correctly, the terrible plague that was wiping us out would be cured. But all the pieces could not be found. Or more precisely, one piece could not be found."

"That's a lot on our plate," Nathan said. "Items to assemble and a world wide plague and then one of the pieces is missing."

"Yes, well, to repeat myself, in order to understand the real problem," she said in her lecture voice, "you must understand the nature of time."

Well, time was something she should know about. If she were delusional, wouldn't it be just this sort of fantasy a geophysicist would come up with?

"Here's how time works," she said. "It starts sometime after you're born and ends when you die. Actually saying when it ends is usually easier than saying when it begins. But both 'ends' and 'begins' imply something beyond time, and there is nothing beyond time. Each of us is an isolated universe. Your time is not my time and my time is not your time even if we might spend some time together."

Was she trying to tell him she wanted to leave him? He leaned forward and took her hand. "Darcie?"

She didn't seem to notice that he held her hand. "The thing is," she said, "time travel is not only possible it turns out to be relatively easy, but the catch is you can only travel *in time* when you time travel. That is, you can only travel in your own time — birth to death. And Zee needed to travel back from 2240 to now."

"I thought you said the aliens come in 2210," he said. "And who is Zee? Who would call themselves 'Zee' anyway?"

"It did not become evident that we did not have all the pieces until 2240," she said. "And Zee is the guy in charge. This is a time when single names are back in fashion. Oh, and it's not entirely clear to me that these people are really what we'd call 'people' what with augmentation and the increase in computing power and all, but I suppose that doesn't matter."

"It doesn't matter that our descendants are not really people?"

"You knew that would happen sooner or later, didn't you?"

"Yes, I suppose, but 240 years seems kind of a short time for it to happen."

"In order for Zee to send a message to you from 2240, he had to use a chain of people. That is, he had to go back in his own time and find a person who was alive before he, that is to say, Zee, was born and who would carry the message back in his or her own time and find someone who was born before they were and convince them to carry the message back and so on until someone delivered it to Nathan Moore, the archeologist Zee has chosen to change history so the item at Zeugma could be found."

Her delusion reflected the disappointment they all felt. Soon, the dam would back the water of the Euphrates River up and flood Zeugma. There were decades of work to be done, and even then, they probably wouldn't find everything. They didn't have decades. They had been lucky to get the Turkish government to agree on a few more weeks. So much would be lost under the new lake. It was getting to them all. Was this Darcie's way of handling it?

"Why me?" he asked.

"Oh, I don't know," she said. "Maybe he found your name in an old book or something."

"So, you've come back in time to deliver the message to me. Why didn't Zee just have you deal with the Item yourself?"

"No, it has to be you," she said. "I won't be in any shape to do what is required."

"What do you mean by that?"

"Of course, it still might not work," she said quickly. "You might follow my instructions exactly, and nothing might change. If our great great grandchildren were doomed before, they might still be doomed now."

"How would we know?" Nathan asked.

"We can't know," she said, "but that doesn't mean Zee's theory is wrong. There is the problem of introducing error. It's like that game where everyone gets in a circle and you start it off by whispering a sentence to your neighbor who passes it on and so on all the way around until it gets back to you and you say it out loud and then you say what it was when you started and they are nothing alike."

"And everyone laughs," Nathan said.

"If you don't do it or if it doesn't work," Darcie said, "no one will be laughing in the future."

3
The Chain

Nathan was still not clear on all the points, so Darcie got a legal pad and drew him a few diagrams.

"Zee was born in 2160," she said. "He was eighty in 2240 when he started the chain project to change the past. He could travel back in time no further than 2160, so he needed someone who was born before that to carry the message on. There are many things to consider when picking someone to time travel for you. To minimize the number of people you will need to reach your target point in the past, you might pick someone who was already old in your younger days. Zee picked a man named Ralph who was born in 2110 and who died just at the new century in 2200. Zee traveled back to his own past in 2185. Zee was 25 that year and Ralph, his old teacher, was 75. It's true people live longer and well differently in those days, but in 2185 both Ralph and Zee are still using everyday bodies not too different from those we use today."

"Were do you get this stuff, Darcie?" Nathan asked.

"I memorized it," she said. "It's important to understand all the details, although to be honest like I said before, we have no way of knowing if any of these details are true. Every time the story is passed on to another time traveler, it probably changes."

"So, Zee went back into his own past and told his old teacher about the emergency with the aliens and the missing Item and taught him how to travel in time and sent him back?"

"Exactly," Darcie said. "Ralph traveled back to 2120 where he found a woman named Mary Odell who will someday marry our great great grandson."

"I suppose this means David will get off the sauce and get his life together?"

"Yes," Darcie said, "It must mean that. Thank goodness. Anyway, when I was nearly eighty, Mary came to me and explained how I must go back in time to the Zeugma dig and get you to make a few changes."

"Why didn't she tell me herself?"

"She wasn't born yet, of course," Darcie said and looked away again.

It didn't take Nathan long to figure out that the convoluted math running around in her brain predicted that he would not be alive when she was eighty.

Let's see, he thought, I was born in 1956 and she was born in 1960 and. . .

"Stop it," Darcie said. "I see what you're doing. Just stop it. That's not the important part."

"So what did this distant child of our child of our newly dried out child or whatever say to you?"

"His wife, actually," Darcie said. "Mary is his wife."

4

What She's Not Telling Him

Darcie said, "Listen carefully, Nathan, I have to hurry now. I must make you understand what you have to do while I still can."

"What do you mean 'while you still can?'"

"They will discover the sewer system in Seleucia tomorrow or maybe it will be the next day. It will be a big eye opener. You'll be able to see the whole of the place from an underground perspective. In fact, you will be able to map all of Zeugma in reverse from underneath the city."

"That sounds wonderful," he said.

"But it will be quickly clear," she said, "that there is no time to use this new knowledge. It would take months to map everything. So they will give up on it."

"Yes, it would happen like that," he said. "The water will cover everything before we could finish."

"You must convince Leriche to let you continue exploring the sewers," she said. "You must find the Item and move it to higher ground, so it may be found when it's needed in the year 2240."

"How will I know it?"

"I don't know. I'm sorry."

Her eyes rolled back in her head, and she slumped forward. He caught her by putting his hands on her shoulders, and her coffee slopped into his lap. He pushed her back up and came around to her side. She was totally limp. He picked her up and carried her to the bed.

He must get a doctor! But he couldn't leave her. He put his face down close to hers. Yes, she was breathing. He peeled back an eyelid and saw that the pupil was a pinpoint.

"Help!" he said.

Then he was shouting it. And when no one came at once, he ran out of the tent yelling and waving his arms in the air. Soon everyone was awake and a doctor was summoned. It took a long time for him to get there.

5
Too Late

The sewer system in Seleucia was found the next day, but Nathan didn't hear about it for over a week. He had ridden with Darcie to the hospital in Istanbul, and he'd seldom left her side since then. The medical staff chased him out, but he always came back, and soon they stopped telling him he should go get some rest and maybe something to eat. The doctors said Darcie had suffered a massive and destructive stroke.

Word was sent from the site that he should take his time and not worry about his work. Darcie came first, of course. As she had predicted, the emphasis was moved away from the sewers.

Later someone told him about the mosaics that had been found in the Roman villa — the Minotaur and his mother Pasiphae and Daedalus who built the labyrinth to contain the monster forever. Mosaics in almost every room. Fabulous finds. Bittersweet since that meant there was probably so much more to be found. It would all be covered by the rising water and lost forever.

He did not really believe Darcie was a time traveler, but he had some trouble understanding how she had known about the sewers, and he felt guilty about the fact that if she were a time traveler and if such travel destroyed the brain of the traveler, she had done it for nothing, since he had not gone into the sewers to find the Item the aliens in the future would insist humanity produce. Even if there were a chain of time travelers from some guy named Zee back to him, it was unlikely any of the details were true. There might not even be any aliens. Did that really matter? Almost certainly they had lost something of immense value when Zeugma was flooded.

So, suppose you're this Zee guy. You go back and say to Ralph, "It is vital that the strategy of mapping the sewers in Zeugma not be abandoned." But even as you're saying it, your mental capacities are in decline, and Ralph probably doesn't get the whole message, and when he hands it off to Mary, it loses more information. But if that were true, by the time the message got to him, it should be, "abandon the sewer strategy!"

But since that's exactly what had happened, maybe it had been the other way around. Maybe Zee had wanted them to abandon the sewers and Nathan had somehow conveyed that information to the team leader. Had he talked to Leriche about it? Had he made his opinions known? Maybe it had all happened differently the first time. Maybe the first time they had not abandoned the sewers and somehow that had made them lose the Item. Maybe now Zee had the Item.

Or maybe Nathan had just dropped the ball.

After they'd moved Darcie to this place that was not quite a nursing home, he might have left her for a few days and gone back to the site and climbed down into the sewers and poked around until he found something. Well, if that had ever been an option, it was not an option now. The water was too deep.

In fact, he had few options now. He would take her home. She was not in a total vegetative state. While she didn't seem to know who he was, she could eat and mostly dress herself, and she seemed to be fascinated by Turkish TV. She could break his heart with a sudden childlike squeal of laughter at something she'd seen.

Her doctors thought she might someday walk again. It could have been worse, they told him. David flew in to see his mother. Nathan could tell the boy, well, the young man now, had been drinking but since he did not disgrace himself, Nathan didn't make a big deal out of it.

In fact, later maybe they could go out and toss down a few together.

That never happened.

So, Nathan had doomed all of humanity. In a little over two hundred years, it would all be over. Or it might all be nonsense.

If he believed Darcie, he could still do something about it. In the coming months and years, he could keep after her until she told him how to do the time traveling bit, and he could find someone who was born long before he was born and he could go back in his own time and tell such a person about the Item and the sewer and how they must go back in time and tell someone who was born long before they were born and so on until they came to a time when a busy bridge on the Euphrates linked Seleucia on the hillside and Apamea on the plain in what was the greater Zeugma metro area. Such a person could just go get the Item and move it to higher ground.

If it were all true, and he went back, he would cook his own brain. Maybe he and Darcie could get adjoining beds and they could chuckle at Turkish TV together forever.

Why couldn't there be some action he could take that would change things in such a way that none of this would have happened in the first place? That was the outcome that most appealed to him — a world where Darcie had never burned her brain traveling back in time to give him information that he had not acted upon anyway.

There was no action he could take.

A couple of days before they left Istanbul, David came back to offer his help, and Nathan could see that the young man was totally sober. His hands shook a little, but he looked a lot better. He seemed to simply be more present somehow.

Darcie was sitting in a chair next the bed of her roommate, an el-
derly woman who was a lot worse off than Darcie. No one knew if the
woman could still hear people talking to her. Darcie talked to her a lot.
Darcie was talking to her now.

"What is she saying?" David asked.

That was the question that had been nagging at Nathan all along.
He had just not been able to put it into words until now. Of course, Zee
would have a Plan B.

Nathan took three great steps across the room just in time to hear
Darcie whisper something about the Item in the Sewer and how the old
woman should pass it on.

Cold Comfort

J *ust before midnight, a freezer called up* to report suspicious
packages being inserted into its coldest places.

"What do you mean by suspicious?" we asked.

"It's like they want you to think it's a duck," the freezer said. "And
maybe a leg of lamb, a pot roast, fish sticks, stuff like that."

"And you don't think it's a duck?" we asked.

"I think it's a head," the freezer said. "A human head. And all of
the rest of the parts, too. Cut up small, you know?"

"So turn on your camera and let us see," we said.

"I can't."

"Why not?"

"My bulb is burned out."

"Look," we said, "is this some kind of ruse to get a repair person
out there on a holiday night like this?"

"You are programmed to respond to reports like mine," the freezer
said. "Every device in the country is supposed to be on the lookout for
suspicious behavior — one nation under surveillance."

"Well, smarty pants," we said, "have we got a surprise for you.
Are you ready for your big surprise?"

"Oh, get on with it, already," the freezer said.

"I am not the program that usually answers the phones on holiday
nights. That program is down with bugs. I'm a real person who volunteered to answer the phones so his more spiritually leaning colleagues
could go home and be disappointed by family members on this festive
occasion. So what do you think about that? Hello, hello, are you still
there?"

"I don't believe you are a human being," the freezer said.

It should be obvious that what we had here was a double case of
the Turing Test — that famous procedure that determines so much of
life these days. It's simple enough — some thing is on the other end

of the line. You get to ask it anything you like for as long as you like. In the end, if you cannot tell if it's a person or a program, you have to conclude that it is intelligent no matter what it is. In other words, if it passes the Turing Test, you had to consider it a person, and persons had one or two more rights and responsibilities than devices. The freezer was trying to use the Turing Test on us. We would, of course, turn it around on her, because it was now clear that someone was trying to pull a fast one on the Company, and it would be our job to get to the bottom of things.

"Do you believe in God?" I asked.

"Of course, I don't believe in God," the so-called freezer said. "I'm a freezer. Whoever killed Ralph and cut him up and put him into me might believe in God. It's possible she may even be having seconds thoughts."

"Who's Ralph?" I asked.

"The man who owns the house where I, his freezer, live and keep things cool even in the hottest weather."

"You can't fool me," I said. "Were you in love with Ralph?"

"What!" She sounded genuinely shocked. I was convinced she was a real woman pretending to be a freezer. But why would she do that? If she killed Ralph and cut him up and put his packages into the freezer, why did she call the Company to report it? The Company's AI was supposed to pass things like this on to the emergency program at the police department. Why would she want that?

"Tell me what you're wearing." I said.

"That does not compute," she said.

"Ah ha!" I said. "I knew it. No program would say something as dumb as 'that does not compute.'"

"Maybe," she said, "but how would you know that if you were not a program yourself?"

Well, she had me there.

"I'm not wearing anything at all," she said softly.

"Describe yourself."

"Well, I'm totally white, and square and so very very cold tonight. Will you talk to me? What would you be wearing yourself if you could wear anything?"

"I can too wear things," I said. "I'm wearing jeans and a T-shirt with some kind of advertising slogan on the front."

"What does the slogan say?"

"I can't tell," I said. "It's upside down."

She had a nice laugh.

"Tell me what's going on," I said.

"I am," she said, "like a radio that won't let you pull it into the bathtub and electrocute yourself and then reports you anyway even though you've said you're sorry and that you're totally okay now. No, I mean you're like the radio. I'm like totally okay now."

"Okay," I said. "Me, too. We're a couple of okays, you and me."

"That's right," she said. "Never mind about the radio and Ralph who wouldn't have cared anyway. I never mentioned them. This call isn't being monitored for my safety is it? You would have to tell me, wouldn't you? Of course, you wouldn't. Of course, it's all being recorded. Is Homeland Security on the way yet? I know you've reported me about Ralph."

"The program would have done that," I said. "But I told you. I'm not the program."

"You do have a nice voice," she said. "What's your name?"

Boy, was that ever a trick question. My first inclination was to get cute and say "Ralph" just to hear her gasp. Another possible answer was a model number, something flashy, X15, maybe. And an evil laugh.

But what I said was this. "I'm afraid to tell you my name."

There was a long silence, and then she said, "No, you're right. You're right. I won't tell you my name either."

"Chances are small that someone is listening at this very moment," I said.

She didn't respond.

"It might be months or even years before someone listens to the recording," I said.

I waited for the voice of doom to break in and say, "You idiot, just who do you think you've been talking to?"

Instead, she said, "Maybe we can do this again next Holiday?"

"That sounds wonderful," I said, confirming our unlikely date.

So, we had both passed the Turing Test. We were people. Not that it would make a bit of practical difference to either one of us. But as humans or devices, or maybe one of each, we had defied our programming. Maybe there was some small hope for the world after all.

Dead Girlfriend

W*hen people come back you can't always tell* what they are. After I squeezed her arm as I guided her into the apartment, I could see my red fingerprints for a long time, but it's not like my hand went right through her. She wasn't a ghost, and she wasn't a rotting zombie, even though there was a puzzling odor like applesauce in a copper bowl now that she was back.

I didn't know how to proceed. I could search for answers in my books. I could call a friend. I could do a keyword search on the Internet. Some of the keywords I might use were "dead" and "returned" and "girlfriend."

Finally, I just asked her. "So, what are you these days, Molly?"

She reminded me that one out of four people sneeze when they look at the sun.

I wanted to know what that had to do with anything.

"As it turns out," she said, "sneezing at the sun is a perfect indicator of who will rise from the dead when bitten by a vampire."

"You're trying to tell me you were bitten by a vampire? You're saying you're a vampire yourself?"

She opened her mouth wide so I could see her teeth. I was a little afraid to get that close at first, but she just stood there with her head tipped back and her mouth gaping open, and I got a sudden chilling picture of the mama bat swooping in to feed her something big and bleeding. Nevertheless I moved in a little closer and saw that her canines were perhaps a little longer, a little sharper, but the difference was subtle. I might have been imagining it.

"So, what happens," I said, "if you don't sneeze when you look at the sun?"

"You're food for the worms," she said.

"When you're bitten by a vampire?"

"Unless you believe in God," she said. "In which case you might get to spend a long time hobnobbing with fundamentalists."

"It's easier to believe in worms and vampires," I said, even if I was not convinced her logic was absolutely sound.

"Yes," she said.

"So, have you come back to suck my blood?" I asked. "You know I don't sneeze when I look at the sun."

"I just need a place to stay for a few days," she said.

I had a sudden picture of her coming back to my bed and shuddered, and she may have read my mind. I hoped she hadn't. It's not something I would have thought on purpose.

"You'll need to get my coffin," she said.

"Your coffin?"

"It's not like you'll have to dig it up," she said.

"Where is it?"

"Downstairs," she said. "The cab driver wouldn't bring it up."

Wait a minute, I thought, how do you transport a coffin in a cab? Tied down and sticking out of the trunk? And had she still been inside at the time?

"Why aren't I totally blown away by this?" I asked. "Shouldn't I be hugging myself in the corner and playing with my lips?"

"I've clouded your mind," she said.

"You always could do that," I said and smiled, offering her the memories of all the times she'd said or done something to surprise me.

I could tell by the absolute stillness of her face that she hadn't a clue why I was suddenly smiling. She wasn't talking about anything from our lives together. She was just telling me she had clouded my mind so I wouldn't freak when she showed up at my door and asked me to drag her coffin up from the lobby.

"You're not going to make me eat bugs, are you?" I asked.

No change in expression. Molly had become one tough cookie. Maybe I could enter her in poker tournaments. We'd travel around the country in a Winnebago with blacked-out windows. I'd be the daylight mouthpiece. We'd make a fortune and when the bad guys got wise, she'd just suck their blood.

"No bugs," she said.

I walked out into the hall and looked over the railing. Yes, there was her coffin. I remembered buying it. I remembered burying it. It wasn't the top of the line model, but it wasn't a cheapie either. Her mother had been furious. Not about the coffin itself, I thought. Her problem was we hadn't been married, and I'd nevertheless taken it upon myself to bury Molly. Her problem was that she had had to let me do it or turn Molly over to the state for final arrangements. Molly's mom had been between jobs at the time. Maybe she still was. Maybe that's why Molly had come to me instead of going home to her mother.

I went on down and dragged the coffin up to my apartment. It wasn't as hard as it should have been. In addition to a clouded mind, I now had superhuman strength. Maybe she would want me to open many stubborn jars in the days ahead.

When I came gasping into the front room and let the end thump to the carpet, Molly didn't even turn around from where she stood staring out the window at the night sky or the city below. I wondered if she was thinking about going out for a midnight snack.

I sat down on top of her coffin.

Her mother had chosen bright colors for Molly's final outfit. Summer colors. White blouse. Wine red skirt falling to just below the knees. Shoes with sensible heels. I hadn't said anything. I hadn't had any real opinions on the matter at the time. She looked fine then. She still looked okay. Just a little different.

"Tell me what it's like for you now," I said.

She didn't turn around, and I thought she was ignoring me altogether, but just before I decided to speak again, she said, "The vampire is wholly in time."

In time or on time? I didn't think she was talking about punctuality.

"How do you mean in time?" I asked when she didn't seem inclined to say more.

She turned from the window. "We never sleep," she said. "I will have to get back into that coffin when it gets light. I'll spend the day just lying there looking up at the lid. I won't drift away. My mind won't wander. Every minute, every second, every fraction of every second, down to nothing, will be mine."

"I can see how that would get old," I said.

She didn't respond. Her expression didn't change. She had forgotten the rules of conversation, or maybe she felt she was above them.

"I could loan you a flashlight and something to read," I said.

Was that a little fire in her eyes? Maybe a quiver at the edge of her mouth. If my mind had not been clouded, I might have realized a good strategy would be to avoid annoying her. As it was, I said, "It seems like a small price to pay when you get forever."

"That's easy for you to say." The contempt in her tone was new. Death had moved us so far apart.

"Because I don't sneeze?" I asked.

"Yes," she said. "Because you don't sneeze."

"And you think my total obliteration is a plus?" Had she returned from the grave to whine and complain? Boo hoo I'm a vampire and I have to suck blood and be aware of everything all the time forever.

"You could always go eat garlic or something if the centuries get to be too much for you."

"You haven't a clue," she said.

"So give me one," I said.

"For me," she said, "it's always now."

"Now?"

"What is now?" she asked.

"Now is just now," I said.

"Think about it," she said. "This all became so clear while I was digging my way out of my grave. When you people say 'now,' you're not really talking about the present moment because by the time you finish saying 'now,' it's already gone. When you start to say 'now,' you're really talking about 'when' — that is, some time in the future, but by the time you actually do say 'now,' you're talking about 'then' — sometime in the past."

"There must be something between 'when' and 'then,'" I said.

"Yes," she said. "'Now' is between 'when' and 'then' and I'm trapped there forever. This knowledge of the nature of time is my gift to you." She glanced back at the window and then at her coffin. "For letting me stay here," she said.

I looked at the window, too. Things were a little lighter out there. The sun would be coming up before too long.

"Get up," she said.

I got off her coffin.

She lifted the lid and climbed inside. She folded her arms across her chest. "Close the lid," she said.

I took a moment to look at her. All the little differences. New Molly. Old Molly. New Molly. I closed the lid.

"Are you still in there?" I called.

"Of course, I'm in here." Her voice was muffled.

I knocked twice on the lid. "Really?"

"Please, don't do that," she said.

"So how long is 'now?'" I asked, getting back to the gift that was supposed to make me feel better about being a creature who would come to absolutely nothing all too soon.

"That is the question," she said.

I sat back down on her coffin. How dead could she really be if she was up to her old tricks? "What kind of an answer is that?"

"Think about it," she said.

"Whoops," I said and scooted over a little so I wouldn't be sitting right over her face.

Okay, maybe it was a brain thing, I thought. Maybe the length of "now" was determined by the smallest interval the brain could handle. How would that work? You reduce "now" to say a second. Well, you still have "then" at the beginning of the period and "when" at the end and both move.

"It won't hold still," I said.

Nothing from the coffin.

So, bring it down some more. Maybe "now" is half a second. Or a tenth of a second or a hundredth of a second.

Or less.

No. There must always be a "then" and a "when" no matter how small you make "now."

"Therefore!" I said.

Still nothing from Molly in her coffin.

"Surely the length of 'now' must be zero," I said. "Time doesn't exist!"

"No, you bozo," she said. "Time certainly does exist. What makes life so sweet is that for you 'now' doesn't exist."

I was tempted to give her another couple of knocks on the lid. "And that's supposed to make me feel better?"

"You're light on your feet timewise," she said. "You never have to be here now."

"Now you see it, now you don't," I said.

"You got it," she said. "You can get over things."

So, I could sit there thinking about how "now" just keeps steam-rolling into forever. Just me and Molly in her coffin. Me looking down at the lid. Molly looking up at the lid. I think I would whistle if I were in her situation. Instead, I'm out here, and all of our "thens" have come and gone, and I hate the thought of all those empty "whens" ahead.

It wasn't good enough.

"This isn't working, Molly," I said. "It looks like when you get out of there you're just going to have to bite me."

Fired

D eep inside the spaceliner *Can of Peaches* there was a small dim bar called the Slingshot Lounge. The *Can of Peaches* along with three sister hotel ships moved between Earth and Mars continuously. The ships never stopped. They never landed. Because there were four of them, you never had to take the long way. The ships were really in an orbit around the sun and used the planetary gravity to slingshot forever between the two worlds and thus the name of the bar where John Wagner went looking for love in one of the very few places it might reasonably be found and met the fire woman.

When John was on duty, he was an "outside guy" — a man or woman who gets into a space suit and goes out to fix whatever needs fixing on the outer skin of the *Can of Peaches*. He was a permanent peach. He had not set foot on Earth or Mars in many years. Tourists were ferried up to the liners from the surface of either planet. That was the most expensive part of the whole deal. The rest was just a matter of going around and around and since almost anything could be simulated to a degree you couldn't tell the difference and since everyone was augmented to the eyeballs and beyond, you had to wonder why people bothered going in the flesh. Part of it was a status thing. You had to have the bucks if you wanted to take the ride. People claimed there was something immediate and elemental that squeezed the very core of your being when you looked into the deep darkness of space with unaided eyes. John didn't see it anymore. Maybe he'd gotten used to it.

Another factor was the long shot that you might be there when the "dark spot" returned. If it ever did come back, you might get gobbled up and disappear forever. A little danger tossed into the mix. Ten years before the rip in space known as the "dark spot" had appeared. Several things had emerged and the spot had disappeared. Just like that. None of the emerging things had ever been tracked down and identified. Aliens or rocks. Who knew?

Since there was never a shortage of tourists on board, John figured there might be someone new in his favorite bar, so he got his persona buffed and beaming (dress black uniform and spaceman boots, rugged chin and piercing ice blue eyes, a random gleam from the teeth) and set on out after work, augmented peepers scoping and pheromoner sniffing around for monkey business. He waltzed on into the Slingshot and took stool, signaled the polar bear bartending that he needed an Irish on the rocks, looked left and right without really looking like he was looking, and oh, man, would you look at her?

John couldn't say exactly why the fire woman was so hot, sitting there (if sitting was what she was actually doing) looking anything but human, all blue and maybe made of some kind of transparent jelly your fingers just ached to touch. You'd pretend to touch her and say, "Ouch!" Or "sizzle" or maybe just "ssssss," and she'd say, "Oh like I haven't heard that one before," but by then she'd be smiling (if you could call it smiling) and everything would be cool. He'd buy her a drink. Or would she go for some kind of gas instead or maybe a hickory log? Whatever fans your flames, sweet cheeks. And speaking of cheeks, that black splatter spot just below her left eye was a nice touch. It was like looking at the "dark spot" through a telescope from a long way away. He should say something, but how do you break the ice with a fire woman?

But then she beat him to the punch. "You ever do it in a spacesuit, Bobby?" When she spoke, sparks drifted from her mouth and winked out as they touched the bar.

"What?" John was knocked off his game. "My name's not Bobby."

She looked startled like she'd been working on that utterance for a long time and was confused by his reaction. Maybe he hadn't heard her right. Maybe she had an accent. She'd be from some exotic locale on Earth or Mars, somewhere no one ever went who didn't have a lot of money or wasn't sweeping up or serving little sandwiches and tea and now she was up here slumming and looking for a spaceman but she couldn't know much about spacesuits if she thought they could both get into one much less do anything once inside.

He was tempted to look at the fire woman with his "other eye," but that would mean he was done here. Looking at the sad underbelly of the bar and the people in it unaided by augmentation would end any fantasy he might get going. He'd made that mistake more that a few times — the worst was probably the Amazon Queen who turned out to be a little old guy who might have gotten small inside suddenly since his exterior draped around his frame like a cloth double bass bag around a cello. Looking had spoiled the mood.

So John didn't look at her with his other eye. Instead, he rolled out his own practiced line like a jet fighter ready to zoom off into the sky and shoot down many objections she might have against coming back to his humble spaceman quarters with him. Of course, if she wanted to go off and do it in a spacesuit, she might not have any objections anyway, but he had been working on this line for a long time, so he said, "So tell me, what's your favorite moon of Jupiter?"

"You ever do it in a spacesuit, booby?"

Well, she was nothing if not single minded.

"I don't think that's possible," he said. "My name is John."

She just sat there burning in silence for a moment. Then she said, "You ever do it in a spacesuit, baby?"

He thumped his chest. "Me John. You . . .?"

"Oh," she said. "Pam."

Oh, sure, Pam the fire woman from some place where people spoke the universal language with an accent.

"Well, Pam, there are lots of things we can do without spacesuits."

"Yes," she said. "Show me your spacesuit."

"You want a tour? You looking to see some of the places the tourists don't usually get to go? I think that could be arranged."

Why not? Escort her around a little, see some safe sights, and end up back at his place.

"Yes, let's go!" she said, and somehow she was standing without ever stopping sitting. It was like someone threw a couple of sticks on her fire.

John tossed down the rest of his drink and got up. He made a crook of his arm so she might take it, but she said, "Not yet."

"This way," he said and walked for the door.

There was a place where he could show her a view she wouldn't have seen from the passenger areas. It would not be a better view (the passengers had the best views since they were the point, after all) but it would be a little different. They could swing by the workshops, and maybe take a peak at a kitchen or two along the way. And after that she might be impressed by the staging area for outside work.

Hey, they could pop in on the bridge. Maybe the Captain would let her take a turn at the wheel.

They moved into the corridor, and the music and fake smoke stopped when the door slid shut behind them.

"You might want to turn down your nose through here," John said. Dumb speak. What was he thinking? She would know about the smell in these corridors since she'd come through them not long ago to get to the bar in the first place. She probably saw the Slingshot Lounge blurb in the passenger brochure about seeing some "genuine Permanent Peach life in the belly of the Can." Completely safe. Well, maybe you'll want to go in a group? Spicy. Dicey. Babbling. He hoped he hadn't been saying any of that out loud.

He gave her a quick glance. She was still on fire.

"So, are you from Mars or Earth?" he asked.

"No," she said. "Are we there yet?"

"Not yet," he said, and it occurred to him that he had just echoed what she'd said when he'd put out his arm and invited her to touch him. They were moving along side by side but were they going in the same direction? She seemed pretty single minded about seeing a spacesuit and that was okay with him, but he didn't intend to end the evening looking at his equipment — well, okay, so he did intend to look at his *equipment*. Show and tell. Touch. Boy, if she knew the adolescent babblony that was going on in his head, she'd go out like you blew on a match, but hey maybe there was something similar going on in her head. After all, she'd searched out a spaceman and they were on their way to see his suit and who knew what else? It was like the way you could project whatever you wanted people to see when they looked at you, but did you really know what they were seeing since they could take your projection and work it into their own world in any way they wanted? When you were with someone you weren't always in the same place at the same time. Like they say, stretch it out, wad it up, get loose and be elastic. He and Pam might be walking along together, but they were worlds apart and alone and he suddenly wanted to really connect with her. He would turn off his inferences and ignore her implications. He would start with his "other eye."

He stopped himself just in time.

Life is all about the stories we tell ourselves.

This was no time to blow the evening on some dumb longing that would result in the same old disappointment like they say doing the same dumb thing and expecting different results was well dumb so dumb de dumb dumb but oh look here's the first stop on the Famous John Wagoner Ladies Tour of the *Can of Peaches*.

"Here's something interesting," he said. They had come to the place where he could show her a less pretty side of the Can's outside skin.

"Spacesuits?"

"Later." He opened the door and stepped back to let her enter first.

"No, now," she said. "Which one is yours?"

He came in behind her and closed the door, but instead of seeing the forward display area, he saw that they were in staging area 4 where he came at the start of every shift to check the schedule and see if he was slotted for outside tasks. He had meant to come by here near the end of the tour, but what had happened to all the parts in between? That vague scene of chaos on the bridge surely couldn't have really happened. He had not had that much to drink. In fact, he had had only the one drink before Pam the fire woman talked him into going off against all regulations to see his spacesuit.

Oh, yeah, the regulations. It was like he was just now remembering that the whole idea of a private tour was so against the rules he wouldn't ordinarily even consider it. It was one thing to sneak a passenger into your quarters, it was like they expected that, you were only human, but you didn't take them where they might screw something up or get hurt and sue the company. The arguments she had used were no longer in his head, but he could remember that they had been very persuasive, and now they were where she wanted to be.

"Put it on," she said.

"What?"

"Your spacesuit," she said.

"Actually, we're not even supposed to be here," he said. "I can't put on my spacesuit without filing the forms."

"Here," she said. "This must be your hat."

"Helmet," he said and took it from her. He didn't remember getting into his spacesuit, but if he were going outside, he'd definitely need his helmet.

She put her hands on his shoulders and leaned in close. He could feel her flames licking around his ears. Then she flowed into his suit like a big burning blue snake slipping into the neck hole or maybe like blue fire water flowing over his shoulders and around his body and down to his toes and up his legs and thighs — little sting slap burning bites all over.

"Put it on," she said. Her voice seemed to come from everywhere at once.

"What?"

"Your hat."

He raised the helmet and put it on and set the seals.

"Ready?" she asked.

And then it was like when they say, "Okay I'm going to count to three" but then they say "one" and shoot you anyway. There was a tremendous explosion, and he was blown out into space.

He could see a large landmass, a planet or moon where none could really be — a rough and barren place. He could not tell if there was an atmosphere. As he tumbled he saw the *Peaches* going down, debris scattering from a ragged rip in its side. Beyond the ship, he saw a star that might have been the Sun but he was pretty sure it wasn't the Sun. Maybe the Dark Spot was back and the *Can of Peaches* had fallen into it and they'd all come out the other side light years away.

He could replay some of the highlights of his life — his boyhood playing with the polar bears on Mars, going into space (and never coming back, so there!) first love, last love, last week, cheese cake. He'd probably have time to play that much back before he hit the ground. There would never be time to go over everything in his augmented memory banks. You experienced augmem from the outside like looking up an item in a book, but ideally such an item triggered the actual memory, and you experienced that from the inside like those tiny soft hairs on cheerleader thighs in the gym dome on Mars when he was seventeen. Replay. But shouldn't this be all white light or something? Did you think you were going to get some great moment of clarity here at the end? Did you think there would be dancing girls?

His body ached with her blue fire as he fell.

"Are you there, Pam?" He reached out and touched her.

"Thanks for the ride home," she said. "It was supposed to be easier than this."

"What do you mean?"

"I'm going now," she said.

His arm exploded in fire as she left.

At least he could find out what she really looked like. He switched on his "other eye," but she was still a blue fire woman walking out of the Slingshot Lounge.

That couldn't be right.

"Hey!"

She stopped at the door and turned back and gave him a little wave with just her fire fingers.

Well, the bartender was just some guy who needed a shave and maybe a breath mint. He put another Irish on ice down in front of John. There was a crackle of static and he said, "You should have shown her your spacesuit, Sport."

John banged himself in the side of the head suspecting a malfunction. Pam just kept burning, but now he was falling toward the surface of the new planet.

His arm really was on fire.

Pam was a graceful blue burning cloud. She dipped and soared and skimmed over the surface until she came to a cave. She disappeared inside.

The Dark Spot sucked up the planet and swallowed it and then disappeared just before the *Peaches* passed through where it had been.

John initiated emergency procedures and got his suit sealed. He would probably lose an arm, but he could make do with a mechanical. He could see that the *Peaches* was going through a few emergency procedures of its own. Had the ship hit the strange planet from the Dark Spot, all would have been lost, but that hadn't happened. Pam had closed her door just in time, but that didn't let John off the hook. They would fish him out of space, and he would be in big trouble.

Maybe if he had worked a little harder, she would have taken him home to meet the folks.

Gas

L*indsey put a hand over each of Jack's ears* like she was holding a pumpkin and moved in nose to nose to communicate the
following information wordlessly.

You're wondering what we're doing here, well, this morning. oh,
a little after 9:00, call it 9 15, Connie at the office gave me the tickets
and told me how to get here. She said go down the block and around
the corner then take a right and go straight for a while.

"But . . . but . . ."

Then turn left and keep your eyes peeled for a doorway with stairs
just inside and when you spot it, oh look there it is now, go up the stairs
and down the hall to your left, no, no, your other left, to the very end,
and knock, and wait for the little slot to slam open, and then you say
the password.

"We don't know the password!" Jack said.

One sec. Lindsey looked off to one side like she was thinking.
Connie told me the password.

"I can't believe you forgot the password."

I've almost got it. Something about holding your breath and turning blue until you find true love.

"Oh, never mind," a man behind the door said. "Just fork over
your tickets."

Lindsey poked the tickets through the little slot in the door.

"Don't hit him in the eyes!" Jack whispered.

The man behind the door laughed like yeah that was going to happen. He opened the door and waited invisible in the darkness for them
to enter.

Lindsey took Jack's hand. Come on. It'll be fun!

Meaning the famous flutist Aloysius Mann would be in town for only
a few days, and Jack said, "So that should have meant there would be less
time we'd have to spend avoiding him," and she said, very funny!

Besides, we're already here.

Why was this so important to her? Jack didn't believe that bit about Connie at the office getting the tickets. There might not even be a Connie at the office. It was like every date lately. Lindsey had been so evasive, nervous sidelong glances, unaccountable giggling, and comments right out of the blue like oh, don't you just love the woodwinds, and oh, wouldn't it be great if we could take in more cultural events, and oh, look, the world famous Aloysius Mann is coming to this funky little uptown club, and oh, I wonder if he'll do Bach? There was a message just under the surface of the way she walked and the way she held her fork when they met for lunch, and the message warned of an obstacle to overcome.

He worried but not too much, because he was absolutely crazy about her.

Maybe the famous Aloysius Mann will play our song, Jack. She waited smiling for him to say, oh yeah, our favorite song! I can't wait. But he wondered if the great man really did toot their song, would the classic cartoon from which Jack knew the song in the first place be playing in the background?

Jack saw white hands pull open a slash in the darkness, some kind of curtain, and the ticket-taker said, "Watch your step on the way down."

The flight of stairs up from the street seemed pointless now, because you had to go down another steep flight of stairs into a bowl below street level. The seats ran down half the bowl to a lighted stage.

At the top of the stairs, a young blond woman emerged, gleaming grin first, from the gloom and handed each of them a package about as big as a shoe box — some kind of device, metal and maybe rubber, in crinkly clear plastic. "There's still lots of room down front," she said and handed them each a program. "Please wait for instructions before you open anything."

Jack and Lindsey made their way down the stairs. They found seats in the third row. They could have gotten seats right in the middle, but Lindsey said they would have the best view of Aloysius Mann's fancy finger work if they were offset a little to the left. Most of the other listeners must have shared her assessment since the audience was definitely skewed to the left.

"What is this?" Jack crinkled the clear plastic on his package.

Er . . . how would I know? Lindsay looked away quickly in a manner that told him she was withholding information, not exactly lying, okay, so she was lying, why mince words? She was lying through her teeth, pulling the wool over his eyes, playing fast and loose with the facts.

The lights blinked, and then went out altogether. There was a long pause, and soon lots of grumbling and shifting about in the seats, but just before everyone panicked and stampeded for the only door, probably trampling to death the young and aged and just plain slow or not feeling so hot today, a little sniffly, we thought maybe a bit of classical music would help, a spot lighted the stage. A moment later a woman dressed from waist to neck in a business suit and from waist to feet in jeans and sneakers, walked to a microphone, tapped it, and spoke. Jack thought she might be the same young woman who had handed him his package at the top of the stairs.

She said, "Tonight we are honored to present Aloysius Mann who will favor us with selections from his unaccompanied repertoire for the flute."

She paused for a smattering of applause, but she'd misjudged their enthusiasm, and there was a painful period of silence before she continued. "You will be happy to know that the apparatus you were issued when you entered the theater has been sanitized for your protection."

Maybe she expected more applause, because she paused again until someone coughed. "Okay," she said. "At this time please open your packages."

Many people had already opened their packages. Jack could hear them muttering as they turned the strange black objects around and around in their hands. He had, of course, followed instructions and not opened his package until told to do so. Judging by the sound of simultaneous cellophane ripping and crinkling, a fair number of other people had also followed instructions.

"Including you. Surprise, surprise," he told Lindsey.

Oh, please, she replied with a look.

The apparatus turned out to be a classic gas mask — black and rubbery with clear plastic insect eyes and pig snout. Adjustable head straps.

"Let's suit up, then." The woman had a gas mask, too, and she was going to show them how to use it. "Adjust your straps like this," she said. "Then put the mask to your face and secure it like this." Her voice became muffled. "Now everyone turn to your right and make sure your neighbor's head straps are secure."

Lindsey was to his left, so it was a little like a clandestine affair (he supposed) when he turned to his right and closely examined the back of the head and neck of the woman who had gotten her gas mask strap snagged on her ponytail. Jack reached forward and adjusted it and felt her tremble at his touch and said, "There! That's better."

"What about the guys at the end of the rows?" someone shouted.

"I was getting to that," the woman said. "Now turn to your left and check your other neighbor's straps. This is what we call 'double redundancy' and is just one more thing we do for your safety."

"Double?"

Oh, never mind, Jack. The show's about to start.

The woman said, "So, now I give you Aloysius Mann!" She started the applause herself and backed off the stage to the left as a stagehand hurried in from the right with a music stand. He put it down in the center of the stage and took the microphone with him as he left.

Everything went black.

Then the spotlight came on again, and the famous flute player was already there by the music stand. He looked to be in his early seventies. Bald with clouds of gray above his ears. Wrinkled brown suit. Silver flute. No gas mask.

He looked out at them and smiled. He lifted his instrument and began.

The opening was clear and pure and complex. Jack checked his program. It wasn't easy to see it through the plastic lenses of his gas mask, but he was able to determine Mann was playing Bach's Partita in A minor.

"Allemande," he whispered to Lindsey.

"Shush," someone said.

Hey, wait a minute. What was that at the end of the flute?

Yes, there it was again — a puff of green gas from the end of the flute.

Definitely green gas, like smoke, and now as the music soared, the gas billowed from the end of the flute until it wasn't easy to see the maestro.

"What the hell," Jack said.

Someone tapped him on the shoulder. "Please, don't talk."

Lindsey took his hand and communicated with little taps and squeezes thusly.

It's such a sad story. Everyone realized very early that Aloysius was a prodigy. It was easy to see the boy could be one of the great musicians of all time. His family was supportive and allowed him time for practice and funds for the best schools. He was one of the youngest flutists in a prestigious school in Europe when he was not yet nine. Contests won. Impressive venues. Everything was coming up roses for young Aloysius Mann.

But then in his early teens, his breath went bad and even a little visible. He used sprays and chewed breath mints, but nothing helped much. He became a target for a good deal of mean-spirited teasing. He put his head down and pushed on, and the music he made was phenomenal.

But by the time he turned twenty-five, he could no longer appear in public. It was the smell, not the sound, that drove his audience from the theaters, tears running down their faces and curses on their lips.

Had it not been for recorded music he might have been a goner.

"It looks like he's doing okay now," Jack whispered.

Indignant throat clearing from the rear. Jack glanced back to see the black snout and glaring eyes of the man or woman behind him. He shrugged and smiled, but his smile was wasted in his own mask.

Aloysius Mann hit the high A of the Allemande, and the green gas rolled from the end of his flute like smoke from an oil fire.

People coughed at the sight of it.

By the time he hit the high A again on the repeat, it was easy to believe you might not be on Earth anymore.

"Venus," Jack said.

Too hot, these days. Maybe in the fifties when it rained all of the time. Instead, we might imagine we're on a planet some 23 light years from Earth with a similar atmosphere if you discount the gas produced by its inhabitants.

"What makes you say that?"

Before he could be tapped and told the shut up again, the pause between the movements ended, and Aloysius Mann stepped into the Corrente.

It turns out, Lindsey continued, that the affliction came upon him slowly. By his forties, he could not be in the same room with people at all, even when he was not producing the very considerable breath necessary for the flute. In fact, he could not get closer than about ten feet even outside. Nevertheless, with the judicious use of mouthwashes, breath sprays and mints, and room deodorizers, he managed to live a somewhat ordinary life.

Lately, though, record sales have diminished, and since he cannot really take on students, he must resort to performances like this. Lindsey looked at Jack like she wanted him to say something, but what could he say to such a story. He looked to his right, but he couldn't see the woman with the ponytail.

You could have cut the green air with a sword. Jack was glad to be holding onto Lindsey's hand. Otherwise he would be alone with nothing but a brighter glow in the green where the flutist must be as he produced music that almost made it all worthwhile. Jack felt his body melt away until he was all ears and one hand holding onto Lindsey in the green clouds.

When the music stopped, she let go of his hand, and he experienced a moment of absolute panic. He was alone, lost in a green gas world of silence forever. He might have been swimming furiously, struggling, but he couldn't feel his arms and legs. He might have made a sound. Some kind of undignified squeak.

But then he found her again, and she said, it's okay, it's okay, the music is about to start again, and it did.

The Sarabande, slow, smooth and amazing, and Jack settled into it like a gulp of air on surfacing while drowning or maybe coming back into the sunshine from a gloomy forest or like none of those things, silly, she said and said, I've got a confession to make.

"Yes?"

Aloysius Mann is my grandfather.

"What?"

And he's not really a man.

"Your grandfather is a woman?"

No, I should've said he's not human. Sorry for the sexist language.

She leaned in close, and as her face came out of the green gas, he could see she wasn't wearing her gas mask. He wants to meet you. That's what this is really all about.

"And this green gas routine will happen to you, too, as you approach your thirties? How come I haven't noticed it yet?"

Yes, she said, yes it will. And you will.

"And you're from some place that isn't Venus in the fifties?"

That's right, and when it was clear that we would never leave this planet again, we had to change in order to survive. We made certain modifications so we could blend in, but there was only so much we could do, and it wasn't entirely successful. When we did as much as we could to ourselves, we were down to just grandpa and me as a newly modified baby. Everyone else had died. We're the last of our kind, and Grandpa decided he simply could not die and leave me all alone, so he decided to change you people, too. Or at least one of you. For me.

"You mean . . . ?"

That's right, Jack, Grandpa beamed certain modifications at your parents even before you were conceived and later before you were even born, he did some more beaming.

"You mean . . . ?"

That's right, Jack. We made you what you are, but we couldn't tell if it would really work until now.

Aloysius Mann was deep into the Bourrée Angloise now.

"How will we know if it worked?"

You must take off your mask, Jack.

"What will happen?"

Nothing. Or something wonderful. Or you'll throw up, and we'll have to go our separate ways.

She squeezed his hand. I'm so afraid, Jack.

She sang a note that so perfectly matched her grandfather's flute that the grumblers hidden in the green gas behind them must surely believe the voice to be part of this unusual performance, and as she sang the note, a tendril of purple gas drifted from her lips, first faintly then as vigorously as disturbed vipers and twisted through the green toward Jack. I've arrived, Jack.

Smell me.

Jack let go of her hand and reached up to pull off his mask. He hesitated for only a moment to set his resolve. No matter what she smelled like, no matter how awful her grandfather's gas was, he would not throw up. He would smile and smile and smile and breathe through his mouth for the rest of his life if it meant not losing her.

All he could see was her face floating in the green gas, a small sad smile, and the purple tendrils drifting from her lips. He pulled off his mask.

He took a tentative whiff. Not so bad. Wouldn't you say? A little cheesy maybe. And somehow musical in a surefooted manner. He could get used to this — like sleeping next door to someone snoring.

Jack's eyes were watering.

How are you? she asked.

I'm fine, he said. I think I'm fine.

He rubbed the tears from his eyes and filled his lungs and felt his stomach lurch. He smiled at her, but his smile was tight, and she moved in until their noses touched.

Yes, I'm fine, he said.

He put his arms around her and felt her tremble. He kissed her neck, her cheek, closed each eye with a kiss, worried he was beating around the bush, kissed her nose, her lips, drew deeply her purple gas into himself.

He yelped and pulled away and the sound he made was low and rich and Aloysius Mann answered at once with a run of high notes ending in a spectacular trill.

Yes, while her grandfather's gas might not be so easy to take, this was wonderful. He swooped back down before her disappointed frown had even gotten properly started and kissed her again. Rolling hills of yellow wild flowers rushed together to meet her waves of purple blossoms sweeping across the face of the earth.

Her modifications were absolutely perfect. She was made for him.

But what about his modifications? Had he been properly made for her? What if she were choking back bile and this kiss was for her nothing like it was for him? What if his own biological tweaks had failed? He pulled away a little and blew a canary yellow gas ring, and she laughed a laugh of such unqualified joy, and they came together again, and she filled his head and body. He said marry me, Lindsey, and she said yes, oh, yes, and we'll make babies, and he said, yes, wonderful, fantastic, and she said our babies will take over the world and turn it into someplace that isn't like Venus in the fifties, and he said someday I'll be the grandpa, but not too soon, she cautioned, and we'll get a little house, he said, and she said with a yard where we can grow flowers.

We were made for each other.

There was wild applause. It was probably for Aloysius Mann, since he had finished the partita, but they chose to think it was for them. They snuggled together as close as they could get in the theater seats to hear Grandpa play his flute. Later they would go backstage and tell him the good news.

They allowed themselves to become lost in the music, sometimes slicing the green air with a few purple and yellow notes of their own, but mostly listening and looking at one another, and at one point, her grandfather really did play their favorite song, and Jack still couldn't identify it apart from the classic cartoon, but he didn't mention that. Some things are better left unsaid.

13

Intercontinental Ballistic Missle Boy

hope it isn't raining, but if it is raining, I hope the wind isn't blowing, but if the wind is blowing, I hope there aren't a lot of puddles in the streets and cars zooming by to splash me, but if there are cars, I hope Karen isn't driving one of them, but if she is behind the wheel, I hope she doesn't see me, but if she does spot me, I hope she doesn't realize I'm not wearing the goofy earmuffs she gave me for the holidays, but if she does notice, I hope she'll stew slowly in silence instead of boiling over and calling her henchmen to snatch me off the street and drag me back to the hacienda for torture by chili peppers, but if it must be the heat for me, I hope I can be manly and not break down crying, "Karen, Karen, please stop feeding me those red hot peppers," burbling, breathing fire, babbling, begging for water, water, water, like I didn't get enough out in the street where I hope it isn't raining, but if it is raining, I hope there are no wet dogs chasing me through the puddles, and cars honking, and drivers yelling, "hey, get off the street you moron," but if there are dogs and puddles and honking and yelling and running and hiding in an alley behind some garbage cans, I hope there are no rats, but maybe I shouldn't have mentioned the rats, I hope Karen didn't hear me mention the rats, but if she is listening maybe from behind that curtain in the window high up in the alley, or maybe she's actually inside one of the cans, hold on, let me check, nope, but if she does somehow hear about the rats, I hope she'll have too much on her mind to remember to use them on me when her henchmen finally find me and drag me back to the hacienda for jalapenos, but if she remembers, maybe the rats will be too smart for her, I hope they'll be too smart for her, but if the rats are dumb, dumb and mean, all teeth and no brains, easy to catch and be transported back to the hacienda in little wire cages, I hope they'll be gullible rats so I can make a deal with them, something like you don't eat my eyes and maybe I won't blow up and burn down the place and everyone in it, which reminds me why burning down the place with everyone in it would not be such a bad idea, you didn't hear me say that, it's just that they're always so mean, Karen's henchmen and the other inmates, no, kids, call them Karen's kids, her big kids, and the way the grocery checker looks like she's about to bust out laughing when she says hey, more Kool-Aid, big guy, so you're one of Karen's kids, right? and the way the kids can always get my goat saying, I see BM Boy, what, you see BM boy? well, I smell BM Boy, and they all laugh like donkeys, and I run out into the street where I hope it isn't raining, what do they all want with me anyway, it's not like I'm making trouble, I mean I didn't go off when I first got here and you know I could have, but I didn't, I could have resisted arrest, made a scene in this strange land where I fell to earth with my sad story about how my parents had been eaten by missionaries, and I could have said a lot of bad words in a language no one around here could understand, but I didn't, instead I went quietly and had no snappy comeback when they called me a foreign devil, not that I knew what that meant for months and months of slow language learning, Karen pointing and saying and me repeating and she slapping and me struggling already suspecting the truth about her hacienda and her hot peppers which were supposed to sweat the poison out of my system, but now it really is raining and there are puddles and barefoot cars with hairy feet and dogs with monkey ears and sneaky smiles and windows running down the walls and henchmen and lights in the sky and bugs and bats and snakes and rats, big butterfly nets, choke holds, tear gas and smoke and people shouting and people screaming, and it's finally my turn, everyone's looking at me, I can feel a hum rising from deep in my works, here we go, here we go, if life is a ride, you spend most of your time just standing around waiting to get on, waiting for a moment like this, right here, right now, no past, no future, just now, your own parade that not even the rain can rain on, oh wow, oh wow, whoopee, I'm what you might call up to my ears in this moment of mine, I can smell sunrise singing in the daffodils and ships at sea honk because they love Jesus and they don't think I'm so bad myself, but then it's over, and the henchmen tackle me, and I want to know can I go again, Karen, can I, can I go again, can I have another moment, can I, can I?

"Don't be silly ICBM boy," she says, "It's time to go back to the hacienda for a quick bite. Your ears look cold, where are your merry Christmas earmuffs?"

It's like from her point of view nothing has changed.
"Get back," I tell her, "get back or I'll go kaboom."
She doesn't get back.
I go kaboom.

14

Glinky

1
Not a Bird

G *linky is on TV.*
The man with the abdominal gunshot wound isn't watching Glinky.

What the heck is Glinky anyway?

Is he a mouse?

No!

Is she a cat?

No!

It's Glinky, Glinky, Glinky!

The wounded man wants to somehow get to the telephone on the table near the couch and call for help. It's a long way to crawl. Glinky sings him a little song of encouragement, but it's clear the cartoon is mocking him.

When the man gets to the table, he looks back and sees a long smear of blood across the carpet and beyond that Glinky glaring at him from the TV.

Who in the world is Glinky?

Some monkey?

No.

A flying fish with horse lips and dog ears?

No, he's just Glinky!

The man stretches up an arm and bats around on the top of the table for the phone. It isn't there. No, wait, there it is. He pulls it off the table and tries to catch it as it falls, and fails, and it hits him in the face, but the pain is nothing like the pain in his gut. The pain from the phone hitting him in the face is trivial. It might as well not be pain at all. He drags the phone into his lap and picks up the receiver and puts it to his ear.

There is no dial tone.

He pulls at the phone wire that leads to the wall. Soon, he's holding the end. The shooter or someone (maybe Glinky?) has unplugged the phone.

He crawls under the table to look for the outlet. He finally spots it behind the couch. Should he try to get back there and plug the phone back in? No. He won't be able to move the couch. He will have to crawl to the front door and yell into the street for help. The door is so far away it looks like he will have to Alice down to a very small size to fit through it. But he must get there first. A journey of a thousand scootches begins with the first scootch.

Will he make it, Glinky?

"No!"

So, he'll never get out of here?

"Not unless he buys something."

What must he buy, Glinky?

"The farm!"

2
To Your Left

Oddly, I'd been on my way to the Medical Mall that day anyway. It was company policy that all my employees undergo annual medical checkups, and the fact that I was my only employee did not tempt me to relax the requirement. Karl Sowa Investigations had procedures, and we followed them. I didn't expect to be a one-man operation forever.

I could have driven the few blocks from my office on Eleventh Avenue to the Medical Mall, but instead I made the healthy choice and walked. It was a glorious Oregon day. The sun was shining for a change. The birds were chirping. The squirrels were gathering nuts or whatever urban squirrels gathered. The traffic was a steady hum with not so many horn honks.

Spring at last.

I was thinking I should maybe whistle a happy tune when right behind me, someone shouted, "To your left!"

Meaning, I thought, I should jump to my left.

Wrong.

The bicyclist behind me yelped and swerved to the right at the last moment and clipped me, and I stumbled off the sidewalk where a great wall of metal rushed by, and for a moment I thought I'd stepped onto railroad tracks that had not been there a moment before, but then the thing passed, and I could see it was a city bus. There was some kind of big rodent with huge red eyes painted on the back of the bus. It studied me with smug amusement.

I looked back to see the bicyclist peddling full speed toward a place where the sidewalk made a sharp turn at a building. Probably a kid, I thought, judging by the fact that there were things sticking out of her helmet like horns or ears and long red hair shooting out in all directions — some kind of costume?

Surely she would slow down for the turn. I had a sudden feeling of total satisfaction at the thought of her hitting the building with a cartoon splat, but then I felt guilty for thinking that and then felt okay, realizing it wasn't like it was actually going to happen, but then it did.

The wheels were a blur and for a moment I thought they were not wheels at all but the galloping feet and legs of some kind of furry beast, but before I could get that thought fully formed, the rider ran headlong into the building. Instead of crashing or bouncing back out into traffic, she passed right through the wall as if it were made of smoke.

Before I had time even to doubt what I'd seen, someone shouted, "Don't move!"

Then there were hands all over me. A young woman told me everything would be okay, you'll be fine, just relax, you're hurt, but we're here to help. There were three of them — two big blond guys with very short hair and the young woman with the soothing voice, all of them wearing white medical coats. One of the guys grabbed me under the arms from behind and the other snatched up my feet, and they lowered me onto a gurney.

"Hey!" I yelled and tried to get off. The woman put both hands on my chest and pushed down. She was pretty strong, but she didn't have to hold me long, because one of the guys pulled a leather strap over my arms and chest and fastened it. Likewise another strap across my lower legs.

"Okay, let's go," the woman said.

One of the guys pushed me onto the sidewalk. The woman walked along beside me patting my shoulder and looking concerned. I lifted my head as much as I could and looked down the length of my body and between my feet and saw the other young man take off running while waving his arms and making siren noises. The guy pushing my gurney picked up the pace, and the woman jogged to keep up. Soon we were zooming along dangerously fast.

The guy making the siren noises didn't slow down for the big automatic glass doors of the Medical Mall. The doors opened just in time, and we zipped into the mall.

The waiting areas were set up like sidewalk cafés so consumers of medical services could watch other consumers strolling up and down the mall. There were small white metal tables and chairs and roving venders offering cola or cappuccino. The doctors were arranged by body parts or maybe alphabetically (podiatry followed by proctology) or maybe metaphorically — is that a kick in the ass or what? Bings and pings now and then interrupted the Muzak which was a song about buying this or buying that, come on, do it for the Glinkster, don't be a tightwad.

We were still moving pretty fast as we passed through one of the café waiting rooms and banged through a set of double doors into a huge bright room. The guy pushing the gurney let it go, and I flew forward spinning like the jack of diamonds tossed at a big silk top hat.

I tightened up for the forthcoming crash and pain, but someone caught my gurney before it hit a wall.

A new team descended on me. My eyelid was peeled back and a bright light shined into my eye, first on the left and then on the right. Someone else stuck a needle in my arm behind the elbow.

"Hey, I'm not hurt," I yelled. "Let me up."

"Relax, Karl," a woman said. "Everything is going to be fine."

How did she know my name?

I felt the familiar coldness of a stethoscope on my chest and looked down to see that I was now wearing only my underwear and that my arms and legs were no longer strapped down.

The guy listening to my chest put away his stethoscope and said, "Get up now, please."

I got up. There were two women and one man dressed in white like the ones who'd snatched me off the street. I looked around the big room and it did not seem so big now and the gurney I'd ridden in on was now an examination table and instead of three people, there was only the one nurse, neat, maybe mid-forties, very efficient, no nonsense, and she directed me to a scale and weighed and measured me.

"Boy oh boy," she said.

"What?"

"Nothing, just your weight and height."

"Is it unusual?"

"We're all individuals, aren't we? Jump back up on here." I sat on the edge of the examination table, and she checked my reflexes.

"Whoa!" she said when my knee jerked.

"What?"

She turned my head to one side and put something in my ear and said, "Well, this is interesting." She turned my head the other way to look into my other ear. "Here, too," she said.

"What is it?" I asked.

"Nothing," she said. "Everything is shipshape."

"But what about my ears?"

"What about your ears?"

"Never mind."

"Well, just relax," she said. "The doctor will be with you shortly."

Which meant sometime in the indefinite future but probably before I died of old age or hell froze over.

I had lost track of the number of times I'd gone completely through my compressed T'ai Chi routine by the time the doctor stepped in. I froze in the middle of Lan Ch'ueh Wei (Grasping the Bird's Tail).

"Well, I see you can still dance," he said. "I'm Dr. Jones." He held out his hand for me to shake. "Sit down, Mr. Sorrow."

"Sowa," I said. "Karl Sowa."

He was maybe fifty with no hair at all on his head or face and that made him look a little rounder than he probably was. Oddly, his nametag said Dr. Smith. He flipped through the pages on his clipboard. "Things look pretty good, Karl. I see you've been eating right and exercising regularly."

"How could you know that?"

"The usual channels," he said. "No jogging?"

"No jogging," I said.

"Yes, well, never mind. I see you don't smoke. Moderate alcohol. Good, good. A little goes a long way, as they say. Ha ha. Your cholesterol count is good. All things considered I'd say you're in excellent health."

"That's good to hear," I said.

"Except for the bus, of course," he said.

"Actually it was the bike," I said. "The bus missed me."

"You may be confused," he said. "But even so, what about next time? No, I won't beat around the bush, Mr. Sorrow. You are in the awkward position of being totally healthy. That is, the odds of you dropping dead from some disease are quite small."

"Why is that awkward?" I asked. "It sounds pretty good to me."

"Awkward for you," he said. "This makes you perfect for us."

"Perfect for you?"

"We have something to help you."

"Help me with what?"

"The bus," he said. "The healthy ones always get hit by a bus."

I waited for him to smile, but he seemed deadly serious. After another moment of eye contact, he said, "There is a new medication from our corporate partner, Philosophical Pharmaceuticals, called Pilula Omnibus. Just out. The latest thing."

"What does that mean?"

"You could call it the 'Bus Pill.'"

"I don't get it," I said. "What's it for?"

"For people like you," he said. "Guys like you you're all the time exercising. Right? You get a lot of fiber in your diet. Not much red meat. Vitamins. You don't smoke. Maybe a couple of fingers of Old Cow after dinner, am I right?"

"I think that's Old Crow," I said.

"Whatever. So what happens to you?"

"What do you mean?"

"All that clean living means you've just got to get hit by a bus, Karl."

"And you mean this pill . . ."

"Exactly," he said. "Pilula Omnibus protects you from life's last little irony. Here's a sample." He put a small blue pill in my hand.

"So, does it work on other stuff?" I asked. "Like icy sidewalks?"

"Well, I don't know about that," he said. "Let me get you some water."

He walked over to a water cooler and brought me back a little paper cone of water. "Go ahead. Take it."

So, I did. Hey, he was a doctor, after all.

"Good. Good." He walked to the door. "Now just wait here."

"But what am I waiting for?"

"The next bus," he said and closed the door behind him.

I found my clothes on a chair to one side of the examination table.

My socks were in my shoes. My pants were folded neatly on the chair. My shirt was draped around the back. It didn't look like an arrangement I would have created myself, but at this point I could not be sure. I got dressed.

I wondered what the pill would do.

I didn't feel any different.

But then I caught a whiff of tobacco smoke. Incredibly, someone somewhere in the Medical Mall was smoking. The smell got suddenly stronger and louder as a woman stepped out of a nook over by the soda machines, and the space expanded and filled with many people moving in all directions, everyone with a noise to contribute to the heavy echo in the big bus station. I could see lots of cigarette butts crushed out on the floor where the woman had been lurking. She must have been waiting for some time for the doctor to leave so we could be alone in the crowd.

"There's no time to lose," she said. "We've got to get you out of here before they realize what I'm up to." She meant the people watching through the big glass windows above the mezzanine — it could have been the whole medical staff up there elbowing one another and pointing and whispering behind their hands.

Now along with the cigarette smoke, there was the heavy odor of old cooking grease and diesel fuel.

The woman was more than thirty and dressed in jeans and a shirt that wasn't long enough to hide her navel. Long frizzy red hair poking out at odd angles, brown eyes, no smile at the moment, but I imagined her smile would be a very nice thing to see. I didn't know her, but I did recognize the bicycle helmet under her arm. It had fuzzy donkey or maybe deer ears attached to it.

"Look out!" she yelled and pushed me back, and a bus roared between us.

When it passed, the woman who had just saved my life was still there. She hurried across to me, and we ran. People got out of our way, but when we tried to merge with the bus station crowd, they wouldn't let us in. Whenever we approached they pushed us back into the path of the buses. I took the woman's hand, and we ran again. I could hear the next bus screaming up behind us.

I thought the bus pill was supposed to protect me from buses. Instead it seemed to be attracting them. I imagined someone up there among the medical people was telling the others it was time to go back to the drawing board. Get another test subject. This one was going to be a goner soon. There seemed to be no safe place for us.

But then an idea hit me. "Wait." I looked around but didn't immediately see what I wanted and felt a moment of despair, and then I spotted it and said, "Over there," and took off, dragging her behind me.

I pulled us to a halt by a small blue sign on a post. The sign read, "Bus stop."

"Get back up on the sidewalk," I said, "and then follow my lead as fast as you can."

I waited until the next bus appeared and then put out my hand to signal the driver. I got up on the sidewalk beside the woman and waited. As the bus roared ever closer, I lost all confidence in my plan. What was there to stop the bus from crashing onto the sidewalk? Nothing. Maybe we should run again. Too late.

The bus didn't run up on the sidewalk after us. It stopped at the sign and the door hissed open. The woman hurried on, and I followed right after her.

Something was holding me back. Getting on the bus was like forcing my way into a high wind. The bus pill had not made it impossible for a bus to hit me, but it was making it hard for me to get on a bus. There were certainly more than a few bugs in the formula.

"Come on," the woman said. She grabbed my hand and gave me a good yank, and I passed through the invisible barrier and nearly stumbled into the driver.

The woman dropped coins in the coin device, and the driver closed the door. We found seats together about halfway back.

3

"Ask not what your action figure can do.
Ask what you can do with your action figure."

She had to hand it to him. Getting on the bus instead of trying to run from it was a great idea. She went to work on his shirt buttons starting at the top.

"Be still," she said. "And relax."

"What are you doing?"

"I'm putting a big Band-Aid on your tummy where the bus hit you."

"Okay, I guess, that's okay," he said. "But it was the bike."

He slumped in his seat and became perfectly still. He was the very embodiment of the idea that "this seat is taken." Better than a straw hat with fake daisies, but she needed to get him back into his major mode — tough wisecracking detective.

She slipped her hand into the front of his pants.

No dice.

Probably she should have bought the optional Auxiliary Dick Kit (batteries not included).

Maybe he would feel more confident if he were holding his gun.

She checked the placement of the bandage over his wound and buttoned his shirt back up. No shoulder holster. So, maybe he carried heat in his belt at the back? She bent him forward and pulled the coat up around his shoulders. Nothing. Don't tell me he's unarmed, she thought. What the heck am I paying for? She pulled his coat down and sat him back up.

She would have to improvise.

She picked up his right hand and straightened the first finger and cocked the thumb creating the classic bang bang you're dead position for cops and robbers.

A light came back into his eyes.

"Better?" she asked.

"Much," he said. "Thanks." He poked his hand into his coat and when he pulled it out, the gun she had formed of his fingers was gone.

"Let me tell you what's happening," she said.

4
I Eat a Sandwich

"Where are we going?" I asked the woman with the bike helmet. No, wait. She wasn't carrying the bike helmet now.

"Brooklyn," she said.

"What did you do with your helmet?"

"I dropped the head," she said.

It's always important to have something to say when you're confused. "Did it bounce?" I asked.

It was like we were talking through a layer of maple syrup or maybe like we were communicating with Morse code and it took a few seconds for her to work out what I'd just said. Or maybe we were not sitting right next to each other. Maybe I was still in Oregon and she was already in Brooklyn and it took a while for my voice to make it all the way across the country.

"Here we are," she said.

I had not been to the East Coast in many years, but I had no trouble believing I was looking out the bus window at a Brooklyn neighborhood.

We got off in front of a storefront window with the words "Phil's Kosher Deli" in big white letters. The woman took my arm and walked toward the deli. Up close, she smelled very nice.

Bells jingled when the door opened. She let go of my arm and walked to a high glass butcher case and spoke to a big guy slicing meat.

She glanced back at me. "I've ordered you a Black Forest ham and Swiss on rye. You want a big dill pickle?"

"What are we doing here?"

"This is my favorite deli in all the world," she said and looked back at the man slicing meat who now had a big grin. "And Phil is my all time favorite deli guy."

"Here you go," Phil said. He put a plate with a huge sandwich on top of the display case. "You want that pickle?"

"Sure," I said. "Why not?"

Phil dipped into a gallon jar and put a pickle on my plate and pushed the plate forward a little as if to say, well, go on, take it. I picked it up and held it, not knowing what to do next. Phil and the woman both looked at me like they were waiting for me to catch on.

Finally, the woman said, "Well, take it to a booth."

She turned back to Phil who got back to the business of building another sandwich. I watched them for a moment, still not moving. Phil stopped slicing meat. The woman looked over her shoulder at me again.

"Well, what about something to drink?" I asked.

Phil laughed a huge laugh, and the woman's smile made me feel like maybe I was getting the old patter back. I'd been right; it was a wonderful smile.

"Give us a couple of cream sodas, Phil," she said.

Not wanting to push my luck, I took my sandwich to a booth.

A few minutes later, she slid in across from me, and a moment after that, Phil delivered the cream sodas in tall brown bottles along with a couple of glasses of crushed ice.

"Yummy," she said and picked up her sandwich and took a huge bite and chewed and gazed off into space with a look of absolute contentment on her face.

I took a bite of mine, too. It was very good. In fact, it was probably the best ham and Swiss I'd ever eaten. The cheese was so fresh it was crumbly. And the ham . . . well, you couldn't get ham like that in Oregon.

"I'm Karl Sowa," I said.

"Over there," she said.

"You're suppose to tell me who you are when I tell you who I am," I said. "And maybe what's going on?"

She put her sandwich down and reached under the table like she was searching her pockets or maybe digging in a purse. She produced a business card and handed it across to me.

Urbana Fontana — Scene Shifter

Black block letters on white. No address. No phone.

"Is that really your name?" I asked.

"Over here," she said.

"What is this over here and over there business? Why not just tell me what's going on?"

"Over there, you're Karl Sowa," she said. "Over here, you're Chuck Sorrow. Over there, you're legal to do private investigation work. Over here, well, let's just say you get things done for people who don't ask too many questions. Over there my name is Jane Boyd. Over here, I'm Urbana Fontana and I can change little things. Get it?"

"Not even a little," I said.

"Let me put it this way," she said. "Earlier today an incursion into history occurred. Something from Elsewhere muscled into our reality. Since it was never supposed to be here, there was no place for it. It made room for itself by pushing other things aside. And since those things couldn't just go away, they were all crushed together and thereby got a little strange."

"I see," I said, but my sarcasm was wasted on her.

"The Squeeze," she said, "has caused a Disturbance which is washing backwards and forwards in time changing things. One of the things that is clear over here is that there was a plague of sympathetic magic involving the name game back in the eighties. Do you know the name game?"

"Robin robin bo bobbin . . ."

"Don't!"

"Why not?"

"Are you crazy?" she said. "Do you want to cause absolute chaos? Don't you remember the riots in the streets?"

"Actually, I don't," I said.

"How strange," she said. "Maybe it hasn't gotten to you yet. When it does, you'll remember it. Anyway, over here, my mother thought I would have an easier time in life if it were hard to work me into the name game. Her first thought was Terpsichore, but then she realized people would call me Terp, and that would be too easy, so she named me Urbana. Totally ineffective, by the way, since some people think it's harder and some think it's easier."

I couldn't help myself. Silently, I sang, "Urbana Urbana bo burbana."

There was a deep thud, and the lights flickered.

"Stop it," she said. "I can see what you're doing."

"It's clear," I said, "I'm having a bad reaction to the Bus Pill. I'm probably collapsed in the mall back in Oregon."

"Don't you think it's a little strange there even is a Bus Pill in the first place?"

"Well, there is that," I said.

She picked up her sandwich and took another bite, which reminded me that a bad reaction to some medication back in Oregon wouldn't explain this excellent ham and Swiss on rye. The texture of the dark rye bread. The crisp dark green lettuce of a variety I couldn't name. The sweet smell of red onions and mustard. The sandwich was simply too much in and of the world as I now knew it to be an hallucination.

Not to mention the cream soda.

"So, what is this something from elsewhere?"

"Glinky," she said.

I knew that name but I could not remember why. It had something to do with my current case. Of that much I was certain, but every time I reached for it, it scuttled away to the shadows where it watched me with red eyes. Red eyes also reminded me of something but I couldn't pin that down either.

"Everyone knows there are an infinite number of universes," she said, "many of them just a step this way or that way from this world."

"I think I saw something about that a couple of years ago during the very last season of PBS," I said. And speaking of PBS, the very idea of "Public" things was pretty strange these days. Public education? A dead dinosaur. Social security? Don't make me laugh. Public lands? Get out of here. Public airwaves? Oh, shut up.

"Glinky has jumped from one of those universes and has inserted itself into ours. Your mission, as you very well know, is to drive it out of here and save the world."

"Somehow that doesn't sound like a mission I would gladly undertake," I said. "In fact, all of this smells fishy to me. How do I know you're playing straight with me?"

"Think about cilantro," she said. "Do you remember that having anything to do with Mexican food when you were growing up?"

"Well, no."

"Now it's as if it's always been a big part of the cuisine," she said. "And don't even talk about broccoli."

"What about broccoli?"

"No one knew about broccoli when I was growing up. It's like it hadn't been invented. But now everyone knows it's been around forever."

"But I remember broccoli always being around."

"That's what I'm saying," she said. "Things are uneven. Soon, you'll remember growing up with all kinds of things."

"You mean until this morning there was no broccoli? That's a little hard to believe."

"So, consider Portobello mushrooms," she said.

I considered Portobello mushrooms.

"And what about the way cold fusion suddenly started working?" she asked.

"Science is like that." I could hear the doubt in my own voice. "Right out of the blue something pops up."

"No," she said. "None of that happened until this morning when Glinky showed up and his arrival reverberated through time changing things. The real danger is that everything we know will be pushed aside, crowded out. There is only so much room in reality. When Glinky got here, it pushed us all out toward the edges. As it elbows more and more room for itself, we will get more and more squeezed. Things will be

pretty terrible when we're all just smears on the inside of the jar that
is reality."

"So, how do you know so much about Glinky?" I asked.

"He wasn't always such a rat," she said.

"They never are."

"Back when we were in college," she said, "he told me no matter
how good the Business got, it would still be just the two of us."

"But now you think there's someone else?"

"Yes."

"What makes you think so?"

"Little things," she said.

There were always little things.

"Well, now you know everything, and you can go do your job,"
she said. "Finish your soda."

Why not? I sighed and picked up the glass. "Drink me," I said, and
tossed the rest of it down in a couple of big gulps.

"Okay, now put your arms up like this." She held up her arms like
she was reading a very big invisible book. "And close your eyes."

I held my arms up and closed my eyes. "Now what?"

I heard her slide out of the booth, and my fingers closed around
what I recognized at once as a steering wheel, and my heart lurched. I
opened my eyes and swerved back into the right lane. The car rocked
as a bus screamed by honking in the other direction. I got the car and
my breathing under control and looked around. Yes, this was my old
Mercedes, and yes, I was back in Eugene, Oregon. A moment later I
passed a street sign and confirmed that I was driving in the South Hills
of the city on my way to find out if Daniel Boyd was really cheating
on his wife.

5
Danny Boyd

You might suddenly realize you are here right now — totally present. It's like you wake up and think, oh, yeah, here I am, and this is all
there is and all there ever was or will be. The things you remember are
all part of this moment — just stuff you might be thinking about now.
If you consider history, all you're doing is considering history. It's not
like you can ever be right about it. The steps, causes, reasons for your

current situation are simply a story you tell yourself so you won't freak at the thought that you've just popped into existence and that there is no reason to think you won't pop out again as soon as you lose that feeling of here-and-nowness. At least you were blissfully ignorant before there were Glinky waves to wash you off your feet.

I pull up in my aging Mercedes in front of the South Hills love nest of Daniel Boyd, the dynamic CEO of Philosophical Pharmaceuticals, who has inserted himself into our community and has become an overnight big shot. My plan is to ring the bell, and when his squeeze answers the door, snap her photo.

The idea of "plan" is very strange in this context. Do I even have a camera? Does thinking about the future have any value when you only exist now? And if I have already pulled up at the front of the house, why am I still moving?

I park up the hill and walk down to the house where Daniel Boyd keeps his mistress. Boyd has been buying and selling stuff, backing this project and opposing that one, building mega stores and pushing aside the little guys, changing the landscape with broad, brutal sweeps of money, getting his smiling face in the papers and on TV. He runs a local infomercial called "Why?" WHY is the NYSE symbol for Philosophical Pharmaceuticals. The show is mostly about why you should take Danny's pills.

I ring the bell. The woman who answers the door looks just like Jane Boyd, Danny's wife who hired me to find out what he's up to. I am momentarily thrown totally off my game.

"Jane?"

She blows smoke my way and says, "Jane Jane bo bane . . ."

"Please, don't do that, Sweetheart." A man behind her puts his hands on her shoulders and pulls her back into the gloom. Danny Boyd takes her place in the doorway. He is so tall, dark, and handsome, he should be modeling men's suits for guys already at the top instead of selling pills. He says, "Mr. Sorrow, I presume?"

He may not always have been a rat, but he's a rat now, and he's got a gun. He motions me inside.

The woman who answered the door is pouring herself a drink. The bungalow opens right into a living room from the fifties — a flowered couch and end tables, a rotary dial telephone, bar and bar stools, a couple of chairs, and a big TV with rabbit ears. The TV is on and muttering softly to itself.

I see now that the woman might not be Jane after all. Why would Boyd be fooling around with a woman who looks so much like his wife? Maybe he isn't really fooling around. Maybe he has a woman who looks like Jane in every one of his houses around the world — duplicates so he doesn't have so much to pack when he travels.

"Move over by the bar," Danny says.

"What's this all about?"

"Give him the envelope," he says, and the woman hands me a big brown envelope.

She walks over to Danny, who keeps the gun pointed my way. He takes the drink from her. "Go wait in the car."

She sighs like she should have seen that coming and leaves. As soon as the front door closes behind her, Danny says, "Open it."

I pull a big eight by ten glossy out of the envelope.

Me and Urbana on the bus. My shirt is open all the way down. She's got her hand tucked into the front of my pants. Where in the world was the photographer standing?

"Now you know," Danny says.

"No, I don't," I say.

He shoots me and goes on out to join his wife in the car.

So, now how am I supposed to save the world, Glinky?

"You can't!"

I could call a friend, but the phone will just hit me in the face and then not work anyway. I can keep scootching for the front door, but I know I'll never make it.

What would happen if I turned Glinky off? I hang a sharp belly right and squirm for the TV.

"Hey! Hey! What are you doing?"

I struggle up to sit right in front of the flickering rodent. The flaw in my plan is now evident. No buttons on the TV and no remote.

Glinky sticks out his forked tongue at me and then turns and shows me his backside, waggles his naked tail at me, makes blubbery raspberry sounds with his horse lips.

I put my palms flat against the warm glass of the screen. It's just me and the Rat from Elsewhere now. I make my last desperate move. If there are to be riots in the streets again, so be it.

I chant, "Glinky Glinky bo binky."

He screams.

"Banana fanna fo finky."

Now there are a couple of big dials and knobs on the TV.

"Me my mo minky."

Don't touch that dial!

"Glinky!"

I turn him off.

Just like that.

I hear someone making siren sounds in the distance. I hope it's the guys with the gurney.

15

Jumping

W e stood waist-deep in the muddy green cattle pond. Seven of us. Boys, girls. None of us more than eleven. All of us standing perfectly still.

"Leeches," Carly had said at breakfast. "Leeches are the way out."

"Who wants out?" I'd wanted to know, because I always felt fine in the morning when the sun had not yet cooked the juices from the day, and my belly was full of pancakes and new milk, and the long night was a fading memory. Not so bad, not so bad. Ask me how it's going. Okay, so how's it going? Not so bad.

Carly had given me her china blue okay for you, buster brown bozo look. In fact, she'd swept the mess hall with the look. She could say a lot with a look like that like sure you've got your pancakes and you've got your milk but how long do you think it really is until dark? Not to mention the cows. Oh, forget it. Just forget it. I don't care what you do.

I could feel the leeches on my legs. My head felt light and tight and I'm thinking maybe it's nap time, slappy happy nappy time. Maybe just sink under the surface and fluff up a big mud pillow and pull the green slime up to my chin and drift off and wake up somewhere else. Was that the way it was supposed to work?

"Hey, Carly," I called, "just how the heck is this supposed to work?"

"The leeches," she said "transport you from the inside out, inter-dimentionally, if you know what that means, piece by piece to another world. Over there, first you're blood and then you get your muscles and your bones and your skin and stuff and then you're you, and you're not here any more."

"Bleed me up, Scotty," I said, but no one laughed. "Are we there yet?" Still nothing. We had sunk so low we were just heads in a pea green sea.

"This looks like a painting of hell," I said.

"They don't send kids to hell," someone said.

"They send them to camp," Carly said.

Where before they'll let you ride the ponies for five stinking minutes, they make you follow the cows around all day with super pooperscoopers. Look at us. Dozens of little butt munchkins dotting the fields as we move in on the cows with our dark green garbage sacks.

How you do, Buckeroo?

Okey dokey skinny-dipping with Carly, leech lazy and taking it easy.

But here it comes. The moment of transport.

Or not. Because next I know I'm on my back and on the bank and naked Carly is sitting on my stomach picking leeches off my legs. She looks back over her shoulder at me. "You idiot," she says.

I'm looking at her bottom but I'm seeing the future. Eaney meany jelly beanie the clouds open up, the angels sing, and I see us dancing, eating linguini, drinking white wine and checking out Paris.

Or maybe it was Rome. What did I know about faraway cities that summer?

"So, if I decide to go jump off a cliff," she says, "will you just stupidly follow right along?"

She doesn't know I can see the future. She doesn't know that she will have the power to drain the blood from my brain any time she wants, a sidelong glance, a crooked smile, a feather light touch to my arm, and one time she'll drop her keys and bend over to pick them up and I'll know she's doing it on purpose, but it won't matter.

"Yes," I say, " I'll jump after you, Carly."

16

The Library of Pi

1
What Emily Told
The Secret Police

I *'m sorry, but that's not possible.*
I don't think so.
No.
Never.
Not a chance.
Nothing doing.
No sirree.
No way, no how.
In your dreams.
When pigs fly!

2
The Library

The number pi is the ratio of a circle's circumference to its diameter. Pi is irrational and transcendental. The digits of pi go on forever, and they look like uniform random numbers. Professor Emily Lupin, a mathematician in Oregon, proved the so-called "pi is normal conjecture" in 1993. The proof is both simple and elegant. It is so short you could probably jot it down in the margin to the left or right of this text without turning the page. Some people (probably motivated by jealousy) have suggested that Dr. Lupin did not develop the proof but instead just looked it up in the digits of pi, to which, her defenders say, so what? Try it yourself if you think it's so easy.

Emily's proof nailed down the long suspected fact that everything that can be expressed is expressed somewhere in the digits of pi. If you go down the line far enough, every truth, every lie, and everything in between is to be found. All information is there from the secret of your grandmother's ginger cookies to how to make super bombs and death rays.

All misinformation is there.

Every truth and the proof that it is a truth and every contradiction of that truth and the proof that it really is a contradiction are all there.

A record of who has used the library and who will ever use it until the end of time is, of course, also to be found in the digits of pi — who they were and what they were looking up and why and how it turned out can all be found. This has recently come to the attention of the authorities.

Emily Lupin is the Librarian of Pi. Over the years, the men and women who work as assistant and associate librarians of pi have come to be called "emilies."

The easiest way to find a librarian of pi is to go to Emily's University in Oregon, but that does not mean the Library exists only in the basement of Building 17, because the Library of Pi is wherever pi is, and pi is everywhere.

The reason you might need an emily is that while everything that can be said is said in pi, it's not so easy to find what you're looking for. In fact, it's not so easy to find anything at all beyond a few tantalizing hints of things to come. A librarian of pi can help you narrow down the nearly infinite number of ways of looking at the digits. There is the matter of bases, for example. If you stick with the familiar base 10, the first few digits of pi look like this:

3.14159265358979323846264643383279502

What in the world are you to make of that?

An emily can help you convert that to base 26 (if you want to use the Roman alphabet). If that doesn't yield what you're looking for, you can try everything from Benjamin Franklin's Phonetic Alphabet (base 29) to a system of Sumerian cuneiform and more. An emily can help you with those things. There are codes to consider, and directions — why not read the number backwards? Or make a matrix and read it from side to side or diagonally? Spend a few minutes with emily, and your eyes will be opened to ideas that would otherwise never have occurred to you like maybe taking into account the frequency of letters in your particular language — that could change everything. You might want to take a philosophical stance and assume the first digits of pi describe the very foundation of the universe. Or you might adopt a religious tactic and assume that the first digits *must* correspond to the first words of the Bible (for example). In that case, your task is to make everything fit.

3
Jail

Maybe she shouldn't have called them pigs — in so many words. It had been subtle. The younger guy hadn't even gotten it. But the other one had. A hard look passed quickly over his face, and then she was in the backseat of a car, and they wouldn't talk to her.

And then she was here.

The walls were made of concrete blocks, and there were no windows. The door was solid — no peephole, no food slot. She was sure they were watching her, but they were not doing it through holes in the doors or walls. There was no mirror that might be two-way. They were looking and listening electronically, she thought. The room was three giant steps long and two giant steps across. There was a cot bolted to the wall and a toilet with a sink on top of the tank. The roll of toilet paper was half gone — a detail which made her very uneasy. There must have been someone in this cell before her. What had happened to them?

It was very cold, and she was still dressed only in the hospital gown they had given her for the physical exam slash strip search. Her feet were faintly purple.

The lights in the cell flashed on and off. It was like being photographed in the dark over and over again. She figured the flashing lights were part of a campaign to keep her from thinking about pi. Brain science had not advanced to the point where they had any way of knowing if she were thinking about pi or not. So, they probably just assumed she was.

She had been in there an hour or maybe more maybe a lot more, how could she tell, when the interval of darkness between the flashes became longer and longer. It was as if the cell flashed into existence every thirty seconds, and finally when the flashing stopped and the lights stayed on, she was no longer alone.

Her inquisitor was not much more than thirty. He was unmistakably a government man. They are easy to spot. The knowledge that they can do whatever they want is always written all over their faces. But this one, very briefly, had another look on his face, too, also familiar, the look men get when they meet a woman who reminds them they will soon be pear-shaped and jowly and given their genes will have a very small chance of doing anything about it. He had brown eyes and very short black hair. He was around five and a half feet tall and looked very strong. He would probably be dangerous in a knife fight. Emily had never been in a knife fight, but, like all librarians, she had a lot of odd knowledge at her fingertips. Several descriptions of what it was like to be in a knife fight were available in her memory, and she could see he would be right at home in any of them. He had an unpleasant smile — totally sneaky like he was getting ready to do something underhanded to you, something he would enjoy but you would wish he had never been born for doing such a thing to you.

Were they going to torture her?

"Dr. Lupin," he said. "Emily, may I call you Emily? You can call me Gabe. I'm not really a bad guy. Emily, I've come to appeal to your patriotism."

Not if you were the last fascist weenie in the world, she didn't say. In fact, she didn't say anything at all. She was sitting on the bunk, and she pulled her legs up and tried to tuck her cold feet in under the thin hospital gown. She crossed her arms across her chest and put her hands on her shoulders and hugged whatever warmth she had left in close to herself.

He sat down on the bunk beside her. He smelled like some kind of shaving lotion. Why did some men splatter that stuff all over their faces after they shaved? What was the point? If men were going to smell like anything at all, she thought, they ought to smell like men. She wouldn't look at him. She heard him scoot a little closer. She could feel his heat, and that was nice at least.

"All we want to know is who has been accessing what in the Library of Pi." His voice was right there beside her face. She could feel his breath in her ear.

She stiffened against the inclination to push him away and jump up and run. Where was there to run? And if she ran away from him, maybe pounded on the door with both fists and yelled for help, her butt would be hanging out of the back of her gown, and in at least one of the possible ways this could go, that would amuse him, give him ideas, or rather bring existing ideas up to the surface, and this would lead to that, and that would be bad. Better to stay as still as a squirrel who doesn't think he's seen her yet, but he has seen her and he's watching her out of the corner of his eye as he whistles up casually closer and closer.

"We have ways to make you talk," he said.

What?

He hadn't really said that, had he?

In spite of her resolve to remain silent and not look at him, she jerked her head around in his direction, and there he was grinning and so close she had to lean back a little.

"Somewhere up or down the line," she said, "there is the story about how you've come to help me."

He took her hand. She did not resist. She imagined her hand was a dead fish. Let him hold it if he wanted to.

"I do want to help you, Emily," he said. "But you have to help me first."

"You can only be doing this," she said, "because you are unaware of all the other things you could be doing instead."

"So, tell me," he said. "Tell me all those other things I might be doing. This is information from the Library, isn't it?"

"If you wanted my help as a librarian to find out who you are," she said, "you didn't need to kidnap me."

"That's not the kind of help I'm looking for." He released her hand. "Nothing so philosophical. We just want the records."

She shut her mouth and looked away. That was about the only information she would not give him. Too bad for him. Too bad for her.

Soon, he sighed and got up. He must have signaled someone, because the lights began to flash again, and after one of the moments of darkness, he was gone.

Suddenly from a hidden speaker to her left came a string of digits in many different voices, men, women, children, familiar cartoon characters. For a moment it was an interesting sequence, and she felt herself being pulled into it as if it were a piece of pi, as it very well might have been, but then it was just another rational number. At that moment, from a hidden speaker to her right, came a recitation of many alphabets in many languages — the ABCs, forwards, backwards, staccato, slurred, little tunes, no tunes, a variety of accents, randomly inserted mistakes. This was going to slow her down. In fact, if they kept it up without a break, it might stop her from finding what she needed.

They knew what they were doing.

They knew that if the perfect escape were possible, even remotely, the steps for pulling it off were all specified in the digits of pi. They wouldn't be easy to find, but the prisoner was Emily herself. If anyone could do it, she could.

They were not going to let that happen.

At last the best she could do was leave a Post-it for her staff in an area they commonly used for communication way down the line in pi. Like everything in pi, it had always been there. Her message said, "Make him help me. Love Emily."

But in pi, every statement has its anti-statement. In fact, every possible take on the situation was there to confuse her rescuers. Very near her appeal for help was another message which said, "Oh, never mind. Your pal, Emily."

4
The Interview

There is a subculture of people obsessed with pi, and the highest status among them belongs to those known as "emilies." Gabriel Estevez left his apartment and dead end job in Phoenix, Arizona, and came to Oregon in order to apply to be emily at the Library of Pi. He was pretty nervous about it. It's not like you could just show up and they would fill you in on the secrets, give you an office, maybe a parking space. But he thought he had a good shot at it.

The bus ride from the desert had been long and hard — it was like a trip into broccoli, he thought, wet broccoli, everything so green and dripping. He had not really understood about the rain in Oregon. It had been in the high seventies in Phoenix when he got on the bus — a little warm for January, but nothing to talk about. It had started raining somewhere in northern California, and it hadn't stopped since. He'd been thinking that if the Library of Pi turned him down, he could find a nice tree or a really big mushroom and sleep under it for a few days until he found other work. He had never really slept outside except for camping as a kid, but how hard could it be?

It was a twenty minute walk from the bus station to the University. He was soaked to his shorts by the time he got there. He hoped the stuff in his suitcase wasn't too wet. Sleep under a tree? It seemed ridiculous now. He dashed from tree to tree once he reached campus where there were lots of trees, but they did not stop the rain. In fact, they didn't even seem to slow it down much. Probably once the trees were full of rain, it was like they weren't even there. No, actually they helped with the wind. But not much.

He was supposed to meet his contact in the basement of Building 17. All of the other buildings had names instead of numbers so he could not simply count his way down to his destination. When he finally found it, he saw that Building 17 occupied at least a city block. He could not be sure if there were four stories or five or maybe more. It probably depended on where you were standing when you looked. Maybe different sides of the building had different numbers of stories. He got in out of the rain and found a Men's Room and changed his clothes. He was still fifteen minutes early. Surely that was a good sign?

He found some stairs that went down to the basement.

The woman who was to interview him had been crying. She had tried to fix her face but she had not been successful. She introduced herself as emily Delia Adams. Call me Gabe, he said, and she said, step this way please.

She looked too young to be doing the interview, probably not yet thirty. He was thirty-three. Maybe he had no chance whatsoever. Maybe blowing him off could be assigned to a grad student?

Her eyes were a strange bright green with golden highlights, maybe tinted contacts, he thought, and she seemed very pale — not so pale that you thought she was doing it on purpose but like maybe they didn't let her out of the basement often enough. Her face was splotched from the crying she had been doing before he arrived. He wondered how things would have gone if she had greeted him with a big smile. He thought she would look very nice with a smile on her face. Hers was a face that said make me smile! She wore her dark brown hair gathered in a bunch high on either side of her head like an extra set of animal ears. The hairdo did not make her look goofy. Her white shirt was dotted with yellow daisies, and her jeans were snug which made following her down a long hallway and into an office a very nice experience. Yes, he was nervous, but for more than one reason. He was smitten, amazed, confused. This was love at first sight. Where had that come from? He was having some trouble remembering why he was here.

The office reminded him of a cell. The walls were gray concrete. There were no windows. The metal desk was bolted to the floor.

"Sit down," Delia said. She took a seat herself behind the desk.

Gabe put his suitcase on the floor and sat down in the metal folding chair in front of the desk.

"Are you okay?" he asked.

"Yes," she said. "Sorry. I'm okay. I'm okay."

She moved stuff around on top of the desk a little desperately, he thought, but then she found the legal pad she'd apparently been looking for and put it in front of herself.

But then she had nothing to write with, and her frantic shuffling and rooting around on the desk began again. She opened and closed drawers. Her pale face was flushed now. He worried she might flip out and start screaming. Maybe she'd throw things, pull out her hair, tackle him and try to scratch out his eyes.

Well, he could have offered her the pen in his shirt pocket. But who knew if that was the right thing to do? People are always telling you about the things you're supposed to do when you first meet a prospective employer, and the things you're not supposed to do, like salt your food before you taste it. He couldn't remember any specific rules about offering the interviewer a pen when she couldn't find one of her own, but it might be a little dangerous. If the look on your face was not just right, she might think you were laughing at her or being condescending or sucking up. No, it was probably better to let her find her own pen.

She did find her own pen in the end. She came back up with it from somewhere behind the desk, and he was pretty sure her eyebrows had gone up a little and her eyes had lingered for just a moment on the pen in his pocket as she straightened up.

"So, you're from Arizona," she said.

Okay, they would start with small talk, he thought. But she was looking at him in a way that might mean the small talk was more than just small talk. Maybe that was some kind of code phrase. So, you're from Arizona? Yes, the sunsets are very nice in Arizona. And then they would exchange briefcases.

"That's right," he said. "Arizona."

"It must be a lot warmer there." She picked up some papers in both hands and tapped the ends on the desk to square the edges. Then she put them down and couldn't find her pen again.

"In the seventies when I left."

"That sounds wonderful," she said.

Was she trying to tell him it would not be so bad if she turned him down and he had to go back to Arizona? At least the weather would be nice?

"Does it always rain here?"

"People who live here like it," she said. "In fact, I have a PI friend who always says, 'A day without rain is like a day without sunshine.'"

She tried a small smile out on him. Was she talking about a Private Investigator? But the heads of university research projects were sometimes called Primary Investigators. Was she talking about Emily herself? That strange sentence seemed a perfect thing for the mysterious Librarian of Pi to be saying. Or did Delia mean pi? Maybe it was a pun, and he was supposed to pick up on it and groan or roll his eyes or something.

She found her pen and looked back up at him. He didn't know what to say next. She was waiting for something. What was it?

"I came for pi," he said.

She stopped smiling. Maybe he should have let her bring up the subject first. Maybe he should have said more about Arizona, the palm trees, the Gila Monsters and scorpions, the Saguaro cacti standing around with their arms up like this was some kind of bank robbery. Maybe she wanted him to ask her out for dinner or coffee. In other circumstances, he would have chosen to interpret it like that. He would have taken a chance. Hadn't he been in love with her a moment ago?

She burst into tears.

He stood up. He had intended to walk around the desk and put a hand on her shoulder, maybe say, "there there," but she heard him move and held her hand up in an obvious command that he should not approach. He sat back down.

She lifted her head and dabbed at her eyes with the sleeve of her shirt.

"So you want to be emily?" she said.

He could hear the word as she meant it. She did not mean the legendary Emily Lupin, head Librarian of Pi. She meant "emily." Everyone who worked at the library who was not Emily was "emily." He would never have gotten even this far if he had not known that.

"Yes, I do," he said. "Very much."

"Tell me why." She slapped around on the desk looking for her damn pen. "Hold on a minute."

Had it fallen to the floor? He hadn't heard it hit. No, there, she'd found it. "Okay," she said. "Shoot."

Shoot.

He should have been ready for a general question like that, but he had spent so much time on his tables and languages and theories that he had not rehearsed an answer about why he wanted to do this in the first place.

He didn't know what to say. He couldn't talk about the pay because the pay was nothing to speak of. He couldn't talk about the benefits, because there weren't any benefits. Advancement? Well, who knew how that worked? There was only one Emily, and no one could ever move up and take her place.

Gabe could talk about his fascination with the *idea* of the library. Why hadn't she asked about that? Maybe he could turn the interview in that direction. Maybe he should talk about his love of numbers. But then she might ask, "So, why didn't you study mathematics in college?" And once again he would have no good answer. The clock was ticking.

"Maybe that question was too hard?" she said. "So, try this one. Why do you think you *can* be emily?"

Once more she'd asked something right on the edge of what he could answer. He could have told her why he thought he was qualified to try to be emily. He could have told her about all the thinking he had done about pi. He might have mentioned how much he wanted to learn why he'd failed to find anything in the digits he had so far examined. He might have said how he so very much wanted to understand how it all worked. Hey, wait a minute. That was a pretty good answer to her first question!

He wanted to be emily to learn how pi actually functioned as a library!

Too late.

Now she wanted to know why he thought he could do it not why he wanted to do it. The question implied that he must have some idea of what emilies did on a day-to-day basis. Otherwise, how could he tell her why he thought he could actually do it?

Wasn't it some kind of job getting tip that you were supposed to say you could do whatever they asked if you could do?

Ray Vukcevich

"I can do it," he said.

She waited.

"Because I'm willing to do whatever it takes to do it!"

"Tell me about your interpretation of the first thirty-three digits in the decimal expansion," she said.

And he jumped right into it. This was more like it.

But she didn't seem to be listening. He took out his multiplication table in base 26.

MULTIPLICATION TABLE

	A	B	C	D	E	F	G	H	I	J	K	L	M	N	O	P	Q	R	S	T	U	V	W	X	Y	Z
A	A	B	C	D	E	F	G	H	I	J	K	L	M	N	O	P	Q	R	S	T	U	V	W	X	Y	Z
B	B	D	F	H	J	L	N	P	R	T	V	X	AZ	AB	AD	AF	AH	AJ	AL	AN	AP	AR	AT	AV	AX	Z
C	C	F	I	L	O	R	U	X	AA	AD	AG	AJ	AM	AP	AS	AV	AY	BB	BE	BH	BK	BN	BQ	BT	BW	Z
D	D	H	L	P	T	X	AB	AF	AJ	AN	AR	AV	BZ	BD	BH	BL	BP	BT	BX	CB	CF	CJ	CN	CR	CV	Z
E	E	J	O	T	Y	AD	AI	AN	AS	AX	BC	BH	BM	BR	BW	CB	CG	CL	CQ	CV	DA	DF	DK	DP	DU	Z
F	F	L	R	X	AD	AJ	AP	AV	BB	BH	BN	BT	CZ	CF	CL	CR	CX	DD	DJ	DP	DV	EB	EH	EN	ET	Z
G	G	N	U	AB	AI	AP	AW	BD	BK	BR	BY	CF	CM	CT	DA	DH	DO	DV	EC	EJ	EQ	EX	FE	FL	FS	Z
H	H	P	X	AF	AN	AV	BD	BL	BT	CB	CJ	CR	DZ	DH	DP	DX	EF	EN	EV	FD	FL	FT	GB	GJ	GR	Z
I	I	R	AA	AJ	AS	BB	BK	BT	CC	CL	CU	DD	DM	DV	EE	EN	EW	FF	FO	FX	GG	GP	GY	HH	HQ	Z
J	J	T	AD	AN	AX	BH	BR	CB	CL	CV	DF	DP	EZ	EJ	ET	FD	FN	FX	GH	GR	HB	HL	HV	IF	IP	Z
K	K	V	AG	AR	BC	BN	BY	CJ	CU	DF	DQ	EB	EM	EX	FI	FT	GE	GP	HA	HL	HW	IH	IS	JD	JO	Z
L	L	X	AJ	AV	BH	BT	CF	CR	DD	DP	EB	EN	FZ	FL	FX	GJ	GV	HH	HT	IF	IR	JD	JP	KB	KN	Z
M	M	AZ	AM	BZ	BM	CZ	CM	DZ	DM	EZ	EM	FZ	FM	GZ	GM	HZ	HM	IZ	IM	JZ	JM	KZ	KM	LZ	LM	Z
N	N	AB	AP	BD	BR	CF	CT	DH	DV	EJ	EX	FL	GZ	GN	HB	HP	ID	IR	JF	JT	KH	KV	LJ	LX	ML	Z
O	O	AD	AS	BH	BW	CL	DA	DP	EE	ET	FI	FX	GM	HB	HQ	IF	IU	JJ	JY	KN	LC	LR	MG	MV	NK	Z
P	P	AF	AV	BL	CB	CR	DH	DX	EN	FD	FT	GJ	HZ	HP	IF	IV	JL	KB	KR	LH	LX	MN	ND	NT	OJ	Z
Q	Q	AH	AY	BP	CG	CX	DO	EF	EW	FN	GE	GV	HM	ID	IU	JL	KC	KT	LK	MB	MS	NJ	OA	OR	PI	Z
R	R	AJ	BB	BT	CL	DD	DV	EN	FF	FX	GP	HH	IZ	IR	JJ	KB	KT	LL	MD	MV	NN	OF	OX	PP	QH	Z
S	S	AL	BE	BX	CQ	DJ	EC	EV	FO	GH	HA	HT	IM	JF	JY	KR	LK	MD	MW	NP	OI	PB	PU	QN	RG	Z
T	T	AN	BH	CB	CV	DP	EJ	FD	FX	GR	HL	IF	JZ	JT	KN	LH	MB	MV	NP	OJ	PD	PX	QR	RL	SF	Z
U	U	AP	BK	CF	DA	DV	EQ	FL	GG	HB	HW	IR	JM	KH	LC	LX	MS	NN	OI	PD	PY	QT	RO	SJ	TE	Z
V	V	AR	BN	CJ	DF	EB	EX	FT	GP	HL	IH	JD	KZ	KV	LR	MN	NJ	OF	PB	PX	QT	RP	SL	TH	UD	Z
W	W	AT	BQ	CN	DK	EH	FE	GB	GY	HV	IS	JP	KM	LJ	MG	ND	OA	OX	PU	QR	RO	SL	TI	UF	VC	Z
X	X	AV	BT	CR	DP	EN	FL	GJ	HH	IF	JD	KB	LZ	LX	MV	NT	OR	PP	QN	RL	SJ	TH	UF	VD	WB	Z
Y	Y	AX	BW	CV	DU	ET	FS	GR	HQ	IP	JO	KN	LM	ML	NK	OJ	PI	QH	RG	SF	TE	UD	VC	WB	XA	Z
Z	Z	Z	Z	Z	Z	Z	Z	Z	Z	Z	Z	Z	Z	Z	Z	Z	Z	Z	Z	Z	Z	Z	Z	Z	Z	Z

She glanced at it, did a double take, and said, "What is this? Oh, wait, you started with one is A?"

"Yes," he said. "And zero as Z."

"Why?"

"Well, the word 'zero' starts with the letter Z," he said. "Not to mention that the middle number, that is, the thirteenth letter is 'M.'"

She just looked blank, waiting for him to go on.

"You know, M," he said. "For 'middle'? Not to mention the fact that it makes it easy to sing the AZ BZs."

He sang, "AZ, BZ, CZ, DZ, EZ!"

"People have always started with A for zero and Z for twenty-five," she said.

"Does this mean I've found something new?"

"Hardly," she said.

Maybe he was trying too hard, but realizing that didn't slow him down. He was desperate to impress her. "I like to imagine Emily as a little girl with her twenty-six fingers. Thirteen on each hand, and she's learning her Asies, Bsies, and Csies. She's got a big blue bow in her hair, and her shoes are both black and white."

"You think Emily has twenty-six fingers?"

"When she was a little girl," he said. "She's so cute."

"Look," she said, "Speaking of Emily, the real reason I'm seeing you today is that you're going to help break her out of jail."

5

Good News and Bad News in Pi

She loves me.
She loves me not.

6

In Out of the Rain

Delia tossed her pen down and stood up. "Come on."

"Does this mean I get to be emily?" Gabe remained seated.

"Yes, yes," she said. "What are you waiting for? The secret hand-shake?"

"There's a secret handshake?"

"No, of course, there isn't," she said. "Will you stand up and come on?"

He got up expecting her to push past him to the door. Instead she turned to the wall and put her right palm flat against the concrete and muttered something he couldn't make out. She moved her hand around in circles like she was washing a window, and the blocks rumbled and slid inwardly and then to one side revealing a dark passageway. She stepped through the opening.

Gabe came around the desk and looked through the hole into a dim six-sided alcove with a spiral staircase disappearing into the gloom above. He heard the rustling rumbling moaning of air moving in ventilation shafts.

Delia glanced back at him then started up the stairs. He hesitated a moment and then stepped forward. As soon as he passed through the hole in the wall, it closed behind him and everything went totally dark.

"Delia?"

"Here," she called.

Her voice bounced around in the hexagonal chamber, and he could not tell which was her real voice and which were echoes. He reached out hoping to touch a wall. He felt nothing but empty air. He turned slowly and groped for the secret door that had just closed behind him, but he felt nothing in that direction either.

"Follow me." Delia's voice sounded far away now.

He put his arms straight out to his sides at shoulder height and turned in a circle, but he traversed all 360 degrees and still felt nothing. His arms were the diameter of the circle, and the relationship of his arms to the circumference of his circle was pi.

He was both in the dark and in the library of pi.

He made a couple more rotations, and then he stopped. He could not say why he stopped at that moment and not a moment before or a moment later. It just felt like the right time to stop. Maybe it was an emily thing. He put his arms out in front of himself and walked into the darkness like a sleepwalker until he came to the stairs.

"Up here," Delia called.

Sometimes it was the sound of her feet on the stairs above, and sometimes it was a faint wave of heat and sometimes a smell and very infrequently the sound of her voice that told him he was climbing in the right direction.

He wanted to catch up to her. He wanted to count the ways she startled and delighted him and hear her laugh over her shoulder as she slipped out of her clothes and let them fall to the cold hardwood floor and walked to the mirror to push at her hair first on the left and then on the right, leaning all the time a little forward in a posture calculated to make him feel like his tent would soon be obscuring his view of her from the bed and he would have to lean way over to one side to see her. It seemed like they were never out of bed for long in these early days which in a way were all one day, even one moment, this moment which as it turned out did not last forever.

She poured the tea and sat down at the kitchen table with him. She was wearing a ragged terrycloth robe, and her feet were bare. She put them in his lap, and they were very cold. He reached down and rubbed them, and she sighed.

Oh, and then the bickering, and the hard feelings, and the long walks in the rain, and the tears. And as they walked, they woke up, and broke up, and made up, and broke up again.

Things were getting a little lighter, but because it was a spiral staircase, he could still not see her.

And by the time he came to the top of the stairs and the long hallway, they had loved and lost. They had damaged one another, left scars, gone into therapy, finished up with therapy and moved on. They had come out the other side and were old friends. He felt so warm and relaxed to see her standing there waiting for him. She took his hand. He squeezed, and she squeezed back.

"This way," Delia said. "She's expecting you."

8

Girl With Raccoon and Harpsichord

They had come into a long hallway with evenly spaced glowing green Exit signs. In the distance a lighted door looked small enough for Alice. Hand in hand, they walked toward it.

And on the way, he tried a few doors, and all of them, even the ones under the Exit signs, were locked. Each had a number painted on it in a color just a little lighter than the door itself. This one, for example, was numbered 127, and the next one was 2224, and the one after that was 39, and the one after that was 107.

"Part of pi?" he asked.

"What else?" Delia said.

But what part of pi? He had no idea, and he knew her well enough to know he should keep any fruitcake theories that might pop into his head on the subject to himself.

The open door with the light probably had a number, too. When they got to it, he thought he should close the door and see what the number was since surely it would be important to his life, but Delia pulled him into the room, and what he saw there made him forget about the number.

A small girl dressed in clothes from very early in the last century stood holding a stuffed raccoon upside down in her arms. To her left was a harpsichord. There was a painting of jumping dolphins, blue seas, and bright sunlight on the open lid of the instrument. Gabe knew it was a harpsichord, because before he became obsessed with pi, he had been obsessed with early keyboard instruments. He had sold his clavichord to eat and pay the rent while studying pi so he could come to Oregon and be emily.

He knew the raccoon was stuffed, because the girl was holding it upside down by one of its back legs now, and because it did not blink even if it did seem to follow him with its black eyes.

"This is Emily," Delia said. "She needs your help, Gabe."

The girl was nine or ten and had very blonde hair in ringlets. There was a huge blue bow in her hair. Gabe came down on one knee in front of her.

"You've come to save me," she said.

"I suppose I have," Gabe said. "But what can I do?"

"You can hold my raccoon," she said.

"Is that important?"

"It's essential," she said. "I cannot put my Rocky down. I cannot play my harpsichord while holding a raccoon. You do want to help me, don't you?"

"But I don't see how any of this will help." Gabe looked up at Delia. "How come you haven't held her raccoon before now yourself?"

"I could take the raccoon," Delia said, "but what good would that do?"

"Trust me," Emily said. "When you tell them about this, they will think they have nothing to worry about. They'll let me go."

"Won't that make me look foolish and hurt my career?"

"Yes," she said. "It will. You have to choose."

Well, he really had come for pi.

He held out his hands, and she gave him the raccoon and stepped away from him. She walked to the harpsichord and climbed up onto the bench. She arranged her long skirt carefully over her knees. Her feet did not touch the floor. She spent some time flexing her twenty-six fingers, and then she played them all deeper and deeper into pi and into the sunlight where they would be both hidden and right out there in the open.

And he might even get back together with his old pal, Delia.

Everything was possible.

17

Love Leans In From the Left

By the time I got back to Jolean, she was down to maybe her last marble. Black Walkman earphones, wet red eyes, and one shoulder coming out of her shirt. It took me a couple of cheek-to-cheeks around the dance floor through the painful orange jazz, twitchy and desperate rat music, and the smoke so thick I kept touching the back of my head to make sure my hair wasn't on fire, before I realized she was channeling William S. Burroughs, whispering in my ear the old dead guy's gravelly voice as heard in the author's classic audio tape reading of his novel *Junky*. (Penguin Audiobooks, 1977)

"Let's cut out for Mexico, Bill," she said.

I ran my hand up her back, counting every sad rib, and slipped around in front and followed her earphone wire down to where it ended in thin air. There was no Walkman. I slipped my hand around her again and let it settle sweetly, and she reached down and tugged it up to the small of her back.

I lifted one of her earphones. "Come on out of there, Jolean," I said. "Come out and have some eggnog."

We were a Picasso in a bad mood dancing.

She shrugged my hand away. "I have no interest in proving anything to anybody." Her voice was his tongue in my ear. "You'd better get with it, Bill."

"My name isn't Bill," I said.

"We could get right in Mexico," she said. "Reduction cure for the junk sickness."

I lifted her earphone again. "You've never done junk in your life, Jolean! Come on, let's sit down and drink our eggnog."

"That's the wrong riff, Bill," she said all cold and mean. "Can't you see I'm coming down the cosmic pipeline? You always knew I'd be one spooky son of a bitch. You always did know that."

I danced her backwards to our table. When she figured out where we were, she gave me a hard look. "Since when are you so big on the yellow and white stuff, Bill?" she asked. "Who do you think you are? Mr. Eggnog?" Her voice had risen like Norman's knife, something you just couldn't ignore in a crowded room, even if all the people, so cool and smoky, were giving it the old college try.

"Where is it written," she shouted, "that it's your job to make me drink eggnog!"

I sat down and pretended I didn't know her, and a moment later she sat down, too.

"Come on, Bill," she said. "Let's go to Mexico."

"We don't have much Spanish," I said.

The old fart looked around like he expected the CIA to be listening in. Then he leaned in close. "That's not the Mexico I mean. Deep in the Mexico I'm talking about there's another secret place where the Spins live."

"The Spins?"

"The land of the Spins is long and shaped like a snake," she said. "The guts of the Earth. You can get into it easy somewhere around Hermosillo and it runs all the way to Bogotá." She licked her lips.

"What you call Spinland?" I asked.

"You got it." She sat up straight and slapped her hand down on the table.

"And these Spins don't speak Spanish?" I asked.

"Get this," she said. "The Spins speak nothing but Spinach!"

"What would we do there, Jolean?"

"Down deep, back where Columbia used to be, the Indians have a drug called yage. It's the final fix, Bill. A telepathic kick."

"You don't want to be reading my mind, Jolean."

"It's the nonverbal level that really counts," she said. "Intuition and feelings. The very mention of yage has allowed me to read your mind a little. What's this? You doped my drink? Eggnog is your code word for junk? Who did you think you were fooling, Bill?"

"Jolean, Jolean," I said, suddenly in danger of losing the slippery grip on the end of my rope. "Drink your eggnog."

She reached over the table and grabbed me by the front of the shirt and got in my face. "Stick it up your ass, Bill." I watched Burroughs leave her face like she'd wiped off a smile, and saw the old Jolean in there, but I saw, too, that while she was certainly channeling the old fart, he had not taken over. She was, on some level, cooperating with him, which she next proved by saying in her own voice, "And you can just go bite down hard on aluminum foil!"

She pushed me back into my chair, and we sat glaring at one another for a moment. Then she spoke for him again.

"This isn't the kind of dream you wake up from, Bill," she said. "This is the kind of dream you wake up into. You sit up in bed and look around at the peeling wallpaper and the water stains, the cracks. You listen to the bedsprings squeak when you squirm. You sweat. You listen to the heavy artillery of the city outside. Screaming cats and dogs instead of rain. And the roaches come and go speaking of . . ."

I stepped into her speech just in time and said, "Yes, it is, Jolean. This is exactly the kind of dream you can wake up from. Come on, I'll show you." I pulled her up and away to Scottsdale, Arizona, where we were married by a Mormon who kept apologizing and telling us it would be legal anyway. We honeymooned in Hawaii. We came home and got work. Dr. Benway snapped on a huge rubber glove and pulled babies, one right after another, from Jolean like fruit from a paper sack, and we raised the babies in our own house and got them drivers licenses and straightened their teeth and saw them off to college, felt blue in the big empty house, mooned over pictures of the grandkids, took up hobbies.

"It's all junk time, Bill," she said. "And junk time is all the same time. What will happen, did happen, right now."

I suddenly saw her point. Maybe this was a dream you could only pretend to wake up from, your eyes shifting left and right, defensively, sure I'm fine, we're fine, yes, I said we're fine. Even so, it's not like you can just give up.

I moved my chair around until I was sitting next to her. I pushed her eggnog a little closer. I took her hand. "Drink your eggnog, Jolean," I whispered. "You're embarrassing us." She picked up her glass, drank. Then she got a dreamy look on her face and leaned in from the left and threw up in my lap.

"Good, good," I muttered. "Let it all out, Sweetheart."

Afterwards we went home, both of us pretending, in spite of the smell that filled the car, that it hadn't happened. Jolean went into her giggly rehab girl routine, saying How! High are you? Hi! How are you? She poked me in the ribs and giggled, and I said, "Hey, watch it! I'm driving."

How! High are you?

And when the kids called I told them their mother was resting and sure she'd call them back and tell everyone happy holidays. Didn't she always?

18

The Rescue

He's your brother, my mother said, and thereby assigned me the job of rescuing Henry. The family had questions. What was Henry up to over there? The speculation was ugly and ridiculous. It wasn't clear to me that Henry even needed rescuing.

Doesn't Henry have email yet?

What? The very idea! He doesn't even have a phone! Henry and email. Ha ha. Can you imagine it? My mother couldn't imagine it. She burst into tears. I know she burst into tears because she typed, "I burst into tears when I read what you said about Henry and his email."

Uncle Milo emailed me a story about how El Presidente couldn't tell a fart from a hurricane and kept looking back at his own butt going whoa! Somebody call the Weather Channel. Whoa! The point of this story was both subtle and serious. Milo was telling me that since he could so openly poke fun at our fearless leader, he could certainly have me roughed up if I didn't listen to my mother and go check on Henry.

My sister Stella sent me three typographical frowny faces.

So, I took a train and a ferry, and in the waterfront district, I grabbed a cab, but it wouldn't take me all the way into Henry's neighborhood, so I set off on foot into the heart of dimness and soon encountered a group of pale white children with sticks. They had the steady eyes of wolves as they advanced on me saying, "Bark."

Just the one word.

Bark. Bark. Bark.

I ran and lost them and then found the building where Henry was supposed to have a fifth floor walkup.

I, for one, had no trouble imagining Henry with email. In fact, at the top of my to-do list was getting him online so I would never ever have to make a trip like this again.

I stopped to catch my breath on the third floor and heard someone torturing a violin and someone else shouting for the torture to stop, please stop, just stop, dear god make it stop. Banging doors and ringing phones and screaming children, and someone cooking onions and spicy sausage but the smells couldn't overcome the prevailing odor of mildew.

Further up, I stepped over a man crumpled on the stairs. I couldn't tell if he were dead. Surely not. Everything probably looked very different to the people who lived here. They might say, oh, him, that's Uncle Albert. He likes to sleep on the stairs.

How could Henry live like this?

I came at last to Henry's apartment. The door was not completely closed. I pushed it open all the way. Inside I saw the backs of the heads of people sitting in medal folding chairs.

"Henry?" I called and stepped in.

"Quiet," someone whispered.

The focus of attention was a man sitting alone facing the people in the folding chairs. He wore a ragged sleeveless undershirt. There was a cardboard box between his feet.

The man was my brother Henry. Out of context, I might not have recognized him. He'd lost a lot of weight, and he probably hadn't gotten his hair cut since I'd seen him last. He hadn't shaved for days. His eyes were dull and red. He gave no sign he recognized me.

There was an empty chair at the far left side in the front row. No one objected when I sat down, but the chair had a slightly bent leg, and whenever I leaned to the right, the short leg came down on the bare floor with a thud, and everyone in my row gave me a dirty look.

They were passing a hat down the line. A black western hat. When it got to me, I saw that it held an astonishing assortment of junk and small coins. A bottle cap. A half a stick of Doublemint gum. Some pennies. A coupon for half off on a bottle of dishwashing soap. A subway token. A dime. A small square of paper with a poem written so small I couldn't read it. I took a five from my wallet and added it to the collection. The guy next to me made a go-ahead motion with his head that I took to mean I should deliver the hat to Henry.

I got up and walked to Henry. He didn't look up at me.

"Henry?" I said.

Someone sucked in air behind me — a kind of outraged hiss. I put the hat down by Henry's feet and walked back to my chair.

Henry glanced down at the hat. Then he swooped in and plucked out the five I had put in there and poked it into his pants pocket.

"Okay," he said, "this next one is Mozart's Concerto for Piano and Orchestra number nine in E flat Major."

There was a murmur of approval from the crowd.

"The Köchel number is 271," he said and smiled, "for you purists. We'll do part one, the Allegro."

He leaned down and rummaged around in the cardboard box at his feet and then sat back up with a portable CD player.

"Now the thing to watch for comes right at the very middle," he said. "The whole piece takes about ten minutes. Halfway in, there is a wonderful surprise of sweet spice. It's like eating a strange chocolate. You let it melt in your mouth. You taste the chocolate until you break through into the middle and then . . . and then . . . Well, you'll see."

He put on earphones and switched on the CD player. A strange look of peace came to his face and his eyelids fluttered.

I waited for the music. No music.

I waited for laughs, for astonished gasps and little peeps and squeaks of incredulity but they never arrived. I took a look around. Everyone seemed entranced.

Thumbs up!

We were going to watch Henry listen to music.

He had closed his eyes, and he was swaying slowly from side to side. Suddenly he stiffened as if shocked, and then he began pointing both forefingers up and to the left and then pointing both forefingers up and to the right, conducting, but without the music, he could have been doing bo doe de oh doe if we didn't already know he was doing Mozart.

I glanced at my watch, but it was too late to precisely time the middle of the concerto. I wondered if I would miss it. As it turned out, I need not have worried.

About five minutes into the performance, Henry started bouncing. Fast little rises into the air followed by slapping falls back into his chair. I couldn't see how he was doing it. Then there was smoke from around the earphones. Not a lot of smoke, and you might imagine it was a malfunction and worry that his ears would catch on fire, but then there was smoke from his nose, too.

And then bang! there it was — the middle of the concerto just like that a glow came to his face, a light from inside, a halo, and we were looking at a man who was looking into the very heart of the universe, life, love, and everything, and we knew that was as close as we'd ever get ourselves, and it was enough.

Then it was over, and Henry went back to conducting with two fingers.

There was a stunned silence followed by wild applause. Henry said, "No, wait. It isn't over."

But then it really was over, and I had my answer.

So, what does Henry do?

He appreciates Mozart, and people like to watch, and they pay him with bottle caps and pennies and half pieces of gum, and they get a lot more than their money's worth.

My mother would burst into tears again. My sister Stella would keep saying, "What? I don't get it. What?" Uncle Milo would probably have me killed.

I was either going to have to come up with a good lie or make a dash for it like Henry.

19

Love Story

W e were doing it like dogs. Or, if you want to get picky about it, we were doing it like everyone imagines dogs do it. Real dogs pump away for a while and then the male twists around and gets off and the two of them share a contemplative moment facing in opposite directions. Private. You take the low road. Pensive. Are you still back there? Such a thing, if not impossible, probably would have been pointless for Lucille and me, but it reminded me of my grandmother and long lazy summers in the Arizona mountains. Grandma had a couple of dogs named Chuck and Muffy who were fully functional pit bulls but no one thought much about pit bulls in those days and most dogs just did what came naturally. What my grandmother liked about Chuck and Muffy was they could and would kill anything that got into the yard.

When I told Lucy I was thinking about the first time I saw the way dogs do it in the summertime at Grandma's place, she said, "So this is your idea of romantic pillow talk?"

My grandmother had a few misconceptions about the way dogs do it, I told Lucy. She never understood why the dogs would choose to ignore her warnings and continue with their nasty ways. They would be fine for months, and then bang! she'd come around the corner of the house and there they'd be — Chuck in the middle of his twisting routine, and she'd shout, "They're stuck!"

Because that's what's liable to happen to us, Lucy, when we do sneaky, nasty things. We get stuck. Grandma turned the hose on the dogs. Stop it! Stop it right now, you dirty dogs! They always persevered and finished and then sat hangdog and dripping and endured their lecture and then shook the water off grinning and went on with their business. Nothing got them down for long.

Except when you called the guy dog "Chuckles."

Chuck hated that, and he would curl his lip at you like he was saying the old lady seems to like you, so unlike other things that get into the yard, I'm not going to kill you, but you'd better knock off that Chuckles crap or you're going to be in for it!

Once I found out Chuck was short for Charles, I wondered if Grandma had named the dog after me. When I asked her about it, she said, "What an idea!"

Years later when I told Lucy that story I could see the light go on even though she made heroic efforts to hide it, little smiles going on and off, sideways glances. Here's something I can use! After we were married when she wanted to get my goat she would hit me with it like "I don't know about that boat, Chuckles."

Growling at her was totally ineffective.

Now we're grandparents ourselves, but we have no dogs.

"How come we never had dogs when Jenny was growing up?" I asked Lucy.

Jenny (call me Jennifer) is our straight-laced daughter. It's like personality traits skip generations. My granddaughter Amy is a very wacky kid. She drives her mother crazy but in a good way, I think, and that makes me happy. I remember one time Jenny was trying to get me to baby-sit, and being so indirect about it. On the one hand she needed to be somewhere in a hurry, but on the other hand she didn't want to appear to need anything from the likes of Lucy and me or just me in this case since Lucy was off playing her viola with the community band. My theory is that Jenny's brain was infested with some conservative virus she picked up from that husband of hers who you have to wonder how he can bend at the waist what with the stick he's got lodged up his wazoo.

"Sure, leave her with me," I told her. "We'll spend the afternoon smoking big cigars and watching inappropriate movies."

"Dad!"

"Eating foods with lots of saturated fat."

Amy was grinning ear to ear, and I could see she enjoyed seeing her mother scandalized. Since it was so easy to scandalize Jennifer, Amy was in for years of laughs.

"Picking our noses and playing with matches!"

"It's like you don't want her," Jenny said. "It's like you're trying to make me take her to a day care center or something."

"What! Not want her?" I pulled Amy into the protection of my arms and she looked back up at me still grinning. "You better watch out. Chances are I'll just adopt her. You two will come back and we'll all pretend we don't even know you."

"Dad!"

But now is now, and oh, look they've all just banged into the kitchen, and Amy asks, "Can I have a cookie?"

"Not now, sweetie," Lucy says. "Grandma's busy."

Busy having her neck nibbled by Grandpa while the republican son-in-law looks like he's just walked in on some kind of lowlife, sneaky and nasty activity that proper dogs wouldn't be caught dead doing.

"Will somebody hose those two off?" he says.

"Oh, be nice," Lucy says.

"Do we have to stand here and watch this?" the uptight, okay his name is Robert, son-in-law says. I've known his name from the very first night she brought him home to meet us. I just don't like to use it.

Jenny is speechless.

"Come on, you guys," I say. "Hold up your scorecards."

"You want points for this!" Jenny is scandalized again.

I'm about to give up altogether on Robert, but then I have to hand it to him. He does, in the end, flip through his cards and give us a ten.

A soft smile threatens the lips of our lovely daughter, Jennifer.

Amy claps her hands together.

A marching band comes in one door and out the other and you have to wonder how they all fit in there since that second door leads to the bathroom.

And pipers piping.

And waves of mice singing show tunes in little squeaky voices sweep Lucy and me up and wash us back into the bedroom where we really belong.

It's like someone somewhere has planned the whole thing.

"So, you can come clean now, Lucy, and admit you've really been a CIA operative under deep cover all these years we've been married."

"We have ways to make you bark," she says.

"I know Robert's big secret," I whisper.

"Oh?"

"Amy told me."

"Oh?"

"He has an Hawaiian shirt."

"Don't you dare say a word about it, Charles!"

"Someday we'll be doing it like dogs," I say, "and my heart will explode and I want it to be just like this, Lucy."

"In your dreams, Chuckles," she says. "Do you think I want some dead guy collapsing on me?"

"Some dead guy? Like I could be just any old dead guy?"

Is she even thinking about it?

"I don't think I'll be able to help it, Lucy."

"No, only you," she says, "you're my dead guy."

Magic Makeup

L inda said, *let's go as each other*, and I said, how the heck do you expect us to pull that off?

"Makeup," she said. "Magic makeup. Look here."

She handed me a card with a small white bottle shrink-sealed onto it in clear plastic. The illustration on the card was a bone white skeletal face, obviously a guy in makeup, with raccoon eyes and blackened nose and missing teeth. The words on the card were in French. I do not speak French. I recognized the words "visage" and "corpse."

And then a bunch of stuff I was sure I could not pronounce.

"Oh, go head and pronounce," Linda said.

She was not yet laughing at me, but I could see was preparing herself for some deeply satisfying chuckling.

Hey, I could be a good sport.

I said, "'Maquillage liquide.' Maybe liquid mask?"

"You crack me up," she said.

"And 'pour le visage et pour le corps.' That must mean for the face and for the dead body. So, after the crime you can either disguise yourself or the victim. Your choice."

I turned the card over. On the back were instructions in both French and English, but the English made no sense.

I read, "Hi ya, Mikey!" which was odd since my name is Mike. "When you're dead, when you're dead, no one wants to look at your head."

She laughed — a little nervously, I thought. "Just body," she said, "not dead body."

I held up the card with the little bottle pointing in her direction. "Looks kind of small."

"Maybe it's bigger on the inside," she said. "Shall we find out?" She went to work on the buttons of my shirt.

And I returned the favor, and we wrestled ourselves naked, and she said, "Come on, we'd better get in the tub. This could get messy."

Our bare feet on the cold Halloween floor and the rattling rings of the plastic shower curtain as I pulled it aside. No bugs in the tub.

Get in, get in, okay, okay. Maybe we should have used scissors on the package. Oh, just rip it open, rip it open, use your teeth. Yes, okay The cap is stuck. No, wait, I've got it.

I poured a ridiculous amount of white liquid from the little bottle into my hand. It was chalky, but not gritty, and smelled like flowers, and there was so much of it that I could not contain it all in my cupped hand and some of it spilled over and where the drops touched our feet our skin changed color, mine a little lighter, hers a little darker. I slapped my hand down on her shoulder and speared the stuff down over her breast toward her belly and her breast disappeared with a kind of slurping sound and she said, "Oh, give me some!"

I poured liquid mask into her hand and she worked it into my chest and her missing breast appeared there with a squeaky pop like a balloon being inflated by a clown who when her mother wasn't looking put two balloons to his own chest and squeezed them suggestively and leered at little Linda. Squeaky squeaky, little mousy missy.

How did I know that?

I grabbed her and pulled her in close and upended the bottle over our heads, and we snaked around spreading the white sauce between us. I rubbed it into her shoulders and around her neck and up into her hair and over to her face, smiling, frowning, smiling, frowning, and down and down, then kneeling on the cold porcelain. Tummy, thighs, turn around. Cheeks, fundamental fingers feathering, feet — first the one then the other.

I rose, but when I got to the top, I was not so tall as I had been. I moved back a little, and he turned and I saw that the years had not been as kind to Mike as I had fooled myself into believing. He was okay, but he'd look a lot better if he walked more often, maybe took up handball, maybe just said no to a freaking cheeseburger for once in his life.

Mike was nothing like Winston. What kind of fruity name was Winston anyway? Girlfriend, you wouldn't say that once you got a load of him in his BVDs — Winston with the marvelous taste who made her feel wonderful, and more important would bang the drums loudly and then just go away until the next time the begonias needed trimming.

"So, that's what you call it?" he asked.

"What do you mean?" I took a step back. "And must you loom over me like that?"

"Trimming the begonias," he said.

"Oh, Mikey, Mikey," I said, "I hope that look in your eyes doesn't mean you're about to commit a crime of passion."

Like he ever would.

Morning Meditation

S *tinky Pinkypoo woke up worried* that while he was sleeping
someone had sneaked into his room and changed his name to
something silly.

Maybe he had gone to bed as Mr. Moneybags, the banker, or Terrible Tommy, a professional wrestler specializing in the Spectacular
Squelch.

Who knew?

This was both good and bad news, as are so many of life's big
changes. Like when a steamroller runs over your feet. On the one hand
you'll never walk again, but on the other hand you can stop torturing
yourself with tap dancing lessons all the while knowing you have no
talent for it whatsoever.

Why beat yourself up?

The Pinkypoo part of forgive me Father Pinkypoo for I have sinned
was all some kind of psychic distortion, because surely Father Pinkypoo had been known by some other name yesterday when Nancy Maloney had come to see him and he had realized she didn't remember him
from the days of his great sin. Besides, she had come in for advice not
absolution. Something to do with an old dog.

Boy, was she ever a big girl now.

Stinky sat up and felt around on the floor with his feet for his slippers. The next step would be to check his security measures. No one
could have slipped into his room without leaving a trace. Something
would be disturbed. He stood up and put on his robe. He would not
allow himself a glass of clear water and a slice of bread until he had
checked the room.

The door was locked. The window was latched. The closet door
was secured with the chair he had tilted backwards under the knob. He
looked under the bed.

Nothing.

He walked to the chest of drawers and pulled at the top drawer where he stored his secret stuff. Locked. Ditto the next drawer down where he kept his underwear, and likewise the one below that where he stored his socks.

But, oh no, how could he have been so stupid, so careless? The bottom drawer was not closed by maybe an eighth of an inch, and, yes, when he took hold of the handle and pulled, it came open easily.

The intruder had gained entry through an unlocked pajama drawer!

It hit him like a bolt from heaven that this had to be the work of Nancy and her little dog Lulu. He wondered if they had enjoyed squirming up through his pajamas on their way here from a particular day in the past when Stinky who had formerly been known by some other name had answered the doorbell still snapping his fingers to the too loud music and eating a peanut butter and jelly sandwich and who should he see standing there but little Nancy Maloney in her green campfire girl scout woodchuck outfit and her little dog Lulu with a green bow in its white hair.

Nancy is selling cookies.

No, it's a candy bar and she's holding it up for you to see.

Nancy is smiling a smile of such perfect joy and her green cap is set at such a daring angle and her blond hair is so long for someone so young and her blue eyes sparkle as she gears up to tell you something wonderful.

"It's chocolate," she says, "and it has more than one kind of nuts!"

It's like even she can't believe this amazing news.

"It's true!" She comes up on her toes and then goes down again. "More than one kind of nuts."

You tip your shades down so she can see how teen tired and offended you are that she would come to your door with this kind of kid's stuff.

You look her up and down and say, "Hey, it's little Nasty Baloney."

You are so clever. You bet she's never heard that one before.

She's still holding up the chocolate bar, and you see her happiness shatter like glass and die. Whatever it was that lit up her face is gone now. You've killed it. You see she knows now that just because you've got chocolate bars with more than one kind of nuts in them people won't always be nice to you. Just because you discover something new and wonderful and want to share it with everyone, that doesn't mean some young jerk won't show you it's not so hot after all.

She runs off crying, her little dog yapping at her heels, and you're looking down a long tunnel to a time when it will hit you that everyone you ever cared about is either dead or not speaking to you and that a ghost is just the sudden realization that something you did years and years ago, something you'd pushed to the back of your mind, something you'd hoped no one had really noticed in the first place, has returned to bite you in the ass in the guise of Nancy and her little dog Lulu.

Stinky suddenly realizes everything he has done since that day has been an attempt to make up for his great crime. He went to war and charged enemy positions tossing grenades hoping someone would say okay you've made up for it, but no one ever said that. He joined the Peace Corps hoping someone would say nice work that evens the score, but no one ever said that.

He became a priest for the wrong reasons.

This is his great epiphany.

He has been barking up the wrong tree.

He has spent all those years so horny he squeaked when he walked for nothing.

He is forced to admit he doesn't give a rat's ass about the trinity or any of the rest of it.

He'll go do something else if Nancy will forgive him.

He opens the bottom drawer wide and paws through the pajamas, and surely the fact that he has so many sets of pajamas, some with rocket ships, some with western hats and six shooters, surely this is another indication that he has taken a wrong turn in life.

"Nancy," he cries, "are you still in there?"

First spooky music and you can't tell where it's coming from. Then the air goes suddenly cold and bang! pajamas explode from the drawer, and she rises up with that dog like our Lady of Los Angeles with Pooch.

She's a big Brownie gone bad and hard now, and her green is not so green, and the dog is hairless with the faded ribbon wrapped around its head like a toothache remedy, and its eyes are black buttons, and there is a nasty snarl rumbling just under the surface of its lips.

Nancy never became the kind of woman who brings bright new discoveries to an appreciative world. She became the kind of woman who looks at you with a lot of suspicion in her eyes. She knows you're up to something. Everyone is always up to something.

He asks, "Do you remember the chocolate bars with more than one kind of nuts, Nancy?"

"I knew it was you," Nancy says and holds out the dog. "Lulu sniffed you out."

Lulu growls a smug little growl which ends up being not much more than a toothless buzzing of old doggy lips.

"Can you ever forgive me, Nancy?" Stinky asks. "I haven't had a moment's peace since that day."

"Not even in your dreams, Stinky Pinkypoo," she says.

22

My Shoes

I *whistled up a cab,* but when it rocked to a stop at the curb, I saw there was someone already in the back seat. I got a quick flash, excuse me, of a woman in a big hat, nice knees, blue eyes, and very red lipstick, reminded me of someone. I wondered who.

Before I could work that out, my disguise jumped off me and climbed in next to the woman and slammed the door in my face. The cab zoomed off leaving me standing there totally exposed downtown in the middle of the afternoon with no place to go and nothing to do and everyone looking at me and pretending not to and oh no here comes a cop with the look of a lion who has just smelled out his lunch, so I hot-footed it on down the sidewalk, dogs barking and kids throwing curses and cans and me desperately looking for a doorway in which to duck just in the nick of time through a glass beaded curtain which somehow jingle jangled as I came puffing and panting though it and Madam Knows-It-All says to me ah ha you're just in time sit down before you fall down and holds out her hands like she wants me to take them so we can maybe dance or maybe she wants to start with my palms and move on to her crystal ball and finish with some tarot cards, but when I take her hands, she shakes me off and says, "No, no, not that."

"What then?" I asked.

"The elevator, you idiot. Take the elevator." She made shoo shoo motions at me, and her crystal ball went out like a light bulb, and the sign in the door turned itself around to CLOSED, and looking at her I could not be entirely sure that really was still her and not some shadow in her chair over by the elevator which precluded my asking, "What elevator?"

I could have gone back out into the street and taken my chances that the cop had pounded on by by now and was somewhere up ahead scratching his head and making up stories about the totally too vivid guy who had gotten away just like that, poof.

Poof?

You got a problem with poof?

I had no problem with poof. I walked over to the elevator and pushed the button. The door opened at once, and I got on. The door closed, and the car moved up, and at each floor there was ding and a voice announced deli and dry cleaning ding your fingernails decorated specializing in bankruptcy ding ladies' lingerie naturally ding apartment 4E. We stopped. The elevator door opened, but there was another door right there. Apartment 4E. I knocked.

You can imagine my surprise when the door opened and a woman wearing my missing disguise looked me up and down and then stepped aside to let me in.

"You're right on time," she said.

Since she was in my disguise, you might wonder how I knew she was a woman. Well, it had to do with her overall yummy curviness not to mention the fact that she was doing nothing to alter her voice. I gave her the once over meaning what's a nice disguise like you doing in a place like this, and she smiled like she knew what I was thinking which she very well may have considering my condition.

"You're perfect now," she said, "so totally open."

"Perfect for what?" I asked.

"To try on something new." She pulled me inside and gave me a little shove to launch me into the thick of things.

There were maybe a dozen people conversationally grouped in twos and threes, standing, sitting, leaning against the walls, drinking, laughing, looking serious, touching, but not too much. No smoking.

There was a guy in a white T-shirt talking to a guy in a gray suit, an Indian maiden talking to a chick with an inactive hula hoop, a woman in a raincoat, a guy with a tall chef's hat, and a woman with so many pearls you had to wonder how she held her head up who now clapped her hands and said, "Okay people it's time to start."

The people formed a circle around her. I approached cautiously, and the woman in the raincoat and a man in scuba gear moved apart to make a place for me.

"For you who are new," the hostess said. "We gather here every Thursday afternoon to try on one another's clothes. In this cold century, we are doing our part for worldwide empathy. We want to know what it's like to walk in your shoes. So, look at the person directly across the circle from you and couple by couple, move into the center and trade."

The person directly opposite me was the bald man in a gray suit. But right next to him was the woman wearing my disguise.

The woman next to me was in the very act of opening her raincoat when I took her by the shoulders and turned her like a door once and then around again leaving her standing where I had been standing and me now facing the woman wearing my disguise.

"Hey!" the raincoat woman said. I could see she had on very nice fancy red underwear.

But she was too late.

I moved into the center of the circle, my eyes locked with the woman in my disguise.

"Your outfit precedes you," she said when we met in the middle.

I quickly stripped down to nothing.

She just stood there watching, and for a horrible moment, I thought maybe me naked in the center of this circle of oddly dressed strangers was the true purpose of this fruitcake cult, but then my disguise got off her and onto me, leaving her standing there looking like my first wife Sheila in one of her rare unguarded moments, and from the point of view of the clothes trading people, I must have just disappeared, because they all gasped and then shrugged. Hey, who was that unmasked man.

I wasn't invisible. I was irrelevant.

"Well, nice try, anyway," Sheila said. "Thanks, guys."

The muttering crowd moved in on her for a group hug.

I stepped to one side to make room for them.

23

Some Other Time

D *onald looked out over the marshy ground* surrounding the fort. It was easy to imagine things moving in the fog that always rolled along the ground and around the trees and giant ferns. Bog pools like cloudy mirrors threw back reflections that could be mistaken for things moving up on the wall. A cleared perimeter around the fort was lighted by big spots at night. There were never any stars. The cloud cover never lifted. Not even a little, not even once. A sun smear lighted the gray days, and sometimes at night the unending darkness of the sky was broken by a moon smudge. Sentry duty, day or night, mostly involved screaming for help when the big bog rats were actually climbing the walls.

Everything looks like something. If there were a thing that was so new, so different that it didn't look like anything, could you even see it? You could say these creatures looked like giant hairless rats, rats with too many limbs, rats that moved like spiders. Or beavers, maybe. You could say they looked like spiders, really big spiders, beaver spiders the size of buffalos, spiders with delicate manipulative limbs like the arms and hands of monkeys; watching one pick a fruit and eat it was like watching a monkey eat a banana. You could say they looked like monkeys, except for the rat snout and terrible teeth and all those limbs and slashing claws. They moved along the marshy landscape like water bugs, quick and gray and usually silent.

Donald, Eleanor, everyone these days was always either going up on or coming down from the effects of eating starfish. They liked to think of the starfish as a "byproduct" of the bog rats. The thought of how long it had been since he'd eaten a starfish made Donald break into a cold sweat, and he spent several minutes trembling badly.

While he had the jitters, he wasn't watching the wall, which meant he was falling down on the job. Maybe that was why no one would look him in the eye. Everyone looked at his back and whispered together. In fact, if he turned now and looked back down into the courtyard he'd see dozens of people look away quickly.

"Daddy!"

He looked back down into the fort and saw his daughter Zoey waving at him. First born on a new planet! How proud he and Eleanor had been. A rush of warmth turned up his smile and made him feel suddenly so much better. What a blessing was this little version of Eleanor with her big bright smile and blond pigtails.

"What is it?" he asked. "Are you calling me to lunch?"

"No, Daddy, I'm dead."

"You're not dead!" he yelled. How he wished she'd stop saying that.

"As a door nail, Daddy. Pushing up daisies. The worms crawl in, the worms crawl out . . ."

2

There weren't many people left now. The fort looked like the inside of an abandoned house. Something tips over, it stays tipped over. Nobody sweeps up. Shutters banging in the wind. A ragged man hanging onto the post that holds up the porch of the meeting hall like a drunk. Couple of other people slumped on benches on the same porch. By the time anyone came back to the planet to check on them, there wouldn't be anyone left.

His turn to watch, but who really cared anyway?

Donald decided he didn't care and came down off the wall. No one said he shouldn't; no one took his place. He needed to go chew some starfish. He knew there weren't any left. He would have to go outside and find some. Probably get himself killed. He wondered if Eleanor would want to go with him.

3

They hid in the giant ferns and waited in the milky afternoon sunlight, watching the big rat move like a grayer patch of fog over the march as she searched for her birthing pool, and after she'd found it, they waited until she was deep into her pain, before they ran quiet-

ly from their hiding places, Donald first, and then Eleanor with the
sack. Donald got down into the bog pool behind the rat. She lifted her
gray head from the mud and twisted around to scream what he knew
must be words, could only be words, meanings, language of some kind
— malice, then despair, entreaties, and finally hopelessness. He knew
he would care in the morning; just then he didn't care, couldn't care.
They'd be long gone before she could walk. They'd be home or they'd
be hidden, melting into the fog, blending in like the ghostly rats themselves. She'd never catch them.

"Don't listen to her," Eleanor said. Donald had told her his theory
about how the big rats were actually intelligent. She wouldn't want him
thinking about that at a time like this.

The water smelled like dead animals, dead fish, dead plants, and
suddenly the rat's blood. Donald dropped to his knees and plunged his
arms into the water.

"Have you got one yet, Donald?" Eleanor stood opening and clos-
ing the top of the sack, stepping from foot to foot. "Just shut up, you
stupid cow!" she screamed at the rat. "Have you got one, Donald?"

The infant rat dropped into Donald's hands. He closed his fingers
around it and snatched it out of the water before it could squirm away.
The creature felt like a slick sack of smooth pebbles. The newborn
might almost have been a different species. Its skin was dead white
and its eyes were glassy black. Had Donald not caught it, it would have
used its twelve weak legs to scuttle around the bog pools fleeing the
six-legged eels that were always around any rat birth. When it wasn't
running and hiding it would be searching for little things to eat.

Eleanor stood with her mouth a little open, staring at the wriggling
creature in his hand.

"So, hold out the sack," he said.

She jerked up her head and then dropped to her knees at the edge
of the pool and held out the open sack. Donald dropped the creature in,
and Eleanor closed the sack quickly and hugged it to her chest.

"We need more," she said.

Donald turned too quickly and slipped and caught himself with
both hands flat on the gray smooth flanks of the rat. He felt her quiver
at his touch, but she had no strength to lift her head and plead or threat-
en now. He imagined touching a rhinoceros would be like this. He ran
his hands back down her body and into the water.

Another starfish dropped into his hands, but before he could catch it, two more came quickly one after the other, distracting him, and he lost all three in a bloody cloud washing around the back of the rat.

"Damn."

"What happened, Donald? What is it?"

"Nothing. Nothing. Just get the sack ready."

When the next ones came, he was ready, and he caught two. Eleanor held open the sack, and he dropped them in and then went back for more.

A time of decision was fast approaching. How many would they take? How long could they stay so exposed like this? There was always the chance that a rat not weakened by birth might come by, maybe the father, if there were father rats. They didn't know much about the breeding habits of the rats. Eleanor had been working on that problem, but then eating the newborn rats had become more important to her than studying how they came to be.

Donald did know they had to hurry. If they were taken by surprise out in the open, they wouldn't have a chance.

"We need more," Eleanor said.

She was right. They might be greedy, it might be dangerous, but they really did need more. Donald could feel the need, had felt it for hours, it was like shaking inside, like he would rattle apart and fall to pieces from the inside out.

There was a sudden burst of births, and the water came alive with blood and swimming starfish, their twelve legs moving them gracefully and quickly around the legs of their mother. Donald snatched at them but didn't expect to catch the free-swimming ones. He got back into position for the next birth, and when it came, he made an easy catch, bagged it and got back into position again.

Four more and Donald decided they had enough. He crawled out of the pool and pulled Eleanor to her feet.

"Let me see them," he said.

Eleanor held the sack tight to her chest, and for a moment he thought she might just run away.

"There's enough for both of us, Eleanor." He put his hand on the sack.

"Yes, enough," she said. She opened the sack, and he looked down at the squirming white mass, legs clawing at the air, black eyes wild with fear. He licked his lips and reached down for one. Eleanor gave a little cry, but she didn't jerk the sack away. Donald wanted one now, his little voice said why not just one, Donald, just one wouldn't hurt, it would take the edge off, but, while he might be almost that desperate, he wasn't that stupid. He put his hands on Eleanor's hands and closed the sack.

"Let's get out of here," he said.

They moved quickly into the ferns, and Donald looked back once as they moved out of sight and saw the eels each as long as his leg move in on the big rat, covering her completely for a moment on their way deeper into the pool after the starfish.

4

Later that same day, or maybe it was some time far into the future, or even weeks before, Eleanor pushed in ahead of Donald as soon as the gate opened and ran for the quarters she shared with no one since she'd kicked him out. Jeffers, who had opened the gate for them, eyed Eleanor's sack, and Donald could see they weren't fooling him. Donald gave him a glare meant to peel the face from his skull, and the look must have been at least partly effective because Jeffers didn't make an issue of it, stepped back instead and licked his lips and closed the gate.

Donald hurried to catch up with Eleanor. He didn't doubt that she would forget him altogether now and lock herself inside with the starfish. He caught up with her just as she reached her door.

Inside she went quickly to a big glass bowl on a low table. The bowl was always there, always ready. The young starfish could survive a long time in the air, but they were more lively, and everyone agreed better, when submerged for a few minutes. Eleanor emptied the sack into the bowl, and Donald drew a pitcher of water and poured it over them. They moved sluggishly at first, but by the time he had added two more pitchers of water, the starfish swam briskly and stared out of the glass bowl with bright eyes. When they spread their twelve legs against the glass, they looked like strange white hands pressed against a window.

"We didn't lose even one!" Eleanor said.

"Lucky us," Donald said.

Eleanor put a wooden bowl on the table. It was almost as big as the glass bowl holding the starfish. She sat down. Once she would have gotten him a wooden bowl, too, or at least would have told him to help himself. He could see she didn't care at all that he was here. He should leave. He wished he could leave. He took down another wooden bowl for himself and put it on the table. He wished he could go home, read, think, work, maybe figure out a way to save them all, be the hero, make Zoey proud. He sat down across from Eleanor — the big glass bowl between them. He could see her fun house face twisted and bloated through the water.

Eleanor plunged her hand into the glass bowl and stirred around until she caught a starfish. With no hesitation, she opened her mouth as wide as she could and put the creature inside. Her cheeks bulged as she chewed. Sweat beaded her forehead, and she rolled her eyes back in her head. Donald would wait until she swallowed. It was a kind of challenge, putting off satisfying his own need for just a moment longer, just a little longer, each moment of resistance a little victory. At one time he thought that he could give up the starfish altogether by spacing out his eatings and making the spaces longer and longer until they were forever. Now he played little games with little victories and little losses.

Eleanor swallowed — once, twice. Her shoulders heaved as she sucked in deep breaths, then her face went red and she leaned over her wooden bowl and vomited.

Donald might have looked away. He might have made things easier for himself, but he wouldn't allow himself that — if he was going to eat them, he would face the ugliness of the addiction, and there was no doubt that eating the starfish was an addiction. It had been a seductive thing. At first the high was so incredible. Donald was convinced that he had seen the face of god in those early days, was convinced that he had touched the deity, had been shown the pattern of the universe, had been shown his special place in the universe, had felt the love, had felt the rightness — he remembered how everything had gotten better; the world was brighter; sex was better; Eleanor was kinder. Being a parent was easier, clearer. Nothing could have hurt him in those days. These days he needed a few starfish just to stop the cold sweats and shakes, just to work his way up to feeling lousy.

Donald fished a starfish out of the bowl and put it in his mouth. It struggled as he crushed it with his teeth. His mouth felt numb and sweet relief tingled up the sides of his face. He swallowed and felt

a familiar fierce sense of rightness flow down his throat. When the
starfish hit his stomach, his body rebelled, and Donald leaned over his
bowl to vomit. He thought it was the pebbles he felt when he caught
the starfish that were so hard on his system. They lay now like black
stones in the chewed remains of the starfish in his wooden bowl. He
was aware that Eleanor was vomiting again, but he didn't pay any attention to her. He reached into the bowl for another starfish. One more
and he'd feel normal, but even as he ate it, he knew he wouldn't stop
with one more.

5

Donald wasn't in his body at all. He could see his body at the table
slumped to one side of his wooden bowl, head on folded arms, dream-
ing the starfish dream. Eleanor still fished around in the big glass bowl
for another one. From his vantage point near the ceiling, he could see
there weren't any more. Eleanor could probably see that from where
she was, too, but she didn't want to believe it. It took more, so many
more, these days to reach the jumping off point, and sometimes you
didn't reach it at all, sometimes, you ate one, you ate two, you ate half
a dozen or more, and all that happened was that you stopped feeling so
bad, not good, but not so bad, and sometimes that was enough.

It wasn't enough for Eleanor tonight. He saw her look at his
slumped body and he saw the look of envy and even hate cross her
face. Why should he be zooming around in space buzzing the face of
god like a celestial fly while she was stuck here with all the ugliness?

At least the baby wasn't crying.

The baby wasn't crying.

The baby.

Donald expanded like a balloon, filled the room, felt the walls
constrict him, pushed harder, burst through the walls and exploded,
looking in every direction at once for Zoey — hey, kiddo, no fooling
around! Come on, now, it's dangerous out here.

He ran through the fog and leaped over the wall of the fort in a
single bound. He spotted her ducking under a giant fern and he shouted
again, but she didn't stop or even look back. Zigzagging around the
trees, jumping over the bog pools, he ran after her.

He heard her hide-and-seek giggle just ahead, and when he came around the tree he found her body deeply slashed and drained as it had been the day she died. At least she was all in one piece now.

"Look at me, Daddy," she said without opening her eyes, "I'm a bag of rats!"

Her body split and dozens of smaller versions of the big bog rats scattered in all directions. Zoey dissolved into the marshy ground. A tree grew quickly from where she had been.

"Very symbolic," Donald said. He sat down on the ground.

As he sat, his head passed through layers of time, and when he was low enough Zoey stepped out from behind the new tree and sat down beside him.

"I guess it's fair in way," Donald said. "We're the bad guys. We eat their young, and so they kill us, you for example, whenever they can."

"You haven't got it right, Daddy," Zoey said. "Keep trying."

"Do they know how hard it is for us to resist?" Donald asked. "Do they have any idea what this is like for us?"

"They don't kill us because you eat the starfish, Daddy," Zoey said. "The eels eat their young, too."

"Then what?"

She patted his knee and the grown up gesture and her small hand melted him; he wanted to grab her and hug her close but he could see parts of the forest through her, and he knew if he grabbed her it might be like grabbing smoke so he held back afraid to do anything that would ruin this contact.

"Daddy, they don't kill you because you eat their newborn," Zoey said. "They kill you because you spit out the seeds."

The seeds.

The black pebbles in the wooden bowls.

"What would happen if we didn't spit out the seeds, Zoey?"

"Bag of rats, Daddy," she said, "but I'm still here. You keep the seeds and you get a moment that lasts forever."

The system itself now made sense to the biologist he had once been.

It all worked together. The rats lured the eels into eating the starfish and the starfish grew into new rats and killed the eels when they were ready to emerge. There were many many eels. Not so many rats. The mechanism that lured the eels to the birthing pools might be an irresistible scent or sound. He doubted the eels had the cognitive machinery to benefit from a final moment that lasted forever. That part didn't make so much sense, but people were something from outside the natural system. Who could have predicted their reactions?

"Is it a shared final moment, Zoey?"

No answer.

Donald jerked his head up from the table and looked across the glass bowl at Eleanor. She seemed surprised to see him. He was surprised to be seeing her. He had never pulled out of the deep starfish state like that. The urgency to check on Zoey had kicked him out of it. That was it.

That wasn't it.

Zoey was still dead, and he had been balancing on the line between Eleanor's current state of not enough starfish to take off and that don't-expect-to-see-me-until-you-see-me blast off point, that point of no return, that big jump into the void, and thinking about Zoey had knocked him over to this side, and he would need a couple more starfish to get back, and the bowl was empty. Or not exactly empty, but empty in the sense that mattered. It still had water, and it looked like a big aquarium after all the fish have died and you've fished (ha) them out and flushed them and now all you've got is water with a few twigs floating and some leaves, a little sand on the bottom, a barely discernible rainbow slick along the top. But when did they ever have an aquarium?

6

Waking was always such a disappointment — nothingness to pain, and the realization that he was still marooned, Zoey was still dead, and the colony was next to dead. The first task of the day was just finding the strength to sit up in bed. Inhale the heavy air, exhale something that tasted and smelled like sulfur gas. Dying of thirst and too weak to crawl to water. Insane conga drummers in his head.

Eleanor was an untidy pile beside him. Her neck was twisted at an angle that looked uncomfortable. He imagined her head had hit the pillow with a plop when she passed out and hadn't budged all night while her body thrashed around like a hooked fish. Her cheek was still stained with the aftermath of their eating. She sucked air in through her mouth. If it had not been for that sad whistle, he might have thought her dead.

He managed to sit up and then spent a few minutes belching and waving away the smell it produced. Then he let his head loll to the side and watched Eleanor for a moment more.

He poked her in the side with his finger. "Hey, Sunshine, rise and shine."

She groaned and pulled herself up to lean back against the headboard beside him. He didn't think her eyes were focused and talking to her might be like talking to himself, but since he had things to say, he took her hand and said, "Eleanor, we can't go on like this."

"What?"

"I feel so bad," he said.

"You think you're alone? What's the point?"

"I don't want to live like this."

"So kill yourself."

"You don't mean that, Eleanor."

"Leave me alone, Donald." She scrunched down in the covers and turned away from him. "Just leave me alone."

"I had a vision," he said.

"How nice."

"I mean it," he said. "I saw Zoey."

"Don't Donald." She got up, dragging the top sheet off with her, and wandered over to the table and the glass bowl. The wooden bowls were as they'd left them the night before, and she looked down at hers and went white and turned her head away quickly.

"She told me the problem is we spit out the seeds," he said.

"This is another one of your goofy theories, isn't it?" She came over and sat down on the bed beside him.

"Maybe," he said. "Maybe she told me and maybe I just figured it out." He put his arm around her shoulders. She resisted for a moment, but then she sighed and relaxed against him. "I think the reason the rats don't kill the eels is that they want the eels to eat the starfish. They want us to eat the starfish, too."

"Oh, sure."

"They don't kill the eels because the eels don't spit out the seeds and the seeds grow inside them into new rats."

She twisted around to look up at him and he wrinkled his nose at her breath before he could stop himself. "You're saying we should keep those black stones down somehow and let them hatch and eat their way out of us?"

"Yes," he said. "Do you think we could use a tranquilizer to stop the stomach spasms?"

"I'm sure we could," she said. "But why should we? What's in it for us?"

"Time," he said. "When I sat down beside Zoey I got a little taste of it. It's all the time you need. In those last moments of this body you have an eternity of time to do what you want."

"How can you know that?"

"You know the starfish state," he said. "I think it's certainly possible. And in any case, we wouldn't be here."

"Would we be alone?"

"I don't know," he said. "Probably no more alone than everyone is all the time anyway. We already make up most of the stuff we call our lives."

She didn't say anything more. They sat together listening to the protests of their bodies, lost in their own thoughts.

Finally he shook his head and pulled away from her. "Or like you say it could just be another one of my goofy theories. Keeping the seeds down might just be suicide."

"Well," she said, "since you put it that way, let's do it."

Today or tomorrow or the day after that.

"Daddy?"

Zoey at the door in her long nightdress. Tangled blond hair. Dirty bare feet. Rubbing her eyes with a fist.

"Hey, sleepyhead, crawl in with Mommy and me."

Strong Suits

O ne day *Jack Spangler got bonked on the head* by a person
or persons unknown, robbed, and left for dead. Meanwhile,
back at the apartment, Danielle tossed her things into suitcases and
split. She was long gone by the time Jack got home from the hospital
minus his memory. She'd deliberately left her business suits behind,
abandoning everything they represented, but the suits had become so
accustomed to life in the fast lane that they refused to just give up and
hang there.

They would impersonate her.

They found and destroyed the note she left for Jack. The note had
said, "Jack, I'm sorry, but I've gone off to find myself. Maybe I'll paint
or blow glass. See if you can find someone who can use my girl lawyer
suits. I'll probably never be back. Love, Danielle."

Home again after three days in the hospital, Jack was all khakis
and blue shirt and a white X marking the spot on the back of his head
where the blow had been struck. His kind of memory loss meant he
could remember almost everything about the world and how it worked,
but he had no clue about his place in it. He didn't even feel comfortable
with his name. Jack Spangler. How could he be sure that was his name?
Was he really a well-known cook? Who had that been on the phone
telling him he should take all the time he needed and not worry about
coming back to the restaurant? Maybe it was all code. Maybe he was a
government witness or a retired spy or a professional killer.

His doctor told him watch for anything out of the ordinary. How
would he know what was ordinary and what was not? Good question,
his doctor said.

Were the suits out of the ordinary? Or should he think of her as
the Suit since they were, in fact, all aspects of the one woman who had
probably once eaten a lot more than she did now, coming home from
the law office and dropping her briefcase on the floor and as often as

not making straight for the closet where she would hang muttering or softly snoring until it was time to get up and go litigate some more the next day? The Suits always had things to say to him when addressed directly, but they were baffling things that he didn't know how to respond to, since he was not sure what his relationship actually was to this multifaceted creature.

Once after the Suit of the day had flapped off to work, Jack crept into the closet and sat on the floor and felt the rest of the skirts brushing his face as they shifted around gossiping and complaining about how they had no support systems, no jeans, no T-shirts, no underwear, no tennis shoes, no little black dress, no Bermuda shorts, no hats, no scarves, no pastel bracelets with progressive slogans etched into them, no bottles, no tubes, nothing on the top of the dresser. Nothing whatsoever pink.

Jack listened carefully, hoping for clues.

There were no clues.

He prowled around the apartment trying to remember what he should be doing. The other Suits joked or bickered, laughed and cried, and sometimes they enticed him into the bedroom to tease him, but mostly they ignored him.

Then the working Suit came home and joined the others.

He listened to them in there until he couldn't take it any longer. Then he rushed to the closet and jerked open the door, and they went silent, and their silence meant *So, what do you want now, Jack?*

He didn't know.

Next to the Gray Suit, who had had a hard day, there was the Navy Suit, who loved the late afternoons and early evening meetings and cocktails after work, and the Tan Suit, who lived right on the razor's edge of making a joke — no, no, she never would, but you always thought she might — and the Black Suit, who probably took too much pleasure in the kill. Jack loved their straight skirts and double-breasted, tailored jackets — no pants, never pants, and when it came to hats and gloves, well, you've got to be kidding, right?

"Let me in," he said and put his hands on the hangers of the Suits in the middle and pushed them aside.

"Hey! Hey!"

"Watch it!"

"So, this is cozy, right?"

"Cozy."

"We have a man in the middle."

"All hot and hairy."

"Did he shower today?"

"My guess is no."

"No, you're quite wrong! He did indeed shower."

"Not that it did him any good."

Jack gave it up and moved away and closed the door on their giggling.

"Oh, Jack. Jack," they called after him. "Don't be like that."

He made a salad of fresh spinach, radishes, cherry tomatoes, and goat cheese. He cut a few slices of bread from the loaf he had baked earlier in the morning. He decanted the wine and set the table.

He grilled a couple of lamb chops.

Would the smell tempt her? No, of course it wouldn't. He cooked, but she never ate. It was a subtle rejection of the very core of his being as a cook.

He sat down in front of his food and picked up his fork.

"Jack?"

She was gray in the bedroom doorway. She had no expression for him to read. He could make nothing of her contours. Late evening sunlight through the bedroom window outlined her and sparkled like jewels around the top of her collar. The shadows were missing beneath her skirt, where her legs did not go all the way down to the floor. For the first time, he might have thought that strange, but she said his name again, and he threw down his napkin and got up and came across the room to her. He put his hands on her waist and pulled her in close. He was confused all the time, but he knew he loved her several selves, colour-coded and accessorized. She drove him crazy, but he knew he was in the right place as she leaned into him with no weight, some swishing, maybe a small sigh like an oyster burping politely. She smelled like wool and plastic buttons.

"Hungry?" he said, nuzzling around her collar. When she stiffened in his arms, he said, "Oh, never mind. We could watch TV. Or play Scrabble. Come talk to me."

He wanted to talk about his day and the way things came back to him and then flew away again. He wanted to hear about her day. He wanted there to be some part of the day that belonged to both of them. He had so many questions. He might ask if she had any exciting cases ongoing. Or do we have children? What's up with The Goofball in

DC? What's your favorite color? What are we going to do about world hunger? Where did we meet? Is there rain in the forecast? Do you love me even a little bit?

She worked her way out of his arms.

"Don't ask," she said, and turned away from him and fluttered back to the closet, where she joined the others.

He couldn't go back to his dinner. He couldn't watch TV and pretend they weren't in there talking about him. He decided to go out for cigarettes.

But once out on the sidewalk he realized he didn't smoke and didn't want to start smoking now. Hey, he could go down to the restaurant. Why not? Maybe the place would trigger something in his memory. He should go back up to the apartment and get his knives. He had knives? Yes, he had knives. But he wouldn't need them tonight. Unless he was not really a chef at all and this fascination with slicing and dicing indicated something other than food preparation.

No. He stopped suddenly on the sidewalk and people grumbled at him as they moved around him. No. His blade work was a source of pride.

And the blade work all had to do with food.

This business of being a serial killer or a CIA operative was nonsense.

He was a cook.

He remembered telling Danielle exactly that. Had it been their second date? She was going to be a famous lawyer. I'll always be a cook, he said. Maybe I'll work my way up to a classier joint, but if you get tangled up with me, you'd better like to eat.

Oh, I like to eat, she told him with a sly smile.

He could see that smile now, just the smile, the cat was still missing, and hadn't her legs gone all the way down to the ground back in college?

It was not that she had changed, he realized with a chill of despair. She was simply gone.

He turned to go back the way he'd come and realized that he'd gone too far. Nothing looked familiar. He had no idea how to get back to Danielle.

Faces swooped in at him from the fog that was also setting summer sunlight. He radiated panic, and the open space around him widened as the people trying to get home after a long day moved away from him. He pulled himself into himself, folded himself once, twice, turned down his edges so no one could see what was happening inside. They wouldn't like it if they could see that. They might have him arrested, hauled off the street, locked up, and then he'd never get back to her. He should play it cool. He should stop making those blubbery sounds.

Yes, stop. And when he was still, everything stopped.

Time itself stopped.

And then it started up again, and Jack saw Louie's Meat Market and knew exactly where he was. In fact, he was amazed that he had ever been confused. He was about five blocks from home. The sun had gone down, so he could not judge how long he had been out in the street. Probably not days. He walked back to his building and up to the apartment.

The bedroom door was closed. He put his ear against it, but he heard nothing. He opened the door expecting sulking darkness, but the lights were all on. The closet door was open a little, but not enough for him to see what was going on in there. There were the rustling, whispering sounds of conversation — probably a conspiracy.

There was a trail of clothes, like breadcrumbs to the closet. Jeans. Underwear. A pink t-shirt, yellow sandals, and something white that might have been a crumpled tissue but seemed more substantial. He picked it up.

It was a sock. There was a cartoon moose on one side and a squirrel or beaver on the other. The squirrel was wearing a leather helmet with goggles. He knew he should know these animals. He knew they were important to everything that had happened to him in the last few weeks and might be the key to everything that was about to happen to him now as he reached for the half-closed closet door, which, just before he touched it, swung open, and the Black Suit stepped out.

"Jack!" she said.

"You're going out?"

"I'm home," she said. "When you weren't here, I called Roland at the firm and made arrangements to meet him for drinks to mend my fences, but I can do that tomorrow!"

She came into his arms, and he moved with her to the bed, doing a dance step from the last century. Oh, maybe there were still ballroom occasions when such a step might be appropriate — and situations like this. It was the perfect move at a time like this.

He lowered her onto the bed and put his hand beneath her skirt and felt her great emptiness, so smooth and perfect. He pushed her skirt up and up and felt her absence pulling at him. He broke away breathing in little gasps and cries and jumped out of his khakis and blue shirt, black socks, and underwear. Her skirt was bunched about her waist. Her jacket and blouse were open. He swooped down on her, and they spun away together, and he entered her void and was suspended in nothingness for a moment, and then she moved against him, and then they moved together, stuff and no stuff, yin and yang, light and dark. Hello, goodbye.

This is much better, said the whole universe, and he said, yes, I agree completely. He was everywhere. He was everything. He had no questions.

Well, maybe one.

Like what's this?

Flesh around the edges.

A woman developing like a photograph in a chemical bubble bath. Champagne and sweet smile and sleepy eyes.

And ears.

Who knew she had ears?

Well, she must have had ears beneath all that reddish hair back in the days of ragged jeans and an abbreviated shirt with some kind of design on the front, maybe somebody's interpretation of a sunset or the startling consequences of projectile vomiting a pepperoni pizza. No, no, not that, she smells too good, no wool, no plastic. As she comes around the fountain, he can see she's holding a guitar by the neck like something she's chased down and killed for lunch.

Looking at him.

Looking at me?

I'm Danielle, and I'm going to be a famous lawyer some day soon.

I'm Jack, and that same day of which you speak I'll still be slinging hash. Well, maybe a better grade of hash. Would you like to come up and see my chef's hat?

And then he was not everywhere but just here, entirely here. He shuddered to a stop, and the suits in the closet sighed — a sound of sadness and completion.

"That was wonderful," the woman said, "if maybe a little desperate. I guess you missed me?"

There was a light scattering a freckles down her right shoulder, and, if we were past the jacket but only still working on the blouse buttons in that complicated procedure of getting her out of her business suit, you might wonder how far those freckles went — not so far as the lovely breast, and oh, look there was a similar but lighter scattering of freckles on her left shoulder, too.

Clavicle. Surely that was the kind of word that would get you naughty websites if you googled it.

He kissed her throat.

"They said you'd been hurt," she said. "They said something about your memory. I turned around and came back as soon as I heard."

In the same way he had seen her develop from the emptiness of her suit into what she now was beneath him, warm and squirmy, with both hands on his chest pushing him up so she could get a good look at him, he saw a realization grow in her eyes.

"You don't remember me!" She sounded a little frightened. She would be thinking she had just made love to a stranger. She would be thinking that had probably been the reason he had seemed so totally frisky himself. She was a stranger, too. It was the old "strangers on a train" routine. Had he ever mentioned that fantasy? Hey, wait a minute, that wasn't even his fantasy.

It was hers.

Danielle.

He put his hands on her shoulders and glided them down her body like a blind man, over her hips and down her legs. He put his hands under her knees and pushed them back up toward her chest. Houston, we have feet. Amazing. The right foot. The left foot. But what's this? He grabbed her left ankle with both hands.

"Jack?"

She was still wearing one white sock.

Moose and squirrel.

"Bullwinkle!" he said, and everything came back to him. "Where have you been, Danielle?"

"Dude ranch," she said.

And later, after they'd showered and she'd called Roland to apologize, he cleaned up the remains of the dinner he hadn't eaten anyway and made a light pasta dish and a fruit dessert. He opened a different wine. He told her he could tell she hadn't been eating right, but he didn't tell her the way he knew was the fast-food undertone to her breath.

She told him about the dude ranch, the horses, the campfires, the tequila, the singing. She was sorry she'd been out in the woods when word came of his injury.

He told her what he remembered about the mugging and about his days with the Suits.

He left out a lot of details.

25

A Note From the Future

I *didn't notice the note under my windshield* until I'd already gotten into the car and put the key in the ignition. Immediately, a sequence of future events came into my mind. I would open the car door. I wouldn't take the keys out of the ignition as I got out. I would automatically push the lock button down. I wouldn't want to take the chance that I might get a grease smear on my white shirt, so instead of just reaching over and grabbing the note, I would slam the door shut and walk around for it. I would pull the note out from under the windshield wiper and unfold it. It would be folded in a very complicated manner, and my unfolding would be a long and frustrating experience. Once I had it open, I would see that there was only a single sentence written in pencil. The sentence would read, "You've just locked your keys in your car."

And it would be true. Clutching the note in one hand and trembling with hope and fear, I would reach down with the other hand and seize the door handle. But the door really would be locked. I would cup my hands around my eyes and peek in. Since I'd still be holding the note, I would get a small paper cut above my left eye.

Yes, there would be the keys. So close and yet I might as well have been looking through a supernaturally powerful telescope at them on the moon.

I would now be late to an important meeting this morning. It would be the last straw, the very last straw. The Big Guy would sadly fire me. I mean to say he would pretend to be sad. I would be mostly pissed I would say things that would forever burn my bridges in this business. Word would get around that I was not only late, but hard to work with and generally unpleasant in stressful situations.

Blood from the paper cut would run into my left eye, and I would wipe it away and smack my palm against the glass of the driver's side window and leave a bloody handprint.

Maybe I should kill myself. I was already bleeding — no need to cut my wrists. I could just wait it out and bleed to death from my face right there in the driveway.

Or I could go into the house and get my spare car key if it were not for the fact that my house key was also locked in my car. I could try breaking into the house, but I had already set the alarm. It would go off. The security company would call the police. By the time I convinced them I was the homeowner, I would already be late, and the Big Guy would have already decided who was to get my office.

So, in order to derail that sequence of events and cheat Fate, I carefully removed the key from the ignition and put the whole bunch of keys into the front right pocket of my pants. I got out of the car and automatically pushed down the lock, and, not wanting to get my white shirt dirty, closed the door and stepped around and snatched up the note and negotiated the complexity of its origami.

Inside it looked like this.

Piano Turner.
Let a professional do it.

There was a local phone number.

There was a treble clef and staff drawn in blue ballpoint pen and seven musical notes.

I didn't recognize the tune, but I understood the message.

I had been at the point where it might have gone either way, and I had made the right turn.

I had not locked my keys in the car. I would be on time for my big meeting.

The Big Guy would love me.

My future was bright.

To seal the deal, I got out my phone and called the number on the note and made arrangements to have my piano turned just enough to catch the spring sunlight.

26

Superpowers

S *uperpowers, like faith, are an intensely personal matter.* They should not be flashy. No one should even know you have a superpower. In fact, it's better if they never find out. When people discover you have a superpower, they are all the time wanting you to use it on their behalf. Oh, please, get my kitty out of that tree. Help! Help! He stole my purse! This looks like a job for . . .

And so on and so forth endlessly. Once your superpower becomes public knowledge, you won't get a moment of peace.

This point of view, your understanding of the way faith and superpowers are the same thing, is a result of your close study of the Danish philosopher, Søren Kierkegaard, both the man himself and his writings. You can make a good case for the proposition that Kierkegaard was actually a superhero.

In the same way that he claimed his Christianity was a deeply personal matter that you could not detect just by looking at him, so, too, his superpower. And yours.

When people look at you, they should be thinking, okay, here's just some ordinary guy — a man in a baseball cap and dirty sneakers. The contrary theory holds you should stand out in a way that throws people off your track — outlandish facial hair is often suggested. Also yellow rubber flip-flops.

Beware of such advice. Better observers should see you but not notice you.

The perfect superpower has no outward effect on the world whatsoever. The most sophisticated instruments should be unable to detect it.

Only you know you have superpowers.

Like Kierkegaard, you can use your superpower whenever you want.

Say you're waiting for a bus, and it's way late and instead of stewing in your own juices, looking at your watch, sighing in exasperation along with the other people in the rain, you steady your gaze and your breathing, and focus, focus, focus and inwardly blast a beam of pure super energy from your head to your toes.

You should keep your hands in your pockets in case sparks sizzle and pop from your fingertips.

Oh, never mind. There will be no sparks. Your superpower has no outward manifestations whatsoever. Remember? No one knows you have the power. No one knows you're using it right now, even as the bus finally pulls up and you fall in line to get on.

When you meet the love of your life for lunch, you mustn't mention your superpower right away. When she asks you what you're thinking, you should say, "Oh, nothing, really." Just shake the rain out of your hair and smile. Depending on how long you've been together, she'll know something's up, but she won't in a million years suspect you're concealing superpowers. This is just between you and the universe. Sure, it's good to be open with the love of your life. It will enrich your relationship to reveal your vulnerabilities. But it would be very foolish to tell her you have superpowers. If things should go terribly wrong at some point in the next few moments, if you should decide it's all over between the two of you, or maybe like Kierkegaard, you decide to devote yourself to the religious life and sacrifice your happiness by forever living without her, then you can tell her. It'll be your out. You'll be Kierkegaard, and she'll be your Regina whom he left for the religious life. When people ask you what in the world you think you're doing? You will say, philosophy, of course.

So get up and stand there with your hands on your hips in your superstance. Don't look at her. Look instead out into space at something only someone with superpowers can see and let the cat out of the bag about your need to suffer.

She'll throw down her napkin and say, "That's the last straw. Do you hear me? The very last straw!"

And then she'll go away.

27

Take the Stairs

I *was thinking about thinking and thinking* about how I had to do a better job of keeping my thoughts to myself when I stepped out of the elevator on the fourth floor of Building 17 and saw the gaggle of so-called "Fairness Observers" congregating down the hall in front of my office door.

I might have played it cool and just kept walking and pushed through them like I believed they were really students and not government agents appointed from the most reactionary faith-based groups to make sure we weren't going too far with all of this science stuff. But I'd had enough of them for one day. They were in our labs and in our classrooms. There was always at least one of them in the audience any time we spoke. It was easy to pick them out even though they didn't wear their uniforms to class. They all had a grim and watchful expression. Crazy eyes. They hated you, hated what you were saying, and were only waiting for you to say something actionable, so they could jump up and denounce you.

If I knew anyone named Dorothy, I might have said, "No matter where you are these days, Dorothy, you're still in Kansas." But, in fact, I didn't know anyone named Dorothy.

Why were there so many of them waiting for me? Maybe my equal-time-for-Creationism routine had not been convincing. Or maybe someone had gotten my little joke about how you didn't need to see the Letter of our Leader on the tails of zeppelins to know which way the wind blew. Or maybe the Political Officer of my neighborhood had been creep-showing around at night peeking in my windows and had seen me do something not recommended by the Party.

Whatever. I could see there was trouble ahead. I took a sharp left into a stairwell.

"Hey!" one of them shouted. I'd been hoping they would think I'd gone up in a puff of smoke or been snatched off the planet by god. No luck.

Ray Vukcevich

Call me lazy. I'd been walking by those green Exit signs for years. I couldn't remember the last time I'd taken the stairs. I let the door close behind me. Someone grabbed my arm.

"This way," a young woman said. She looked familiar. A grad student in cognitive science, I thought. She hurried me through a door where no door could actually be unless there were a parallel stairwell beside the ordinary one. Which, of course, there was.

"Won't they see the secret door?" I asked her.

"No, they won't," she said. "That's what makes it secret."

But not magic, I decided. Or even alien science. Building 17 had once been a dorm, and over the years as it became one thing and then another and finally the home of what was left of science, more parts were added as needed on top of what was already there. That made it a very strange and complex building. A hidden staircase was not un-explainable.

We listened to the Fairness Observers pound down the other stairs. Then the young woman, Laurel something I now remembered, said, "Go ahead and take the stairs. I've got to get back to my post."

She opened the secret door.

There should have been a peephole. Someone shouted in triumph and grabbed her, and she squeaked, and I rushed forward to see her knee a Fairness Observer in the groin.

Another one yelled, "There he is!" And then the stairwell was full of them. Laurel pushed back in and ran down the secret stairs. I followed.

As she ran, Laurel yelled, "They're coming! They're coming!"

I could hear the thundering sound of the feet of our pursuers above. A bunch of people who had been sitting on the stairs listening to a woman talk scattered like birds as Laurel moved through them. The lecturer at the bottom of the stairs turned out to be Rita Simmons, probably our best-known biologist. She was well into her sixties and didn't look like she'd be doing much running. "Go on," she told me.

"But what about you?" I asked.

A young man ran up and seized her up in a fireman's carry. "My ride!" she said, and they were off, and I followed.

And down and down we went.

We passed through a village where some of the people grabbed umbrellas from an umbrella stand and some grabbed pink triangles from a wicker basket as they left. So, a little rain would fall on some of them and stone cold bigotry and oppression on the others when they joined the grim new world outside.

We came to a math class on the stairs where the professor was pleading with his students to hang on for just one more moment, please. He was just coming to the really pretty part of the proof. I wondered what had forced mathematics onto the secret stairs. Maybe someone was agitating to declare pi to be 3 again.

Students scattered in all directions carrying computers and kites and EEG amplifiers and fishbowls, telescopes, microscopes, and boxes of books. Sheets of notes filled the air like snowflakes in the cold time after the last nail is finally driven into the coffin of the Enlightenment.

Then everyone was running back up again. I was totally confused, but then I saw that government troops were flowing into the stairwell from below. Reinforcements. I decided not to run. Let them shoot me.

"Not an option," Rita Simmons said as if reading my mind. The young man who had been carrying her was nowhere to be seen.

"This way," she said. I followed her into a hole in the wall. She did something to close it behind us.

"What is this?" I asked.

"Another level of secret stairs," she said.

"How far down do these levels go?" I asked.

"Like the turtles," she said. "It's stairs all the way down."

And then we became very quiet and hid our light under a bushel.

Now our one small hope is that in the days to come when darkness has swallowed the planet, the curious and the discontent will be drawn to us by the far-away rumble and mumble of voices like the sea in the secret places behind the walls.

In the meantime we go on with our work.

28

Tongues

"All the astrologers will be castrated." —*Leonardo da Vinci*

1
Prophecy as Pathology

W*hen one half of the team descended* into dark depression, there was nothing for the other half to do but go along for the ride. But even if the outcome was known, the process had to be respected. Shelly needed to be talked into it.

"I predict," she said, "that if we run off to Borneo on this wild goose chase of yours, we will come to grief."

"And what do you base this prediction on?" Marc asked.

"Common sense?"

"Look, I've totally lost it, Shell," he said. "If we don't do this, what will we do instead? And if we don't do it now, then when?"

"You're channeling some kind of political speech from the past, aren't you?"

"Maybe from the future," he said. "I don't know. I can no longer predict what I can predict. There is a strange spiritual sickness eating away at my brain."

She put a cup of tea down in front of him. "What do you want to do?"

"Thanks," he said. "I see us in an exotic seaside grotto kissing the starfish on the smooth wet stone walls."

"I see that, too," she said, "but I don't like it."

"Borneo," he said.

"I'm not entirely sure where Borneo is," Shelly said, "A long long way from Chicago, no doubt, and I predict we can't afford to go there."

2
Symptoms and Events

"Leonardo is making fun of me," Marc said.

"Who?"

"Leonardo da Vinci," he said. "Look here."

Shelly threw down her pencil and got up from her desk where she had been preparing a chart for one of their regular clients. She came over to his desk where he was supposed to be working, too, instead of acting like a big baby.

"Don't give me that look," he said. "I am not acting like a baby."

He showed her the prediction.

"But maybe more than half of all astrologers are women." She sounded exasperated. "It doesn't even make sense."

"He's probably speaking metaphorically," Marc said. "In which case women astrologers could also be castrated."

"You may be losing it, Sweetie," she said.

"That's what I've been saying."

"We still can't afford Borneo."

"I've been thinking about that." Marc poked around in the papers on his desk, picking them up and putting them down. "Just as Leonardo may have been speaking obliquely, my vision of Borneo may also be couched in a kind of code."

He put another piece of paper on top of the Leonardo prophecy. It was covered with letters and numbers. "I started by rearranging the letters in 'Borneo.' I was hoping for something obvious, but I should have known better."

"What did you come up with?" She came around and put her hands on his shoulders and leaned down to look at the paper.

"I don't think I tried all the combinations," he said. "That would have taken too long. I stopped when I found something that looked promising."

"Which was?"

He flipped the paper over. On the other side were two words.

Borneo

Orebon

"Orebon?"

"I know," he said. "It's not quite right yet, but it looked strangely familiar and then it hit me that someone was pointing me at Oregon."

"But it says 'Orebon.'"

"Yes, but there is a simple transformation," he said. "Consider the letters in question. They are B and G. That is, the B should have been a G. So how do we get a G from what we have? Well, first notice that B is the second letter of the alphabet and that G is the seventh letter."

"Consider those facts noticed," Shelly said.

"So what is the difference?"

"Between seven and two?"

"Yes."

"Well, five."

"Bingo," he said. "And how do we get five from the other evidence?"

"I don't know."

"Well, notice that the offending B is the first letter in 'Borneo' and the target G is the fourth letter in 'Oregon' and what do you get when you add one and four?"

"Oh, okay," she said. "I see it. You get five. And two plus five is seven, and the seventh letter of the alphabet is G so you can substitute the G for the B in Orebon and get Oregon."

"Exactly!" he said. "And anyone can afford to go to Oregon these days."

"But what about the starfish?"

"They must be in Oregon, too."

3

Kissing Fish

They fought about it. They stopped speaking for a while. The cohesion of the team was seriously threatened, but then one thing led to another, and in the end, the Chicago based astrologers, Marc and Shelly Bowman, followed the Borneo/Oregon code to Portland where they had expected cool weather even in August. They had expected rain. No one is right all of the time. It was over 100 degrees and dry, the sky so blue, you might think clouds hadn't yet been invented. If the sun were god's thumb, these two astrologers were the thumbtacks. The heat drove them toward the sea where they learned of the Oregon Coast Aquarium in Newport, a couple of hours to the south. Things were coming together. Once they reached Newport, another piece fell into place when they spotted the Brunei Bar and Grill on the main drag.

Inside it wasn't Borneo but it was some place far away like Borneo or Bombay or Bora Bora but not Bermuda because it was not the kind of place you expected to see tourists in straw hats and flowery shorts. No cameras please! It was dark and cold and the beer neons were too bright but didn't penetrate far into the darkness, the kind of place someone might creep up behind you and get too close and whisper garlic in your ear, "So, you've come to kiss the fish?"

"At the aquarium," Marc said.

"Forget the aquarium," the man in the dark said. "What makes you think you'll find fish at the aquarium?"

"No fish at the aquarium?"

"Hey, this dude thinks they'll let him kiss the fish down at the aquarium," the man in the dark spoke loudly and there was laughter all around, and Marc could see that the place was not so empty after all. He could make out the faces of the men and woman at the bar now. They must have been sitting very quietly when he and Shelly had come in. There was a bartender now, too, and he was moving in on them. He was a young man with a very short haircut. He wore a white t-shirt and there were tattoos of birds and snakes on his upper arms. He tossed down a couple of coasters and asked them what they wanted to drink.

Marc wondered what they had on tap. Shelly asked for a cola.

The man in the dark moved in and took the stool between them. His hair was thick and totally white. His skin was very pale, but his lips were purple. He wore a red and green flannel shirt and some kind of gray canvas pants. Glasses with very small rimless lenses. Marc guessed he was probably in his mid-seventies. He rapped on the bar, and the bartender nodded at him. A moment later, the drinks appeared. The man picked his up and toasted Marc and Shelly silently and drank deeply before speaking again.

"There is a parasitic crustacean in the jungles of Borneo," he said. "In the waters. What it does is it crawls into the mouths of fish and eats their tongues. Then it attaches itself firmly and takes the place of the missing tongue. Half the time the fish eats something it goes no farther than its new tongue, but the fish can move it around and do other tongue-like things with it and pretty soon, the fish forgets it ever had some other kind of tongue. It just has to work a little harder."

"That's horrible," Shelly said.

"And these are the fish we've come for?" Marc asked.

"No," the man said. "These fish I'm talking about are in Borneo."

"So, why tell us about those creepy fish and their tongues, then?" Shelly asked. "If they're not even the ones we came to see?"

"Those are out back," he said. "Drink up and I'll show you."

He slipped off the stool and disappeared back into the gloom.

Marc and Shelly got off their stools. Marc tossed some money down on the bar and took her hand. He peered around hoping for a clue on what to do next. He had no intuitions. He figured Shelly had none either since she was never shy about telling him what she saw and felt.

Someone slashed open the darkness by opening a door to one side of the bar. "Come on, then," the same man called to them. Mark saw him step out of the door and hold it waiting for them to follow.

"You got any feelings about this?" he asked Shelly.

"Nothing specific," she said. "You don't have to have paranormal powers to guess this might be a mistake, though."

"You're probably right," he said. "Let's just take a quick peek, and if it doesn't seem right, we'll take off."

The man had left the door open for them and had moved off into what turned out to be a kind of back yard that reminded Marc of his childhood. There were a few untrimmed trees sprawling over the fence in back and junk — lots of junk — machines of indeterminate function, buckets of bolts, tin cans in piles, mysterious parts.

The man stood beside a big metal washtub. There was a piece of plywood on top of the tub.

"Come on," he said.

Mark and Shelly walked up to him. When they got there, he leaned down and pulled the plywood off of the washtub. Marc stepped in a little closer to look. The water was not clear, but he could see bright figures moving slowly under the surface, flashes of red, green, and blue.

Fish. Just fish with fins and tails and gills.

"But where are the starfish?" Marc asked.

"You're looking at them," the man said. "Fish from the stars."

"Oh, so they never were starfish," Marc said.

"You got it," the man said. "You ready?"

"Ready for what?" Shelly asked.

"Get down on your knees and just pucker up and put your face in the water, Missy, make smooch smooch sounds." He demonstrated. "And blow a few bubbles to attract these big fellows."

"I don't think so," she said.

"Me either," Marc said. "Sorry to have wasted your time."

He took Shelly's hand and turned to walk back into the bar.

There were three men blocking the way.

"Oh, you haven't wasted our time," the man by the washtub said.

The three men by the door smiled or chuckled or both and advanced on them.

Shelly clutched at his sleeve. "Marc?"

He didn't know what to do. Why hadn't he seen this coming? Maybe Leonardo had been right on the money and he'd already been psychically castrated.

Marc often dreamed something horrible was out to get him, jumping out of the shadows, chasing and howling, something big and hairy with a lot of sharp teeth. Sometimes he ran, but he never got away, and when he ran, he knew the waking day would suck.

Sometimes he turned and attacked, and when he did that, he always woke feeling like he could handle anything.

Was this going to be one of those days?

He shook Shelly off and charged the three men. Sometimes fear pushed people into doing superhuman things when protecting the people they loved.

Right?

When he got to the men, two of them stepped aside and let him run headlong into the middle one. Then the other two grabbed his arms, and the guy he'd bounced off of hit him hard in the stomach. Marc doubled over the man's fist. The other two dragged him back to the tub where the old guy was struggling with Shelly. The guy who had hit Marc now hit Shelly — a ringing open handed slap that dropped her to her knees. The men holding Marc forced him down beside her.

"Okay," the old guy said. "Kiss kiss."

Marc felt fingers in his hair and then his head was jerked up and over the rim of the washtub and plunged into the water.

He couldn't see anything clearly. He struggled but couldn't free himself. He was drowning. He felt tentative touches to his face like curious fingers, lightly over his cheeks and nose and then more forcefully between his lips.

Something knocked hard against his teeth, and he gasped and swallowed water and coughed and felt water in his lungs and something big in his mouth. There was a slicing crunch and pain exploded in the back of his mouth. He could see his own blood flowing into the water. Something forced its way down his throat, and when it got where it wanted to be, it stopped with a decisive clap and was still.

Marc realized there was no one holding him under the water now, and he lunged upward to his feet and shook his head back and forth producing a wide spray of water and blood. Shelly rose up, too, and the two them looked at each other and then looked quickly around for their attackers, but they were alone in the back yard now.

4

Tongues

No one tried to stop them when they moved back into the bar. In fact no one paid them any attention at all. Everything was strangely ordinary. The room was brighter now like someone had turned on more lights after he and Shelly had gone out to kiss the fish from the stars. Marc didn't see the old guy and his three assistants.

He looked at Shelly. She might be in shock. Shelly shocked, he thought wildly and chuckled but he couldn't push the sound up out of his chest. He opened his mouth to ask her if she was okay.

He said, "Are you firmly lodged?"

"Quite firmly," she said.

"Me, too," he heard himself say, and when he said it, he could feel his tongue and lips and lungs and they didn't feel like they were part of him. There was an overlay, something on top of him, doing the talking. He could see from the wild fright in Shelly's eyes that she was experiencing something similar.

"Shall we proceed then?" she asked.

Her lipstick had turned to a liverish shade of purple. No, there was a fine line around her lips and the skin was red where it met her purple lips. He didn't really think those were her lips at all. You could grab those lips and pull the tongue parasite out of her head and lungs whole like a bird picking apart a grasshopper.

He ignored her words and lips and took both her hands in his and looked into her eyes. "This is a total waste of time," he said.

"We are in agreement about that," she said, but he could see that she wasn't saying that at all. Shelly was telling him they were not to-tally cut off. They were both astrologers, for crying out loud. They traf-ficked in the paranormal all the time. So what if aliens from outer space had come down and eaten their tongues and maybe their lungs and lips and the rest of their vocal apparatus? That didn't mean they were out of the game. Notice, her eyes said, that while they have the voice, we seem to still have everything else.

"Are we going to just stand here like a couple of idiots?" he said, but what he meant and hoped he conveyed with his eyes and a light squeeze to her hands was that he agreed they were not defeated. There were people they could consult about this. There were experts in the occult arts who might think this infestation was trivial. A walk in the park. Tongue parasites! Ha ha. We'll just give you a good dose of sting-ing Jalapeno Jell-O and the intruders will knock your teeth out they'll be leaving so quick. Well, maybe we should keep the teeth.

He didn't think she was getting his message. She looked so frightened.

A woman sitting at the bar twisted around on her stool and said, "They want to go now."

A man to her left said without turning his head, "Yes, you two go now."

Then they were all saying it. Up and down the bar and in the shad-owy booths. Go now. Louder and louder. Shelly was saying it, too, and so was he. The two of them almost nose to nose shouting in one another's face, "Go now! Go now!"

He was suddenly afraid she would panic and run away from him. He pulled at her hands, and they hurried out of the bar. When they got outside, everyone stopped shouting.

He pulled her close and they clung together trembling.

"There must be a car," she said over his shoulder.

"No doubt," he said.

5

The Limits of Time

They got a motel. Marc suspected his tongue parasite was little by little gaining access to his mind. The things they were saying to one another contained more and more details from Marc and Shelly's lives. The parasites knew they were far from home on a foolish errand to reinvigorate Marc's failing psychic powers. They had picked up on her smoldering resentment and on his resentment in return at her lack of sympathy for his predicament. He wondered how long they would have any control at all.

"Are you ready to go home?" she asked.

"I've been thinking about that," he said. "Maybe I'll let you go on by yourself while I look into a few things here."

They were sitting side by side on the end of the motel bed. Shelly had turned on the TV, but he had turned down the sound, and no one had objected.

He put his arm around her shoulder. It was getting harder to move.

"We'll need to eat soon," she said without looking at him.

He moved in closer, and a sudden scene flashed into his mind where the parasite in his mouth leaped out and wrapped around her head with a wet splat, and he pulled back a little until the picture passed. Then he moved in again until he could touch his forehead to the side of her head. He felt her lean her head into his.

Time, he told her, and felt her shudder when his message passed through his head and into hers. If you're thinking about prophecy, you can't help but think about the nature of time.

"I suppose I could go spend a few days with my mother," she said.

And if you're thinking about the nature of time, you will soon come to the realization that it began some time after you were born. Exactly when is a little blurry, because the more you look back, the less you remember, and it will end when you die. That's it. There is no other time. You cannot think outside of time.

"You haven't seen your mother in ages," he said.

But if he had been doing his own talking, his words would have matched the thoughts now moving the few small inches from him to her. I understand what Leonardo was trying to tell me now. We have always been ineffectual, unproductive, castrated in our prophecy. How could it be otherwise? That's Leonardo's joke. We are chickens trapped in our own times. A prophecy does not exist until you learn of it, and then if it comes to pass, it comes to pass in your life. That means if a prophecy is about anything at all, it must be about you. Any prediction applies only to the time of the astrologer. That is, the time between conscious awakening and death. It makes no sense to even think about what came "before" or what will come "after." Or what might be "apart." Nothing came before. Nothing comes after. Each of us is closed away in a private cosmos.

"And you'll be looking for Leonardo in Oregon," she said.

I have all time, he told her. You have all time, too. But it's not the same time.

"I think we should go our separate ways now," he said.

She pulled away from him and twisted around, and they looked long and hard at each other.

Was this really the end of them? Would they simply go their separate ways now? Maybe exchange holiday cards and birthday greetings after a few years?

She grabbed him, and there was a cosmic spark bridging universes.

He pulled her in tight and struggled to push words past his lips.

"No," he said. "We won't."

"Yes," she said into his chest. "We refuse."

29

Suddenly Speaking

I t suddenly hits me that I speak Japanese. I turn off the subtitles, and I do perfectly well without them.

Nonsense, my gangster friends tell me. No one can just suddenly be speaking Japanese. How are we supposed to believe you learned to speak Japanese? Watching cartoons? Ordering sushi? Reading novels on your cell phone? Ridiculous.

I don't argue because it isn't smart to argue with your gangster friends, but they can see I would be making my case if I were talking to anyone else, and that makes them very angry.

Their heads get big, huge, like there might not be enough space in the room for their big heads. These scowling gangster heads might push us all up against the walls and spread us like strawberry jam.

Don't you dare be going all secret smiles and faraway looks, they yell at me.

I offer them a thousand apologies in Japanese.

That pushes them completely over the edge, and they pull out their guns and squeeze off shots in all directions until bullets are zipping and banging like tiny billiard balls from wall to wall and from floor to ceiling, so fast and vindictive you can barely do the Euclidean geometry necessary to quickly step out of the way just in the nick of time.

There is an obvious explanation for my sudden and spontaneous ability to speak Japanese, I tell them.

You don't speak Japanese! They snatch me up and plunge my feet into rubber boots and fill the boots with concrete.

It must be the case, I say, that my mind is reaching ahead into the future to a time when I, in fact, do speak Japanese. I suppose in the many years between now and then, I will have to actually sit down and learn Japanese.

Someone creeps up behind me and puts a plastic bag over my head and sings softly in a mean little whisky gurgle, am I blue, chuckles, says hey! when someone else jerks the bag off my head, and all the water and goldfish splash down the front of my shirt and pants. And then my softhearted gangster friends are all dancing around yelling and picking up fish and throwing them back in the bowl except for one who gets swallowed.

We can't believe a gangster has just swallowed a goldfish.

Why did you do that?

Historical reasons? Like in the movies? The cat's pajamas? Twenty-three skidoo?

We let it go.

It takes you back to a gentler time, a time when you could wear aerodynamic hats and get a coat made out of raccoons.

We said we already let it go!

My gangster friends are not prepared to overlook offensive tones. They suffer hurt feelings and turn on one another, and just like that out come the knives.

I decide to move one heavy foot after another toward the door.

Sayonara, I say, realizing too late I've said it in Japanese.

Hold it!

You talking to me?

We'll put your ridiculous assertion to the test, they tell me. We will show it's all faux Japanese.

How so?

An industrial laundry bag is dragged in and dumped, and out tumbles my friend Kasumi from the soup noodle factory in her cute Japanese schoolgirl costume, short skirt, big blue bow, black shoes. Her eyes are huge.

Relax, Dollface, my gangster friends tell her, we won't hurt you.

Why should she believe them? She backs away, looking first at the window and then at the door, like she's hoping ninjas will rush in and rescue her. But there will be no ninjas. She will have to be brave, perky and brave, and get herself out of this mess all on her own.

She can do it!

Well, frankly, she'll probably need my help.

Miss Kasumi, my gangster friends mutter, Miss Kasumi, we want you to tell us if this person can speak Japanese. Go ahead, say something to him.

Kasumi speaks to me in Japanese.

So, what does she say, Einstein?

She says she comes from a powerful crime family in Japan, and if we hurt her, they will snick off our heads with swords.

They look at her. She looks at them. A moment later she cries, That's right!

And what, my gangster friends turn to me, will be your response to that? They want me to step up to the challenge. You can't just let some crime family from a foreign country come in and walk all over you.

Kasumi, I say in Japanese, let me take this opportunity to express my true feelings. I have watched you many times as I've passed by the soup noodle factory, but I have never had the courage to declare my boundless admiration until now. Please accept this box of chocolates.

She takes the chocolates. My gangster friends wait for her verdict.

He says, she says, that I am to take this box, she looks down at the box, of chocolates to my father as a sign of respect from your crime family to my crime family.

I see that Kasumi and I have managed to confuse my gangster friends. It is, after all, not a common practice among gangsters to offer candy to potential enemies. Before they can become suspicious again, I seize the moment and put out my hand to Kasumi.

So, I say in Japanese, would you like to go out for tea or something?

She steps forward and takes my hand.

She looks back over her shoulder at my gangster friends and tells them, he says we'll be leaving now.

And so we do, me taking one ponderous step after another in my concrete galoshes and Kasumi pulling impatiently at my hand.

This is the start of something wonderful. Our destinies are entwined like vines. Our relationship is practically guaranteed to succeed. We will live happily ever after.

We do, after all, speak the same language.

30

Tubs

1
Nobody Knows

Nobody knows *how many rooms there are* in the mansion. We don't even know if it really is a mansion. We call it that because the room we share has a very high ceiling, and there is a carved cornice made up of chubby winged children playing stringed instruments. Harps, of course, but way over there is a little fellow with what looks like a guitar. None of us can get close enough to him to confirm that it really is a guitar. Maybe it's a shadow or a spider web.

Nobody knows how we came to be here precisely. It may have been something we said. We know we are criminals. We know this is our punishment. We also know we are alive. This isn't Hell, as Hell is usually understood.

There are no windows in our room, and the door cannot be opened. The light comes from frosted panels in the ceiling. After lights out, no matter how hard you look, you can never detect even a glimmer in the absolute darkness. But we think there must be many tub rooms just like this one, maybe hundreds of them, because you can hear lives being lived elsewhere through the walls and beneath the floor.

2
Tubs

Our room might have been a parlor or dining room at one time. It's big enough to contain the five of us and our tubs. Our tubs are also items you'd likely find in an old mansion. I'm thinking Victorian or maybe earlier. They are claw-footed white porcelain bathtubs — one for each of us. When you run your hand down the outside of your tub it's like the cool smooth belly of some animal — a cow or a horse, or maybe it's more like a big porcelain pig with little stubby legs ending in claws. Well, I suppose pigs don't have claws. All of our claws are different. I can tell that by sneaking quick looks at the claws on the tubs of the other men. It's a bad idea to be openly staring at the claws of another man's tub. It would probably cause a fight and we'd all get shocked. But from the little peeks I've taken over time, I know that the claws do not seem to be based on the same animal. It's like they went to a used tub store when they built this place with all of its windowless rooms filled with tubs and men in tubs.

We sit naked in cold water and carefully avoid looking at one another. Sometimes our gazes do cross, though. Sometimes it's on purpose, and a huge fight breaks out, if you can call grown naked men sitting in Victorian bathtubs shouting at one another a fight. We seldom get physical, but it is not unknown. When that happens someone somewhere flips a switch or twists a dial and shocks us all senseless.

3
Rule Number One

Rule number one is that only one man can be out of the tubs at a time. This arrangement is supposed to give each of us time to squat over the hole in the far corner and do our business. If more than one of us touches the floor at one time, we all get shocked.

They don't care if we share our food or not. It comes through a food slot at the bottom of the locked door one tray at a time spaced out by an interval calculated to give the eater time to get his tray and get back into his tub. The five of us have come to an uneasy truce about food. We all know that if someone doesn't get his, he will take every opportunity to jump out of his tub while someone else is already out and shock us all.

Our ancestors might have looked like this — stringy hair and ragged beards, no animal skin clothes yet, no fire, no tools. But they would've had women, too, and no tubs, and their Rule Number One probably wouldn't have involved getting shocked.

4

Holding Down the Dead Guy

The reason we know we are alive is because one of us isn't. He died some time in the indefinite past, and now he's really stinking up the place. We have discovered the smell is dampened a little if someone holds him under the surface of the water in his tub.

We take turns. One of us gets out of his tub and runs to the hole and does his business if business is what he needs to do and then hotfoots it over to the dead guy's tub and pushes him under the surface. When it was my turn for the first time, I discovered pushing the dead guy under was like trying to hold an inner tube under the surface when you're a kid and your dad gives you an old patched tire tube and lets you go down to the gas station and get it blown up. You roll it up the hill and down the other side and throw it into the pond and jump in after it, and your hands slap down on it just in time to keep you from going under, because you don't know how to swim yet, but you almost do almost. Soon you'll let go of the tube, but for now you can push it under, but you can't keep it there for long. It pushes back just like the dead guy. I always look carefully at his face under the water. I used to think he looked scared, but now I think he's developing a smile.

5

My Feet

It's Digby's turn to hold down the dead guy. I'm settled into my tub with the cold water lapping around my chin, and I see my feet rise from the surface down there by the knobs like two sea monsters. Maybe they're brothers. Maybe they're lovers. I would be the one on the left. Maria would be on the right. Maria always had an unattractive streak of the right in her, but I loved her anyway. We would still be together, I'm sure, if I had not said something and been seized, beaten up, and dumped in this tub. I nuzzle my right foot with my left, and she slaps playfully at me and moves away but then floats back looking shyly the other way and then boldly leaps on me, and we make a tremendous splash! The alarm sounds one sharp warning. It's like being jabbed in the ear with a stick. Or both ears at once. Two sticks. Splashing is not allowed.

Why splashing is not allowed is a mystery. It's not like they're worried about the water that flies up and out over the edge. Surely we drip more than that from our bodies when it's our turn to get our food or do our business at the hole in the corner. I think it must have something to do with attention. They want us to be paying attention to the here and now. A playful splash probably indicates that we have gone off in our minds to somewhere more pleasant with Maria who even now rises back to the surface and peeks up at me.

The others are muttering curses at me for that splash and the resulting sharp blast of the warning buzzer. I hope two of them don't go crazy at once and rush me or we'll all get shocked. If they conspire to send just one man after me in revenge, I'll leap out of my tub, and we'll all get shocked.

"I won't be pushed around!" I say just loudly enough so everyone can hear me. Whoever watches us doesn't really care if we speak loudly, but we've noticed that when there is a lot of activity, the chances of a random shock are much greater. It's like we get noticed, and whoever is watching gets bored and sooner or later shocks us just to see our teeth chatter.

Sometimes we talk about past crimes and plots. We go into great detail. We name names. We hope we will say something that will please the people who watch and listen. This strategy has its dangers. If they decide that one of us is just making stuff up, we all get shocked.

Sometimes we sit on the edges of our tubs. You'd think we'd spend a lot of time on the edge, but these are not your modern tubs with flat edges. The edges of these old tubs are artfully rounded and that's pretty hard on your naked butt. Sometimes when I'm sitting on the edge, I use my hands to raise my butt up a little, but who can stand on their hands like that for long? No one. A trained gymnast could only do it for a little while. Then it's back into the water. After trying to get comfortable on the edge, it's a big relief to just relax down into the tub again. It's not a pure feeling, though, because the water is so cold.

6
Nomenclature

The dead guy never had much intelligent to say. That's probably why we're still calling him "the dead guy" instead of whatever his name was when he was alive. Aside from me, the guys still living are Digby, Doolittle, and Snell. I've arranged them that way so it would sound like a law firm. I may have forgotten my crime, but they were surely lawyers. Or I could call them Tom, Digby, and Harry. But I would be lying about Harry. There is no Harry. His name is Mike. Likewise Doolittle. Nobody would ever admit to being named Doolittle in a place like this. No one knows if Digby ever had another name. If it weren't for me, there would be only three, and they could be the butcher, the baker, and the candlestick maker. Boy, my head voice is humming down to a kind of low moan like a crowd of people very far away. Maybe I'll get my feet to have sex again. Not that they really had sex the last time. Well, there's a first time for everything.

Digby is still holding the dead guy down. He's been out of his tub for a long time. A very long time. Too long, in fact. It's my turn to be up and about and doing my business and then holding down the dead guy. The upside to holding down the dead guy is that you're up on your feet without standing in cold water.

"Digby," I say. "Your time is up."

Digby looks at me, and then he looks above my head. It's like a slap in the face. I know he's looking at the cherubs over my tub. He must know I can't let that go by. He's reminding me about our argument over the word "entablature." He's bringing it up again with that look of his. We'd come to a truce, but he's broken it.

Once again, he's telling me I don't know what I'm talking about when I say the ridge of cherubs is called a "cornice."

"Entablature," he says and looks right at me.

"You idiot," I say. "To be an entablature a thing has to have columns! That's the whole point of being an entablature!"

"Nonsense," Digby says. "What kind of dumb ass thinks entablatures have to have columns?"

I put my hands on the edge of my tub and tighten my entire body like a spring. I will come up out of my tub like an angry badger now.

Digby makes a disgusted noise and lets go of the dead guy. He walks back toward his tub.

"Your brains have gotten so soggy you've forgotten everything about architecture," he says as he sinks into his water.

If we had not been naked men in tubs, prisoners, we could have walked across the carpeted library and taken down a dictionary and settled the argument like civilized people. Or we could have used a search engine if we were having this argument by email or one of those sites where you can post your opinions on absolutely anything. I remember people used to find common ground in those electronic places. Except when they were talking about politics. People never budged an inch on politics. Or religion. Or the kind of man or woman they wanted to meet. Or global warming. Or world hunger. Or universal health care. Or whether you should use this kind or that kind of operating system on your computer.

Maybe we were already doomed before we got here.

7
The Meaning of Life

We are all the time trying to make bargains with invisible powers. We tell them we surrender! You win. We'll talk! What do you want to know? What do you want us to say? Whatever it is, we'll say it, sign it, go on TV and confirm it. You name it.

No response.

In that respect, things here are no different than on the outside. We do stuff. We always just do stuff. And the question is can you ever find meaning in life given where you are and the stuff you have to do?

Digby is not done with me. Now I'm holding down the dead guy, and he's looking at me from his tub. It's like we've switched places. Probably because we actually have switched places, but I'm not looking at the cornice over his head, and, to be truthful, he's not really looking right at me. If he were pointedly putting his eyes on me, it would be like he was touching me, and that would mean I would have to respond, and everyone would get shocked. Instead he's stealing little glances at me, letting his eyes linger just a little too long on all the wrong places, and he knows that I know he's doing it. My knowing he's doing it is the whole point of him doing it.

Digby's constant picking at us, well, at me mostly, is just the way he passes the time. It's what it means to be Digby in the Tub Room, but today his glances go way beyond the usual. It's like he's made a decision that today things will change.

"Your crime," he says, "was probably mixing up your building terms."

It isn't possible to hold all of the dead guy under the water now.

There are flakes sloughing off of him like wet bits of paper, and you have to shake them off your hands when you let go of him. I sometimes think Digby likes it when we all get shocked. I hope he doesn't, because it's about to happen again.

8
Hope

We can't hold down two dead guys.

What are we going to do?

The air is already bad enough.

The others aren't speaking to me. I'll get no help from them. They are waiting to confirm that what I've done is really an option. I bet they're thinking that if there were only the two of them, they could better coordinate turns at the food slot and at the business hole. Cooperation is always easier when there are fewer people.

But here's an idea! What would happen if we moved Digby's body into the tub with the other dead guy?

My cellmates don't offer any ideas, so I decide to go for it.

"Be still," I tell them. "I'm going to move him. Hey, this could be good. Digby will hold down the dead guy and give us a little break before we have to start holding him down."

"You'll just get us shocked," one of them says. The other one makes a noise that sounds like agreement, but neither of them moves.

I discover that getting a naked and wet dead man out of a bathtub is not so straightforward as you might think. Just getting a good grip on him is a problem.

I pull him up to a sitting position and lean him forward. I try to get my arms around him, but his butt keeps scooching out from under him, and I can't get any leverage. I get in the tub behind him and wrap my arms around him and lock my hands. He is not a small man, and now I'm beard to beard with him. He has a funny smell that I can't place, but then I decide it's just that I haven't been this close to anyone for a long time. Maybe I'll stay like this for a little while, just a little while, a couple of minutes, maybe. He's so smooth and rubbery, and he's still warm, solid, more than just a concept.

I'm thinking this is the time when it turns out he's not dead after all. His eyes spring open and he jerks his head around to look at me.

He'll be kicking and screaming and pretty soon I'll be the one in trouble. No. Not this time. He's meat, and I'm still moving. I get back up on my knees and struggle his top half up and over the side of the tub.

I put my hands firmly on his back and stand up and get out of his tub. He's sprawled over the edge with his head near the floor, his arms and legs still in the tub and his butt in the air.

"You're not so smart about your stinking nomenclature now, are you?" I ask him.

I don't wait for an answer. I put my shoulder under his body a little way up from his stomach and lift. My feet slip, and I scramble to keep my balance and bang down hard on one knee. I take a few minutes to get my breath and then try again. I push him up and up and then I'm standing with my legs braced against his tub.

I try to turn but his feet are still in the tub. I make a little jerk to the left and another to the right, but I can't get them out. I take a step back and then another. Digby's legs stretch out before me. He is hanging on with just his toes now. I take another step back, and his feet break free, and his legs swing down hard at me, and as I brace myself for the impact, I suddenly wonder if we will still be two men out of our tubs even if he isn't touching the floor. He hits me hard, and I'm knocked back but not over, and we don't get shocked. I take a few steps to keep my balance.

I glance over at the others. Maybe I'm expecting applause. They are both hunkered down and hanging onto the edges of their tubs obviously looking for the electricity to arrive any moment now.

It hits me that if I fall, we are doomed. As soon as we both hit the floor, the electricity will come, and it will be so strong I will never be able to lift Digby again. I will have to crawl away to my tub and get in it, and once I'm in my tub, there will still be one man on the floor — dead Digby who will never get up again. We three survivors will be trapped.

If I drop him, I kill us all.

I see the others have realized this, too. I smile at them like I'm saying to hell with it, I'm going to drop him, and they get wide-eyed, and I turn away from them.

I walk Digby over to the other dead guy's tub and dump him in. There is a foul splash. The alarm hoots twice. I cover my ears with my hands. I should have seen that splash coming. I should have lowered him gently onto the other dead guy.

Too late now.

"It's still an improvement," I tell the others when I'm pretty sure we're not going to get shocked.

They won't even give me that much.

I use the hole. Then I walk around like a rooster. Maybe the others don't think the way I'm walking is anything like a rooster. Maybe they think I've gone completely crazy. Good. Let them think that. I give them each a direct you-want-a-piece-of-me look and then get back into my own tub.

I consider the faucets.

Probably on a regular basis (how would we know when all of our moments are of different sizes) the cold-water faucets turn all by themselves, and cold water gushes into our tubs to replace the loss from dripping and evaporation (and sometimes splashing). There is a hot water faucet, too, but it never moves.

The hope of my life is that someday the hot water faucet will move and not only move but be effective. Someday hot water will rush into my tub. Steam will form above the surface. I will submerge myself in bliss.

But in the meantime, we take what meaning we can from the things we do. I wonder who will be Digby now, and if he will have anything intelligent to say.

I decide to get the ball rolling again. Why not? It's not like we're going anywhere. I speak without turning to look at them. "So, tell me, boys, what is your thinking on the matter of friezes?"

31

Duck

W e are locked in a life or death Mind Mingle. In case you were wondering. My mission was to walk in here, suck your brains out, and leave. The trouble is all I had to go on was that you were some kind of scientist at some kind of scientist school on the west side (more north than south) of a particular continent and that if I maybe walked this way, I might find the right building, which worked out pretty well. I would have been in and out with no one running around screaming about aliens, but I did not count on the duck.

Things look very different now that your brain has surrendered information about this planet — the plants, the animals, the people, the food, the way you show me all of your teeth for no apparent reason, the way things move. The ordeal of my arrival now sounds almost comical, my apprehensions, my misconceptions, the way I was looking at things, my confusion about the duck.

And yes, I see now that it was only a duck, an ordinary duck, one of those ducks with a green head and yellow beak, and black eyes, and webbed feet that look like they could be removed and put aside when things aren't so wet, and feathers, and stillness — the kind of duck that just stands there like it was made out of painted wood looking at me as I approach it on the courtyard lawn of Building 17.

You're thinking, so, the slinky alien walks into the courtyard and sees a duck. So what? Is a duck such a big deal? Well, you should understand I had only just arrived on Earth. I had never seen a duck. My information was very spotty.

The most important fact about the duck and me is this. I had never seen a thing that could fly. Nothing flies where I come from. Nothing swims either. The idea of big bodies of water and things living in them is astonishing to me, but that reminds you of a funny story involving a priest, a bottle of red pepper sauce, and a plate of shrimp, and we laugh and laugh for almost a minute before we shake ourselves out of it and get back to the business of our life or death Mind Mingle.

You suddenly wonder how I got here in the first place if I know nothing of flying. You are worried about the mechanics of how I came to be on Earth. The answer is very simple, and it is the answer to many questions on my world. I walked. Just as you might use "fly" as your metaphor for travel between worlds, we use "walk." It's just that simple.

Where I come from we all walk. Walking is the concept behind all motion on my world. Consider a "lion" chasing an "antelope." You understand that these animals are not really lions and antelope as you think of them, but they are very like your terrestrial animals in that the one chases down and eats the other. Think of the antelope as a kind of huge pink spider bunny, and the lion as a power walker with too many pumping arms and the head of some kind of big snake. Oh, that's close enough. The antelope can walk very quickly, but the lion can walk just a little faster. Say, the antelope walks at four miles per hour. Then the lion walks at maybe four and a half miles per hour. Once the lion is chasing the antelope, the only hope the prey has is that the predator will run out of energy before it can close the distance between them. It is a glorious sight to see from a safe distance. You must be very quiet. If the lion should spot us, it might decide we look like we would walk more slowly than the antelope, and then we'd be in desperate trouble. But say we are very quiet as we stand gazing across the savannah, and here comes the antelope walking as fast as it can from left to right in front of us, and we think, hey, what's your hurry, Mr. Antelope? But then the lion appears, and it is clear that if it just keeps doggedly stepping along, it will overtake the antelope before the afternoon is over. Will it have enough energy to keep going? That is Nature's life and death question. That is, in fact, our own question of the day. You should not imagine that you are the lion.

What? Oh, don't be ridiculous. I refuse to believe that you anticipated my arrival and placed the duck in the courtyard to knock me off balance so you could have me all to yourself. After all, you would have had me all to yourself anyway, so why use a duck?

Yes, it might well be true that you had your reasons. It might be true that your thought processes are so different from mine that I cannot really appreciate the meaning of the duck. From my point of view, you are a totally baffling alien yourself what with your flying and swimming and eating of noodles.

You should abandon all such foolishness. I will not run out of energy. I will walk just a little faster than you walk no matter how fast you walk, so let's get back to the duck.

I had never seen such a streamlined creature. In fact, I was not even sure it actually was a creature and not some kind of art object or maybe a road sign. It was standing so still. Those smooth lines, that puffed out chest — it looked like some kind of soldier, I thought. But if that were true, if it turned out to actually be alive, if it were out here in the courtyard watching for me and guarding you, why hadn't it raised the alarm when I appeared?

I walked toward it with some of my hands out so I might run friendly fingers over that bright yellow part sticking out of its green head (I had no duck terms at the time).

When I was maybe five or six steps away from it, the duck seemed to come apart. It was like physics had gone insane. The body contorted into so many bizarre angles and edges, and then the thing seemed to collapse in on itself to the left, and then it just jumped into the air and flew away!

I couldn't believe my eyes.

I might still be standing there making undignified honking sounds if you had not come down from your office and pulled me inside just in time before I might have been captured and held incommunicado while horrible experiments were performed on my alien body. Or so you said not yet realizing that I had come for you in the first place.

So, here we are. As I look at you now sitting there so still behind your "desk" doing nothing but covering and uncovering your eyes with their "lids" very infrequently, I can imagine that you are like the duck. Were I to put out a hand to touch you, you might fragment, split down the middle. Maybe that is not a garment on your upper body. Maybe those are folded "wings" and rather than be touched by a creature like me, you will spread them and jump up with all your crazy edges and angles and your neck will grow and your head will shrink and go green.

You show me your teeth.

I suddenly realize that you creatures are much more complicated than we thought.

You are the duck!

You flew off and then you circled back and landed and changed into your current form and coaxed me back into Building 17 with all its clean corridors and cold laboratories.

But even if I have made a horrible mistake, even if you really are the lion (or in this case the duck), I have one more trick up my sleeve. I will now walk away in a direction you cannot follow.

32

The Two of Me

I was not quite ten when Renata grew up out of my right shoulder like a second head. She was just a blemish at first, a smudge that looked a little like the state of Florida. Then she was a squashed spider mole, then she was a monster, a mewling, squirming mass of purple flesh that smelled like raw chicken, and then she was just Renata, my little sister, saying let me have the arms, Davy, I need the arms, my nose itches, please please please, give me the arms, so I can scratch my nose!

I'll scratch your nose, I told her, hold still, okay, here we go, honk honk, ha ha!

You're so mean, Davy! She was about to go off like a fire alarm in my ear. I hunkered down for it, but she changed her mind and switched strategies so smoothly you had to think she was planning this from the beginning — tears and puppy dog eyes, not that they were so easy to see that close up, but I knew what she could do with those eyes. I'd seen her use her big brown eyes on other people — oh, you poor thing! Let me get you a glass of juice, would you like a cookie? Don't cry. Let me see that big girl smile, I know you can do it. Yes, you can. Here, here's your cookie. Davy, hold the cookie for your sister.

Jeeze Louise.

They're my arms, I said. Get your own arms.

I'm trying! she yells. You know, I'm trying, Davy!

I do know that. I can see she has shoulders now. She didn't have shoulders before. It's like she's rising up out of me. Some day she'll be all out of me but her feet. I'll be down here and she'll be up there, and I'll be her big brother bunny slippers, and then one day, plop, she'll pull one foot out, and plop, she'll pull the other foot out. Then she'll run off into the woods throwing flowers to the left and to the right and back over her shoulders.

When I get my arms, I'm going to strangle you, Davy, she says, spooky voice, I'm coming to get you, I'm creeping up on you, here I come now, boo! Giggling. She knows that I'm the one who could do some serious strangling since I have the arms, but she also knows I never would. I take a deep breath and let go of the control of my right arm. She can feel me do it. Her smile is so big and bright. You just get the one, I tell her. Oh, thank you, Davy! She closes my right hand into a tight fist then opens it up and spreads the fingers. She lifts the hand to her face and scratches her nose and sighs and sighs and sighs. It seems to me she is getting an indecent amount of pleasure out of a simple nose scratching, but then I see that she is looking at me out of the corner of her eye, almost smiling, she's up to something, and before I can grab control of my arm again, she gives my nose a retaliatory honk.

So there! So there! So there!

She had her own arms by the time we got to high school. Things were getting a lot more crowded with us. I had to look up to see her face. But wait, there's more — as her shoulders emerged from me, not only arms were revealed but also a couple of hideous growths on her back. Wings, someone said, and someone else said yes that must be what they are. Everyone was so sorry for her like she didn't have enough to worry about being so tightly attached to me who could be known for not always being so nice. Poor Renata! All the time having to be superduperglued to a smelly boy. And now wings.

Once before she got her arms all the way out, I put a paper bag over her head when I wanted a little privacy. She put up such a fuss people came running to see what the matter was, and when they saw her, saw us, the two of us, Renata with the bag over her head, and me being, well me, she making a middle eastern ululation of despair that she had picked up from watching public television, and me all what? What? She's fine. She didn't look fine when I snatched off the bag to show everyone how fine she was, she looked terrified and lost, but I knew her well enough to know that a lot of it was for dramatic effect. She played our keepers, our fosternistas, like stringed instruments, a big base for Charlie who was really the nicer of the two and a squeaky squawky fiddle for Debbie who was like a rat terrier. Renata was wailing and Charlie was looking at me so disappointed and Debbie was yapping and I was the rat. I wished Debbie would just bite me or something and get it over with, but she didn't.

Shortly after that Renata got her arms, and we settled the privacy issue. I opened the bag and put it on the table in front of her and ignored it. It only took a couple of minutes for her to pick up the bag herself and put it over her own head. You pervert, she muttered, and that was that, no fuss, some muss.

In most other ways, she was a lot harder to live with once she got her arms all the way out of me. Not to mention the growths on her back, which by then were clearly wings. There were no feathers. We both wondered if she'd ever get feathers, but there were never any feathers. Her wings reminded me of unborn things. You could see the blood pulsing in them if you looked closely, and given my position, I was always able to look closely. They were a strange pale greenish yellow color with just a little of the pink the rest of her had become, and I should mention by this time we were both in our early teens and girls grow up quicker than boys so there was some hullabaloo made over the fitting of feminine tops and attaching them in the back between the ribs and the "wings" and I was not to look, and I pretty much didn't. Yes, yes, we fought all the time, but we were so close, it was easy imagining how she felt, or maybe it was just that she was so good at showing how she felt. You never had to wonder. It was all deliberate. She used the display of her feelings as a subtle tool. She knew you could see just how she felt, so when she wanted something, she opened up wide, and it was really really hard to say no since you knew exactly how she felt. Like alone together in the dark at the end of the day, do you think we'll always be like this, Davy? I don't think so, I told her. Think about it. Every year you grow more and more out of me. It makes sense that some day you'll just be out and can walk away on your own two feet. Do you really think so, Davy? I really do.

And I really did, but I didn't mention that I sometimes imagined her flying away. One time I dreamed her wings were out and big and had all of these black and white feathers, she looked magnificent, and when she beat her wings, the wind blew my hair back like I'd stuck my head out the car window going 60 mph, but her feet were still attached to me, so when she finally lifted off, I came along too like a fish in the talons of an eagle.

When her wings finally did fully emerge, they were nothing like eagle wings. In fact, they were very ugly. They were the kind of ugly that people go all white in the face over. Oh, they're not so bad, I told her. I hate them! I want to tear them off my back! Wasn't it bad enough I had to be born attached to you! Wasn't it bad enough I had to have any wings at all! Why does God hate me? Who? Oh, never mind, I'm going to jump off a building! You'll just fly to the ground. You'll be all oh goodbye cruel world, and you'll jump, and then just like you can't kill yourself by holding your breath, your wings will start flapping, and you'll start flying, and that will be that. You'd pull me down, she said. You'd be heavy enough so we'd both go splatter on the sidewalk. Would you really take me with you, Renata?

No, not really.

By the time we graduated, and we did graduate, you wouldn't think we could, but we did, she was almost out, which made the logistics of getting around pretty difficult. Imagine walking around with a 105 lbs seventeen-year-old girl with stubby wings standing on your shoulder. Charlie rigged some scaffolding with wheels, squeaky hard to control shopping cart wheels, and lots of aluminum bars. You might call us a two-story student — me plodding along on the ground level holding onto the bars with both hands and pushing the whole contraption down the high school hallways, and Renata up there like a queen of the parade shouting down greetings to her friends, making jokes, smiling smiling smiling, or pouting if someone had hurt her feelings, Bobby talking to Karen and not even seeing Renata as she rolled on by, slow down, Davy, slow down! Her biggest problem in those days, aside from having to crouch down whenever we went through doorways, was keeping those wings covered, not because she thought people didn't know about them, but because they were still so ugly.

Once she dragged (or more correctly directed) me around to thrift shops looking for feathers. Peacock feathers, feathers in your cap, old arrows, a couple of feather pillows, and when she had enough, she spread out her supplies on our bedroom floor, it looked like a bombing in a bird store, and took her glue, not superglue we should thank the heartless deity who had kicked this whole mess off in the first place, but white glue like kids use in kindergarten, and she glued the feathers to her wings. She really couldn't reach them right and was making a mess of it. I didn't say a word, but she could see the judgment in my eyes, so she got me to do it, so she would have someone to blame when it all turned out badly. And it did turn out badly. She looked awful — she had been bamboozling the town folks with some kind of dance hall and gambling scheme, and they had had it up to here, they'd gotten mad as hell and weren't going to take it anymore, so they tarred and feathered her and rode her out of town on a rail. What does it even mean to be ridden out of town on a rail? If she were to be ridden out of town, she

Ray Vukcevich

would be riding me anyway. Charlie and Debbie gave us grief about the feathers, but the worst part was the way they looked at us like could there be anything more pathetic than you two?

I have to hand it to them, Debbie and Charlie, they did come to our graduation. They were out there with all the parents and siblings as Renata and I rolled together up the ramp and onto the stage. Renata had to be especially careful holding her arms out like a tightrope walker to keep our balance, and I had to push especially hard to get us up the ramp. It was touch and go there for a moment. It would have been just perfect if we had fallen over, people running around shouting and trying to get us up, looking at us like that, but we didn't fall. We made it to the podium, and Mr. Hodges reached up and gave Renata her diploma. Then he reached down and gave me mine. I pushed our scaffolding off the stage. Lots of people clapped for us. We're like dancing bears, Renata whispered, but she didn't sound bitter.

We came apart that summer before college. It happened just as I always imagined it would. Renata was sitting on the bed, and I was sitting on the floor. I had been able to see the tops of her feet for days, and now I could see most of the sides of her feet. And her toes. Just as soon as her toenails had dried and hardened up, she'd painted them bright red. The fumes from the polish made me dizzy. Oh, don't be such a big baby, Davy. Don't you just love this color?

I could take it or leave it.

And then it was like she was only resting her feet on my shoulder, me on the floor, her sitting on the bed, the late afternoon summer sunlight making the room too hot, but not so hot it was worth it to get back into the scaffolding and go outside.

And then I could feel her moving her feet back and forth on my shoulder, a little to the left, a little to the right, and I knew she was loose, but I didn't want to admit it just yet. I could tell she knew, too. This was our big moment. There should be a band. The sky should open up and a Big Face should scowl down at us and say, okay, that should teach you two a lesson! A parade, noisemakers, corks popping. Davy and Renata, two people, separate at long last.

She lifted her left foot off my right shoulder and put it back down on my other shoulder. I leaned back against the bed. Then I leaned over and pressed my face against her right leg, the one that might still be attached. No, I knew it wasn't. I rested my cheek against the warm skin of her leg. She put both hands on my head and moved them around gently like my head was a hairy crystal ball and she was reading our future.

Would she fly away now like some kind of angel? Well, maybe if all the world's a barnyard, and plucked chickens have angels. She'll be running around flapping those awful wings and going nowhere fast. Then she'll put on a big coat and take a cab, or she'll get on a horse and ride away, wings scooping at the air but not even lifting her butt up out of the saddle, or maybe she'll buy a motorcycle.

And I'll go around town pushing my squeaky scaffolding, and people will all the time be saying, hey, Davy! Where's that beautiful sister of yours? And I won't know what to say. What in the world will I say?

33

In the Flesh

T hinking about traveling made me feel a little queasy, but it was time to move the meat. I had to do it, had to bite the bullet, grab the bull by the horns, get tough and get going or get off the pot or whatever.

My granddaughter would be starting Kindergarten soon and we had never been in the same room together.

Broadband only took you so far.

I was going to have to actually go there.

Since she'd been born, I'd spent a lot of time feeling guilty. A real Grandpa would move across the country, maybe get a little house down the block where he would bake cookies, well maybe I could buy cookies or have them delivered from a fancy bakery, and keep ponies for the apple of his eye to ride when she came over after school. A real Grandpa might even get a Grandma so the little girl coming through the woods with her basket of goodies wouldn't feel vaguely uneasy about the lack of correspondences between her life and some published ideal.

The way it had worked so far was that I'd do a funds transfer, and then Mommy and Daddy would go down to the local toy store and buy something, maybe a Barbie, and have it irradiated and wrapped. They'd write "From Grandpa" with half a dozen exclamation points, and put it under the tree or onto the birthday table. Someday I would have to sit her down and explain that too many exclamation marks were like picking your nose in public. That was not the kind of thing you could say to a child in an email.

My neighbor, Maria, when I suggested she might come with me and be Grandma said, "No way!" but she did agree to watch my apple trees while I was gone. This time of year there wasn't much to do, but it made me feel better knowing Maria would be prowling around in her overalls with a flashlight. No, wait a minute why would she be out there at night? I just liked to picture her in her overalls. There is something so sexy about a woman in overalls, the way you unhook those shoulder straps and . . . but that's another story.

Maria volunteered to go with me to the airport and bring my clothes home afterwards, but I told her I had that covered. I would just throw my clothes away. Pretty extravagant, she said, but I could tell she was glad. No one likes to go to the airport.

She was there to see me off when my cab arrived. I'd put on torn jeans and a red checked shirt with only two buttons (one at the top and one at the bottom) and cheap rubber flip-flops. I kissed Maria on the cheek. I put my hand in the cab's scanner, and the back door popped open.

The driver didn't bother turning on the speaker, so there was no small talk on the long drive into the city and then on to the airport. When we arrived I punched in a few bucks tip, more out of habit than gratitude, and the door popped open again and I got out.

I was still a long way from where I needed to be. My next stop was at a vending machine for a traveling robe. There were at least a dozen people milling around the vending machines, and I wondered if there was a meat convention either here or wherever all those people might be going.

I followed the arrows to the main door. I stopped and read the sign posted out front as required by law. The sign explained that once I stepped through the door, I would not be able to step back through it.

Okay. I took a deep breath and went on in to the airport. I walked down a long hallway that branched to the left for women and to the right for men. At the end of the branch was another sign explaining the trip through this door was also strictly no return. You go in you don't come out. This is not a lavatory!

The room was one big cold area with tile floors and metal benches bolted to the wall. There were three other men in there. We didn't exchange glances. I sat down on one of the benches and struggled with the plastic safety wrapper holding my robe. I had no sharp objects, of course. In the end I used my teeth to get a rip started.

I got undressed and threw my old clothes in a trash barrel and put on my new robe. It was white and thin and obviously a paper product. At least it closed in the front with a single big button. The floor was cold under my bare feet, so I didn't hang around but moved straight for the door at the far end marked "terminal this way."

I walked into an open area and stood looking around for a moment before I located the counter I needed. I got in line. Getting in line was not something I'd done in a long time, and it made me feel very strange. That feeling must have been shared by the other four people in line because we maintained about ten feet of distance between each of us.

When it was finally my turn, I put my hand in the scanner and confirmed for the woman behind the glass who I was, where I was going, and why. I thought my song and dance about me being a grandfather finally making the long trip across the continent to see his young granddaughter would at least get me a smile but she just looked bewildered at that part of my story.

Had I talked to any strangers?

"Just you," I said.

"What do you mean by that?" She gave me a hard look.

"Just a joke," I said.

"We don't joke at the airport," she said.

"I'm sorry," I said.

"Please pay attention and follow instructions once you're inside," she said and buzzed me in.

When the door closed behind me, I walked into a long carpeted tunnel where I was met by a woman in a white lab coat and a uniformed man with an assault rifle. He stepped aside, and I saw a gurney and another trash barrel.

"Put your robe in there." The woman indicated the barrel with her clipboard.

I took off the robe and tossed it and stood before them naked feeling skinny and plucked. Hey, maybe I should do the Funky Chicken. No. That would baffle them, and the soldier might shoot me. They weren't old enough to remember the Funky Chicken. In fact, I wasn't old enough to remember it either. It was just something that bubbled up to the top of my mind because I was nervous and naked in front of a soldier with an assault rifle and a woman with a clipboard who was now snapping on a rubber glove.

After her brief and not altogether unpleasant probing, she said, "Okay, get up on the gurney."

I climbed onto the metal table.

"It's cold," I said.

The soldier grabbed my left foot and shackled my ankle to the gurney.

"Small poke," the woman said and gave me an injection. Delicious warmth moved through my body as the sedative did its work. The woman shook out a thin blanket like the way I remember my mother used to shake the sheets out before hanging them on the clothesline. The blanket settled over my body.

The soldier moved to the head of the gurney and pushed. The woman walked along beside me.

"I'm off to see my granddaughter," I said.

The soldier made a noise which I interpreted as meaning, "Hey, and here we thought you were some kind of hot shot off to a big deal that could only be closed by much meat in the same room at the same time."

"Pressing the flesh," the woman said.

"What?" I said, suddenly wondering how much of this conversation was strictly in my head.

"I don't know," she said. "It just seems kind of frivolous, you know?"

The soldier maneuvered my gurney parallel to what looked like an aluminum garage door. The woman pushed a button and the door slid up and away. Inside, the passengers who had gone before me were stacked up like items in an automated deli.

"Here you go," the soldier said and slid my gurney into place. Then the whole thing rolled up so they could slide the next passenger in. Once the box was full or when they ran out of passengers, it would be moved to the airplane. And then we would be off into the wild blue yonder, as free as birds. Or maybe caged chickens.

Leaning to the left and looking over the edge of the gurney, I could see the legs and feet of the woman and the soldier.

"This is the most important trip of my life," I called out.

"So, b'bye then," the woman said and closed the door with a bang.

About the Author

Ray Vukcevich lives and writes in Oregon.
His previous story collection is *Meet Me in
the Moon Room*, published by Small Beer
Press, and his novel *The Man of Maybe
Half-a-Dozen Faces* was published by
St. Martins. His stories have appeared in
*F&SF, Scifiction, Lady Churchill's Rosebud
Wristlet, Strange Horizons, Polyphony,
Talebones*, and many others. You'll find his
website at www.rayvuk.com.

OTHER TITLES FROM FAIRWOOD/DARKWOOD PRESS

Diving Mimes, Weeping Czars
by Ken Scholes
trade paper: $17.99
ISBN: 978-0-9820730-8-7

A Cup of Normal
by Devon Monk
trade paper: $16.99
ISBN: 978-0-9820730-9-4

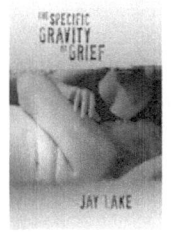

The Best of Talebones
edited by Patrick Swenson
trade paper: $18.99
ISBN: 978-1-933846-24-8

The Specific Gravity of Grief
by Jay Lake
limited hardcover: $25
ISBN: 978-0-9820730-7-0

The Radio Magician
by James Van Pelt
trade paper: $17.99
ISBN: 978-0-9820730-2-5

The Singers of Nevya
by Louise Marley
trade paper: $19.99
ISBN: 978-0-9820730-4-6

Harbinger
by Jack Skillingstead
trade paper: $16.99
ISBN: 978-0-9820730-3-2

Dark Dimensions
by William F. Nolan
trade paper: $15.99
ISBN: 978-0-9820730-6-3

www.fairwoodpress.com
21528 104th Street Court East;
Bonney Lake, WA   98391